Voices Behind the Curtain

by

Gordon Zuckerman

OTHER TITLES BY GORDON ZUCKERMAN

Fortunes of War
Crude Deception
Matter of Importance

PREQUEL

FAREWELL SPEECH:
President Dwight D. Eisenhower
January 20, 1961

"The conjunction of an immense military establishment and a large arms industry is a new American experience. The total influence—economic, political, even spiritual—is felt in every city, every state house, and every office of the federal government . . . In the councils of government, we must guard against the acquisition of unwarranted influence, whether sought or unsought by the military-industrial complex. The potential for the disastrous rise of misplaced power exists and will persist.

"As we peer into society's future, we—you and I and our government— must avoid the impulse to live only for today, plundering for own ease and convenience, the precious resources of tomorrow."

PREFACE

IT'S JANUARY 1948. THE SECOND WORLD WAR CONCLUDED MORE THAN 2 years ago. Believing the world has fought its last Great War, and unaware of or unconcerned about Russia's potential emergence as a new world power, the American public is preoccupied with getting married, having children, spending its pent-up wartime savings, and looking for peacetime work.

Meanwhile, defense spending has dropped by $400 billion, or 67 percent of peak wartime spending limits. It's a drop that has some powerful people concerned. In recent years, New York commercial and investment bankers and military contractors have been convening regularly in secret. Carefully guarded meetings have been conducted to discuss how to cushion the adverse economic effects of America's shift from wartime production to the manufacture of consumer goods.

Not even the most optimistic among the Wall Street investment managers believe proposed solutions—selling off surplus capacity, retooling plants to manufacture peacetime consumer products, and generating postwar demand—will be adequate to offset the economic consequences. Something has to be done. That's why, on this bitterly cold day at the start of 1948, they decide to retain the law firm of Southwick & Cornforth. They expect its managing partner, J. Jordan McWilliams, to develop an imaginative and comprehensive plan needed to address the urgency of the situation and present it for their approval at the earliest possible date.

PROLOGUE
The Sentinels Gather
(Ten Months Later)

NEW YORK, NOVEMBER 1948

The jungle drums registering concern over the latest developments in the fast-rising world of anti-Communist campaigning are beating more loudly. The tide of the public's growing fear of the spreading threat of Communism is rapidly rising.

Jacques and Mike, the European and American Sentinel leaders, via transatlantic telephone, have been exploring possible corporate agendas in play and the evidence that a new Power-Cycle type threat may be forming.

Mary Wheeler Clarke's sources—former generals now consulting with military contractors—continued to give her reports on the ramped-up plans for increased defense spending.

Marco Tancredi has reported on the situation from his unique vantage point: Members of his late-night office cleaning staff have been separating the discarded executive notes of the members of Manuel's Club they have discovered in the trash they are required to remove each night.

Walt Matthews, the nationally syndicated columnist for the *New York Times,* has been reporting the activities of the House Un-American Activities Committee with increasing frequency . . .

Natalie's transatlantic casting program, "Natalie's Bridge," widely regarded as a brave effort to identify English employment for out-of-work, blacklisted Hollywood personalities, has caught the attention of the American public.

PROLOGUE

It had been decided that an all-hands meeting of the Sentinels was needed to organize a plan of opposition. The scheduled dinner in the Stones' spacious Upper Eastside New York apartment represented the first time all 14 would be called together.

By seven o'clock on the appointed evening, everyone had arrived, been offered their drink of choice, and had sampled Cecelia's magnificent array of Oriental hors d'oeuvres. With drinks in hand and nibbling on the marvelous finger food, the battle-hardened Sentinels stood around talking. The affection, admiration, and respect they held for each other was apparent.

As involved in their own conversations as they were, they couldn't help but notice that Mike and Jacques had made their way to the outside balcony. Trying not to appear obvious, the others would periodically steal quick glances through the big plate-glass window. Judging from the body language of the two leaders and the intensity of their facial expressions, the other Sentinels concluded that their leaders were having a serious, do-not-disturb conversation.

* * *

JACQUES WAS TALKING. "I'M GUESSING THIS SITUATION WITH THE military budgeting represents a serious threat to the congressional appropriations process and demands our attention. When the Founding Fathers set up the checks and balances of your remarkable government, I wonder if they anticipated that these concentrated pockets of wealth and influence would become so dominant. Unfortunately, it's not just a problem for American citizens. Many people in other countries are depending upon the generosity of the American people to help them reconstruct their local economies. Already, they're starting to worry about how the cost associated with rearmament might interfere with their own needs."

Responding, Mike said, "We may not like what McWilliams and his cronies are attempting, but at least we know what it is. Now that we have two sources of confirming information, I wonder if we really have any alternative to becoming involved."

Jacques was about to respond when Cecelia announced, "All right, everyone, dinner is served!"

CONTENTS

CONTENTS

CAST OF CHARACTERS

Jordan McWilliams: Wall Street Attorney-In charge of Manuel members plan

Manuel Rodrigues Arena-Friend of McWilliams, Acapulco Host, Mexico City movie maker

Richard "Slick" Bailey: California congressmen, member of HUAC committee

Mercedes Ordonez Velasquez: Former Miss Universe, under contract to Arena Movie Studios

Mike Stone:/Original Sentinel, Executive V.P. Scone City Bank

Jacques Roth: Original Sentinel, Head of Roth Bank in Geneva

Claudine Demaureux Roth: Original Sentinel, daughter of Henri Demaureux, wife of Jacques Roth

Mary Wheeler Clarke: Former Administrator, CIA, Bern, Switzerland

Henri Demaureux: Fifth Generation family President of Demaureux Bank of Switzerland

Cecelia Chang Scone: Original Sentinel, Born in Hong Kong, married to Mike Scone

Southwick & Cornforth: Powerful Wall Street, New York City law firm

Marco Tancredi: Second generation, Sicilian immigrate, former garbage company executive, founder and owner of American Building Maintenance Company

Armando: Marco's partner

Gordon Newell: Monterey sculptor, Scone family friend

Don Cerreta: Marco's oldest and best friend, Federal Prosecutor, Attorney General Office

Natalie Cummins: Retired star of New York and London's musical Stage

CAST OF CHARACTERS

David Marcus: Visiting Fellow, University of California, Owner-founder of Great Britain's "International Petroleum Investment Advisors"

William W. Wey!, "Mr. Bill": Successful author, playwright, and screen writer, former World War II highly decorated naval aviator. Target of HUAC anti-communist investigations

Mrs. Cyril "Gloria" Adams: Retired Hollywood actress, former wife of Hollywood Black Listed screen writer

Dr. Tom Burdick. Professor, University of California, doctoral advisor to the "Original Six Sentinels"

Juan Pablo Perez: Venezuelan Petroleum Engineer, consultant co Middle Eastern, oil rich country governments

Tony Garibaldi: Original Sentinel, founder and managing partner Sentinel Vineyards

Walt Matthews: Senior reporter New York Times and long-time Sentinel friend "Voices behind the Curtain Attorneys"

Ben Holt: represents implement Mid-West manufacturers

Ken Hoffman: represents steel maker from Pittsburg

Dale Pennington: represents Oilmen from Los Angeles

Bert Damner: represent aircraft manufacturers from Seattle

Pere Scott: represents oil companies from Houston

Sir Colin Meyer: Duke of Trafalgar, father of Ian Meyer, an original Sentinel

Stanley Victor: McWilliams' Georgetown friend who hosts weekend cruises on his ocean-going yacht

Pete Ferrari: President American West National Bank

Frank Majors: Foreman, night cleaning office maintenance crew

CHAPTER 1

Manuel's Club

J. Jordan McWilliams was standing in front of Acapulco's international air terminal, enjoying the warm tropical breeze. Waiting next to him was Señor Manuel Rodriguez Arena, a Mexico City movie producer. The two longtime friends were silent as they watched the landing of the first of six flights that would arrive that afternoon. Each plane had departed from a different major city in the United States. On board each craft were the chief executive officers of many of the country's largest military-industrial corporations. These men were accustomed to making difficult decisions, solving complicated problems, and ensuring important things happened.

Responding on short notice, they had immediately accepted the offer of Señor Arena's Acapulco hospitality. They understood what appeared to be an innocent invitation was, in reality, their notification that J. Jordan McWilliams was preparing to present his plan for restoring American military spending.

To provide sufficient room for all of his invited guests, Señor Arena had arranged for the exclusive occupancy of Acapulco's finest boutique hotel. As the only guests, they would be able to listen, discuss, and hopefully, approve McWilliams's plan.

As Jordan watched the first plane taxi along the tarmac, he reflected on the events that led up to this day. Anticipating the government's sudden cancellation of military procurement contracts might cause problems. He and his friend Señor Manuel Arena, for the prior 2 years, had been periodically inviting different combinations of these powerful industrialists to his 10-room beachfront villa in Acapulco, where they could discuss postwar problems on a confidential basis. Each time before they departed, the invited guests would make handsome contributions toward the next movie Manuel was planning on producing. Those who appeared to be the most interested in finding some way to extend government spending on military contracts had been invited back. Each time a returning guest was preparing to depart, he was handed two envelopes. One contained the dividends from his previous investment, and the other contained an invoice for the next-to-be-produced movie. The dedicated group that ultimately emerged had come to call themselves members of "Manuel's Club."

These Manuel's Club members were masters of personal compartmentalization. At home, these powerful, respected leaders were active in local politics and charitable causes. They prided themselves on being supportive, loving husbands and caring fathers. They were men of trust and responsibility.

Away from home, however, they were accustomed to "relieving" some of the pressures of their demanding lives. The males-only club indulged themselves with the attentions of their personal secretaries, mistresses, or the fetching local female "cousins" who were frequently present during the less formal parts of the gatherings. Excessive drinking and unexplained absences were never questioned.

The time for talking had passed. Existing government contracts would soon reach maturity, and other contracts were being canceled on a somewhat regular basis. The need for restoring government military spending was fast approaching.

Within an hour, the line of chauffeur-driven limousines was transporting Manuel's guests to Acapulco's Villa Verra, the long-recognized exclusive resort hotel of choice for Hollywood's film colony. Perched high on a hill overlooking Acapulco and its crescent-shaped turquoise bay, Villa Verra enjoyed a fine reputation for luxury. High-profile patrons gushed about the elaborate tropical character of its rooms, the excellence of its cuisine, and the privacy it afforded celebrity guests.

On any given night, the menu, printed daily, featured the finest local seafood, wild quail, and gourmet French and Italian dishes. The six-page leather-encased wine list featured the finest vintages from each of the selected appellations in Italy, Germany, and France. A knowledgeable sommelier stood by to help guests with any unfamiliar selections.

Despite the seriousness of this meeting, Jordan knew that the first night's dinner needed to be a relaxed, friendly gathering. By early evening, voices and laughter filled the main dining room of the villa's restaurant. Accustomed to Mexico's custom of long cocktail hours and late-night eating, Manuel's guests stood in groups of two or three chatting with old friends. Waiters served exotic drinks in large, interestingly shaped glasses; others carried platters of shrimp, caught that same day, and folded minitortillas stuffed with cheese and jalapeños. A local mariachi band stood off to one side, blaring festive music on trumpet, guitar, violin, and a huge and well-worn string bass.

Their appetites whetted and their spirits buoyed, no one objected when the dinner gong was finally sounded. Once they were seated, everyone's attention was drawn to their host, J. Jordan McWilliams, who rose from his seat. "Gentlemen, if the situation weren't so serious, I would not have found it necessary to prevail upon you to join me and your fellow Manuel's Club members on such short notice. It's no secret that my colleagues on Wall Street, as well as most of us in this room, are convinced that the cancellation and expiration of so many government contracts could materially affect your ability to maintain current levels of employment and purchase of products and services. Over the next 3 days, my colleagues and I plan to present a three-part plan for you to consider, discuss, and, I sincerely hope, to approve. It's one that we think could encourage our government to renew military contracting well into the foreseeable future."

"And exactly how do you intend to do that?" one of the well-oiled guests asked. His tone was sarcastic, his voice slurred.

Unfazed, Jordan responded with vigor, "We are planning to scare the living hell out of the American public over the threat of spreading Communism. At the same time, we are going to introduce a national publicity campaign designed to convince them that improved military preparedness is our best defense! And, we will be electing a candidate to Congress who will decide close votes in our favor."

His words hung in the silent room. "But I'm getting ahead of myself here," he said. "I have been told the management has gone to a great deal of trouble to prepare a marvelous meal. Let's relax and enjoy the evening. We will have ample opportunity during the next 3 days for discussion. Bon appétit!"

* * *

T HE NEXT MORNING, THE VISITING EXECUTIVES AWOKE TO BRIGHT sunlight on their balconies. Cool ocean breezes and the smell of hot coffee and frying bacon permeated their elegant open-air suites. One by one, they struggled out of bed and into hot showers. They shaved, slipped into tropically patterned sport shirts, white linen Bermuda shorts, and sandals before making their way down to the poolside veranda where breakfast was being served.

At precisely nine o'clock, J. Jordan McWilliams opened the meeting. "Considering how long some of you stayed at the bar last night, I'd say you all look rather presentable!"

Pleased with the men's laughter, he continued. "I might add, however, that if people back home could see these outrageous shirts and all these pale, hairy legs, they'd never recognize you for the all-powerful executives they know you to be. Just take a look at Peter, standing over there by the pool; his white legs look like two white out-of-bounds stakes!" That drew an even bigger laugh.

"Okay, gentlemen, enough levity. Let's get down to business! As I'm sure you all know by now, we're here to talk about one thing: how to persuade the government that our country needs to adopt a more aggressive military posture if it is to protect itself from the spreading threat of Communism. Our work starts with encouraging the American public to support the rearming of America. This will not be an easy task. Poll after poll indicates that a significant majority of American voters believe we have fought our last Great War. Our most loyal congressmen are convinced that without a material change in public opinion, the introduction of a more aggressive military budget would prove fruitless."

"Jordan, I don't want to appear negative," an automobile executive from Detroit said, "but nearly every major economy besides ours has been severely wounded. Does any country, even Russia, really pose a threat credible enough to encourage such a drastic change in public attitudes?"

"I've been hoping someone would ask that particular question," Jordan said. "We may have won the war, but we have to still prove we can manage the peace. The severe damage so many economies have absorbed suggests that regional governments' efforts must be focused on solving more immediate local problems required to feed and employ their people. Unless solutions are found for these problems and hope is quickly restored, redeveloping economies will remain vulnerable to external threats.

"Meanwhile, a well-equipped victorious Russian army remains in Berlin, the back door to a deeply wounded Western Europe and a front door to Eastern European countries. The United States is the only viable remaining source of opposition to prevent an ambitious Soviet government from expanding its sphere of influence.

"Our best information suggests the Russians are developing their own atomic weapons, and they are reverse engineering American B-29 bombers capable of delivering atomic payloads across oceans and attacking America.

"As long as the probabilities of intercontinental atomic warfare exist, we have convinced ourselves that it should be possible to persuade the American public of the importance of a major increase in military spending. No matter how remote the possibility may be, it's our job to further convince them that it represents a risk we aren't prepared to accept."

"Are you suggesting, Jordan," the automobile executive said, "should we accept the foundation of your entire plan, we will be able to modify public attitudes, pack Congress with a sufficient number of members loyal to our cause, and introduce and pass needed legislation required to raise military procurement spending levels?"

Smiling, the cagey veteran Wall Street attorney answered, "I guess that pretty well sums it up. There's nothing like a good dose of preventive medicine to cure what doesn't ail you!"

The audience, unprepared for such a flip answer to such a penetrative question, carefully reflected on the implications of what they had just heard.

McWilliams broke the silence. "Fortunately, gentlemen, we have a special guest who has come to Acapulco prepared to address this particular problem. He is California's freshman congressman, the Honorable Richard Allen Bailey. You may have heard of Dick. In college, he was an all-American quarterback at USC. He is a graduate of Loyola Law School and a member of the California bar. Since his discharge from the army, the well-decorated war hero has become a practicing member of Bean & Bean, a highly respected Southern California law firm that specializes in all things political. Dick is also a highly decorated war veteran. While he was stationed in England—and for reasons he refuses to reveal—he gave up his cushy, safe position in the

Judge Advocate General's Corps and asked to be assigned to the infantry. According to our review of his war record, Dick volunteered for the most dangerous assignments, beginning with his landing on Normandy, France's Omaha Beach. He also served in Patton's Third Army as it made its way to Berlin.

"Shortly after his return, working at Bean & Bean, his father-in-law's law firm, Dick began to exhibit a strong interest in the political side of the practice. Despite his fashioning an outstanding record as a political lobbyist, Dick realized he both needed and wanted to be more engaged in the political process than his current position allowed. Approaching Southern California's Republican Committee, he inquired about the feasibility of his running for the vacant congressional seat. Thoroughly vetted, he became the committee's unanimous choice. With the support of his father-in-law, Bean & Bean, and their conservative friends in Southern California, Dick was elected as his district's representative to Congress. More recently, he has been appointed to the House Un-American Activities Committee.

"In the coming days and weeks," Jordan continued, "you'll be hearing a great deal about Dick and this committee. They will be conducting hearings into the subversive Communist activities of certain members of the State Department, government officials, higher-ranking military officers, and high-profile Hollywood film producers, writers, and actors. We anticipate that the committee's investigations will create an enormous amount of publicity, fan the public's fear of Communism, and make people more aware of anything else they see or read related to the spreading threat of Communism."

Jordan paused as he noticed the highly respected aircraft manufacturer from Seattle rising to his feet. "Jordan," the man said, "before you bring Mr. Bailey out here, perhaps you wouldn't mind if we asked a few questions of our own."

Jordan, anticipating the question, said, "Of course not, fire away."

"That is one hell of an ambitious program you just described. How confident are you of Bailey's ability to complete the task, particularly if the going gets tough? He's young and inexperienced. He may be a decorated war veteran, but what about his legal skills? From what I've heard from opposing counsel, he doesn't seem too concerned about the accuracy of the accusations he enjoys making. Clearly, he depends on the fear created by intimidation to win cases. Is he really someone with whom we want to be associated?"

Jordan smiled. "You've heard right. Mr. Bailey isn't known for establishing rock-solid foundations for his accusations. He prefers to rely on his use of intimidating courtroom tactics."

"Perhaps I'm confused," began the tool manufacturer from Oklahoma City, "but how in a high-profile arena like a congressional hearing can a young and inexperienced attorney expect to succeed by relying on his use of intimidating tactics?"

"Good question!" Jordan responded. "Our review of prior questioning of witnesses has revealed that they are not confident or well prepared. They wish to avoid any possible confrontation and exposure to contempt of congressional citations. Bailey's intimidating practices may be perfectly suited for his new role."

"It's been reported Bailey has never seemed too concerned about personal values or ethics," the tool manufacturer said. "He just wants to win."

Jordan smiled and nodded. "I commend you on the accuracy of your homework. We are convinced as long as Bailey is convinced that his political future depends on continued support of party leaders, he can be controlled. Let me assure you that he is *precisely* the kind of person we want."

"What about his personal life?" a chemical manufacturer from Delaware asked. "Anybody who is going to be dishing out so much dirt has to be able to withstand the heat in the kitchen. Does he have a drinking problem or gambling habits? Does he have an eye for the ladies?"

"More good questions," said Jordan. "When his friends were questioned, almost to a person they admitted they were never quite sure if Dick earned his nickname, 'Slick,' for his skills on the football field or his ability to bed beautiful, rich women or his adeptness at talking his way out of trouble. The one thing they all agreed on was his demonstrated fondness for a good time, which generally included liquor and adoring women. That said, I don't think we have to worry; these indiscretions appear to have been confined to his behavior before the war and before he was married.

"From what we have been able to learn, something happened during the war to radically change him. I personally spoke with his father-in-law, the managing partner of Bean & Bean, and he told me Dick returned from war a far more serious man who's devoted to his family and the practice of law. He also told me he had every reason to believe that it's a sensible proposition for us to believe we can depend on Dick."

Jordan scanned the group of men. No one stood to speak. "If I've adequately addressed—and allayed—your concerns, gentlemen, I'd like to ask Mr. Bailey to join us. Once you hear him talk and answer your questions, you should be able to judge for yourselves."

Jordan excused himself from the veranda and reappeared shortly thereafter. "Gentlemen, may I present the Honorable Richard Allen Bailey."

After waiting for the polite applause to subside, Dick Bailey took the podium, and with an air of command, said, "Gentlemen, thank you for inviting me to speak. I'm deeply honored to stand before a group of such powerful leaders. I'm also honored to be speaking to you about such a serious matter.

"As my friend Jordan has no doubt told you, the House Un-American Activities Committee has faced some pretty evil foes and achieved an admirable track record. Originally organized back in the thirties, the committee started looking into reported subversive acts of Nazi agents and certain activities of the Ku Klux Klan. During the war years, the committee lay dormant. It has been recently reactivated and is already busy working to investigate the activities of Americans suspected of having subversive affiliations with the Communist Party or the Soviet Union."

"Excuse me for interrupting," said the chemical executive. "How will you identify your prospective witnesses? How well founded are the charges you expect to make?"

"Our investigators, along with agents of the FBI, will be questioning prospective witnesses. Targeted people will be given the choice of either signing specially prepared affidavits or appearing before the committee. I have been told that in the past, most witnesses subpoenaed to testify in person chose to sign the affidavits, even if they didn't believe all of the content was accurate. With regard to the evidence we will be using, we will be relying on material provided by the FBI and the information extracted from the signed affidavits."

A raised and waving hand in the back caused Bailey to stop. He nodded toward the man, the steelmaker from Pittsburgh.

"Excuse me, Congressman," he said. "To what standards of law are those affidavits, and the evidence you present, expected to comply?"

"Sir, you are thinking in terms of a court of law. We're talking about congressional committee hearings, organized for the purpose of gathering information. Since none of the witnesses will have been charged with a crime, nothing compels the committee to follow the rules of evidence. If I might add, should the witness refuse to testify, invoking his First or Fifth Amendment rights, he will be informed that the exercise of those rights is specifically reserved for those who have been charged with a crime."

The steelmaker frowned. "Congressman, it sounds very much like you're suggesting that people come before the court of public opinion and be expected to answer questions that could incriminate them or their friends. Aren't you concerned about what the public will say? What could happen if the public becomes concerned about the possible infringement of their civil rights? Might a groundswell of negative opinion prevent the achievement of our objectives?"

Bailey laughed. "By the time we finish questioning the witnesses, it will be too late. The threat of Communism will seem too real, and the witnesses will have already been convicted, if only in the, as you put it, 'court of public opinion.' Witnesses refusing to cooperate will be charged with contempt of Congress and held over for trial."

The faces in Bailey's audience registered shock, and there were a few seconds of silence before another executive spoke up.

"If you are going to interfere with people's lives, how are you planning to distinguish between the people with a purely intellectual interest in the politics and economics of Communism and, for example, a secret agent of the Russian government?"

"We don't plan to make that distinction," Bailey responded. "By the time we get through, we hope to convince the American public that improved military preparedness is our best and possibly our only course of defense against the growing threat."

* * *

LATER THAT SAME AFTERNOON, THE FRESHMAN CONGRESSMAN WAS comfortably settled into his first-class seat on a plane flying back to Los Angeles. He leaned back and waited for takeoff.

Once they were airborne, he allowed himself to take his first deep breath, relax, and reflect on the meeting. *I wonder how the rest of the world would react were it to find out some of America's most powerful industrial executives had convened in Acapulco for the purpose of approving and funding a plan designed to compromise the integrity of the U.S. congressional appropriations process.*

* * *

AFTER REMOVING HIS SHOES, HE LEANED BACK IN HIS RECLINING SEAT and began to think about the possible implications of the secret meeting. *That's a dangerous game they are planning. By including me, have they extended their exposure . . . or have they just provided me with my just-in-case-get-out-of-jail-free card?*

CHAPTER 2

Mike Stone &
Jacques Roth

The regularly scheduled board of directors of Stone City Bank required Cece-lia and Mike to return in time for Mike, the bank's executive vice chairman, to be in attendance. The meeting had already started and was well underway when unexpectedly, the big, heavy wooden door of the executive conference room slowly swung open. Mike's secretary, trying to remain as unobtrusive as possible, walked down the far length of the room, passing behind the padded leather chairs with the brass grommet edging where directors were sitting, to the far end of the highly polished, very old conference table where Mike was sitting.

* * *

Joe Wright, one of the senior directors, who was in the middle of attempting to make what he considered an important point, was notice-ably annoyed by her unexpected intrusion. However, along with the other directors, Director Wright was curious. *What could be of such importance to warrant such an unexpected interruption? Has some emergency occurred with one of his family members?*

* * *

IT WAS A BRIEF NOTE THAT READ: *IMPERATIVE WE TALK AT YOUR EARLI-EST opportunity. We are in possession of new information strongly suggesting a highly threatening new Power-Cycle type problem may be about to appear.*
    Jacques.

* * *

NOTICING MIKE'S REACTION, DIRECTOR WRIGHT INTERRUPTED WHAT he was saying to ask, "Mike, would you prefer to adjourn and reconvene at a later time?"

Mike shoved the note into his pocket as he stood to speak. "No, I don't think that will be necessary. If you wouldn't object, however, why don't we take a short break while I attend to what appears to an urgent situation."

* * *

AFTER EXITING THE CONFERENCE ROOM, WALKING DOWN THE WIDE corridor that led to the offices of the bank's most senior executive offices, he entered his office located on the southeast corner of the building. After crossing the large office, he plunked himself down in his big leather executive chair, located behind the big mahogany desk in the far corner. Pausing to collect his thoughts, an extremely curious Mike picked up the receiver of the transatlantic telephone and politely informed the overseas operator he was ready to accept the call.

Mike's mind was racing as he waited for Jacques to come on the line. *It has been less than 5 years since the six of us decided to oppose the efforts of German industrialists to smuggle their "fortunes of war" out of Germany. During that time, we have already dealt with two Power Cycles. Now, Jacques is waiting to explain why we may be faced with a third threat. Could it be what we thought were merely isolated efforts to abuse the privileges of "Free Enterprise" are becoming part of a continuous process?*

After a series of clicks and scratches, the strong, deep, heavily accented French voice of Jacques could be clearly heard. Jacques thanked Mike for taking his call and immediately began to explain the urgency of the call. "Mike, have you heard anything strange or unusual about a secret plan to escalate the rearming of the American military?"

Not waiting for an answer, he continued. "Mike, do you remember meeting Mary Wheeler Clarke?" he asked. "She attended one of the parties Claudine and I had in our New York apartment just before we returned to Geneva. She is the woman who worked for the OSS for 7 years in Bern, Switzerland, before and during the Second World War. It was her work that provided her with the opportunity to meet Henri when he was serving as the head of the French Resistance in Switzerland. Apparently, they had reason to work together on a highly interdependent basis for several years. In the process, it was only natural that she and Claudine would become friendly. On more than one occasion, Claudine would tell me how reliable Henri regarded Mary's work and her instinct to sense what might be happening well before it actually occurred.

"Following the conclusion of the war, after her longtime boss was reassigned to Washington to help with the conversion of the OSS into what we now refer to as the CIA, she returned to New York and is teaching at NYU, lecturing, and when time allows, is working on writing a book about her World War II experiences.

"Mary, for some time, over the course of several conversations with Henri, has reported receiving invitations from a number of her former military associates. They all want to talk to her about a secret military-industrial plan that may be in the works to accelerate the American postwar rearmament. The people supposedly involved in this plan are the chief executive officers of prime military contractors who would be the principal beneficiaries of the increased military contracting."

Biting his lip, Mike hesitantly asked, "And why do you think the restoration of military spending might represent a new 'Power-Cycle' type threat?"

"It's not the proposed increase that concerns us. From what little we have been able to learn, it's the way they are going about it that has us so upset. There are rumors floating around about a series of supposedly secret meetings that have been convened over the last 2 years. According to the reports, these meetings have been organized for the purpose of developing some kind of a plan to accelerate increases in government defense spending. These executives and their investment bankers have convinced themselves the revival of Defense spending is necessary to cushion the transition of the American industrial complex from a wartime posture to a peacetime footing."

Quick to respond, Mike said, "From what I have been hearing, they have good reason to be concerned."

"Mike, it's not those meetings that have us concerned. Mary has recently received information suggesting there is a secret gathering of corporate executives currently taking place in Acapulco. The purpose of the gathering is to approve a three-part plan, and the funding of an offshore industrial-military war chest needed to support the implementation of their plan.

"Our concern runs deeper than the possible implications of their secret plan. We think it may be possible their plan calls for the coordination of corporate resources, cooperation of government, and Wall Street—all the essential ingredients of a 'Power-Cycle' type threat. The details are still hazy, but based on Mary's information, it doesn't look like the proposed rearmament has anything to do with responding to some new foreign threat—plain and simple. We think these industrialists are attempting to take advantage of the possible threat of spreading Communism to advance their own self-interests.

* * *

"THERE IS ONE OTHER SITUATION THAT COULD OCCUR THAT HAS US even more concerned. There are many Europeans who are worried about the possibility should America decide to initiate a new round of rearmament. It could alarm the Russians and cause them to react accordingly. If the two countries, Russia and the United States, were to become involved in a reciprocal military spending conflict, the offered generosity of the American people needed to rebuild the war-torn economies of Europe and Asia could be interrupted or substantially reduced."

"Jacques, are you basing your concerns on anything other than what Mary has related to Henri?"

"Well, it's true she's our main source of intelligence, but Henri is convinced when Mary Clarke thinks we may have a problem, the probabilities are very high that we have a problem."

After thinking for a moment, Mike asked, "Did Mary mention any specific names?"

"Only one. Supposedly the group has retained J. Jordan McWilliams of the New York Wall Street law firm of Southwick and Cornforth as a sort of advisor-leader."

"I can understand the urgency. McWilliams has no shortage of government relationships. How long has it been since he coupled American companies and members of New York's investment community to participate in the prewar organization of German cartels? Could it be that we are talking about the same man, the same story, but different players?

"Jacques, do you realize we are talking about challenging what has to be the country's largest and most powerful combination of industrial corporations? Are you sure that is something we should attempt?"

"Mike, challenging seven oil companies may have appeared impossible, and maybe we got lucky. Opposing an industrial network capable of supplying a multifront war on three continents could be entirely different. All I am suggesting is that you make a few calls, and then we will talk again."

* * *

MIKE, STILL SITTING IN HIS HEAVY LEATHER CHAIR, WAS STARING OUT at the city whose lights were starting to appear. On a normal day, he would have enjoyed watching the spectacular view transition from day to night, but he was too preoccupied to appreciate what he was seeing. He had the sick feeling that Jacques's concerns might be true.

CHAPTER 3

Richard Allen Bailey

Los Angeles, California, February 1948

As soon as the plane reached its cruising altitude and leveled off, the charming young stewardess began to take drink orders. Admiring her slim, tight figure as she moved on, he thought, *I love it when people recognize me. The life of a congressman may have its limitations, but I certainly seem to enjoy the notoriety.*

* * *

Savoring his first drink, Bailey began to reflect on this past morning's meeting. *Pleasing this group of corporate executives can't be the dumbest thing in the world I have ever done . . . How many congressmen, particularly ones early in their career, have the opportunity to meet these men who are considered to be the true "Voices Behind the Curtain," much less, to have the opportunity to win their approval and support? Who knows where all this could lead.*

* * *

After ordering his second drink, he began to speculate, *I wonder how long it took, after I departed, for them to get around to discussing my personal life. I would hope any suspicion about the true basis of my marriage would have long been forgotten. If they knew or suspected anything about my tattered past, why would they have supported my candidacy for Congress? Hopefully, all my past indiscretions are behind me, and I am free to concentrate on my political career.*

* * *

Deeply etched in his mind were the events of 3 years ago when he returned home from the war. *No one has questioned the problems regarding Barbara's and my marriage. If they knew or suspected anything about our strange arrangement, I would have to believe someone would have mentioned it by now.*

* * *

Sometimes, I wonder why I wasn't more surprised when I received *a letter in England from one of my old friends and teammates reporting Barbara was openly conducting an affair with an old friend of hers. Being so strong willed and so committed to pursuing our individual interests, I couldn't remember her objecting to the long hours and my abstraction with the early stages of my law career. I don't recall paying any particular notice to how much time she was devoting to playing tennis, playing bridge with some of her Kappa-Kappa-Gama friends from college, and showing me off at the Friday night dinners at the Los Angeles Country Club. Somewhere along the way, we must have lost interest in each other.*

* * *

I wonder if I will ever really understand if my deciding to *enlist in the army didn't represent the path of least resistance that would allow me to remove myself from an impersonal marriage. Rather than react, from 7,000 miles away, I decided to leave the entire matter alone, at least until I could return home and judge for myself what had really happened.*

* * *

Expecting to see Barbara waiting when I disembarked from *the train in Los Angeles's Union Station, I was surprised to see my father-in-law patiently standing on the crowded platform, one car up. Why would he come to greet me? Outside the office, as long as I showed up for our Saturday morning golf games, I sometimes wondered if he really approved of me and wanted to spend as little time with me as possible.*

* * *

N OT KNOWING WHAT TO EXPECT, *I WAS SURPRISED WHEN HE SHOOK my hand and proceeded to engage me in a strong hug and whispered in my ear, "Welcome home, son. The ladies are waiting at home, excited to welcome you back. It's been a long time."*

* * *

M Y INTUITIVE SUSPICION THAT SOMETHING MUST BE VERY WRONG *was confirmed when he turned right on Wilshire and headed downtown in the opposite direction from where we lived. He then announced, "I've made reservations at Brown Derby."*

* * *

W E WERE SEATED AT HIS REGULAR TABLE, THE FIRST DRINK HAD BEEN *barely served, when he said, "You may need that drink after you hear what I have to say. Barbara is 3 months pregnant. As strange as it seems, she claims she still is in love with you, and has asked me to try to find some way of convincing you to remain married and agree to raise the child as if it were your own. She doesn't know what to say or how to face you. She has asked her* old man *to do the dirty work."*

As braced as he was for talk of infidelity, Dick was caught completely by surprise. Taking a minute to collect his thoughts, he decided to wait before saying anything. Almost immediately, his father-in-law continued.

"Dick, you have a brilliant political career waiting for you. With the support of my friends, me, and the clients of our law firm, you could become the man that we have been waiting for to represent our interests inside the government at the state level, and someday, possibly, at the national level. We have the wealth and influence to help you make it happen. All you have to do is remain married

to my daughter and stay out of trouble. Perhaps I need to be more specific. I am prepared to place $5 million into a trust account in your name that will mature in 10 years, providing you and Barbara are still married and you have avoided embarrassing her, your family, or any of the people who have faithfully supported you. After that, you are free to do as you wish. Obviously, this arrangement has to remain secret. Not a word to my daughter—not to anyone. Any hint of our arrangement would destroy her, your career, and your $5 million."

* * *

Sᴛᴜɴɴᴇᴅ, ɴᴏᴛ ᴏɴʟʏ ʙʏ ᴛʜᴇ ɴᴇᴡ ɪɴғᴏʀᴍᴀᴛɪᴏɴ, ʙᴜᴛ ʙʏ ᴛʜᴇ ᴀᴜᴅᴀᴄɪᴛʏ of his father-in-law's proposal, Dick couldn't help but think, *Am I being asked to commit myself to a marriage, to a child, and being an obedient servant of the "Voices Behind the Curtain"? Dick, ole buddy, you better think fast. You are being given a choice. You can walk away, use your military savings to help start that new law firm you and your friends have spent so much time discussing, and be free to pursue a new way of life. Or, you can accept his offer of financial independence, making a family happy, and enjoy the opportunity to pursue a high-profile political career. Talk about selling your soul to the devil . . .*

When his thoughts were disturbed by the sound of lowering flaps and descending landing gear, he shifted his thinking back to the present. *Today has been a pretty good day. I wonder if the day will ever come when I regret my decision.*

CHAPTER 4

Movie Night

ACAPULCO, FEBRUARY 1948

The 3 days of meetings passed quickly. J. Jordan McWilliams made his case, and as the end of the retreat neared, even the most cynical of the executives had to admit that if they put their collective effort behind his imaginative plan, they might have a chance at revving up the American war machine. One thing was certain: this plan allowed them to accomplish together far more than they could accomplish individually.

On the afternoon of their last day together, Jordan stood before the assembled executives, his hands resting easily on the podium. "My friends, over the last 3 days, we have attempted to convince you of the importance of our fanning the public's fear of spreading Russian Communism to modify public attitudes about the need to restore America's military preparedness. We've also discussed the necessity of us adjusting the membership of Congress to better support the programs we will be introducing. And, last, we will introduce an intense public relations plan together with a more aggressive Washington-style lobbying program to ensure the introduction and passage of the new legislation needed to increase the levels of Department of Defense appropriations.

"Gentlemen, now that you have had the opportunity to digest our three-part strategy, it is my hope that you all agree it presents a realistic plan for preserving and enhancing the profit potential of each of your companies.

"Tonight, you'll each be handed two envelopes before you leave—a tradition that is familiar to all of you. One envelope contains the distributions from your previous investments in Señor Arena's production; the other, a request for a contribution to his next film. You will observe that these requests are substantially greater than the prior year's requirement. This time, we're asking you to help fund not just Manuel's next film but also the war chest that will support our upcoming campaign. It will be kept here in Mexico, under Manuel's care, to be used as we direct." A low murmur of approval rose from the group.

"And now, on a more casual note," Jordan said, his voice lighter and seemingly more amusing, "I am told that Manuel has planned something extra special for your evening's enjoyment. Tonight, if you make your way to the hotel front lobby, we will have limousines waiting to take each of you to Señor Arena's spectacular seaside home. Tonight, my friends, is Movie Night at Manuel's!"

* * *

ONE BY ONE, THE LIMOUSINES CARRYING EACH OF THE EXECUTIVES pulled to a stop under the canopied porte cochere marking the front entrance of Señor Arena's majestic beach house. As each guest stepped from his limousine, he was greeted by Señor Arena, J. Jordan McWilliams, and the gorgeous Mercedes Cardona Velasquez, the celebrated former winner of the Miss Universe contest.

For days, photographs of Mercedes had been filling the Mexican newspapers, magazines, and posters, promoting the release of her forthcoming film. None of these images truly captured the beauty of this striking, sensuous woman. Mercedes was an imposing figure, seeming much taller than her 5 feet 10 inches. She wore 3-inch high heels. Her jet-black hair was curled into a glossy French twist arranged on the top of her head. Beautifully arched eyebrows and high cheekbones framed her wide green eyes. Her aquiline nose and strong chin perfectly complemented her broad jawline, her wide mouth, and full lips. Her flawless facial beauty was further enhanced by her buxom figure, broad hips, and long legs. Mercedes could always count on being the center of attention.

This evening, she was exquisitely dressed and lavishly bejeweled. She looked stunning, and her artfully applied makeup gave her an unusual, almost catlike appearance.

Mercedes stood between the two cohosts as they greeted the arriving guests. She had studied the name and background of each of the executives.

After shaking each man's hand, she asked a knowledgeable question about his work, company, or about the generosity of his latest charitable gift. Flattered by the attention of this radiant, celebrated, and remarkably beautiful woman, the guest would only offer modest resistance as Mercedes offered to introduce him to his personal dinner hostess for the evening.

The dinner hostesses, all of them young actresses from Señor Arena's movie studio, were a longstanding feature of Manuel's "Movie Night." Most of them were, like Mercedes, models and former beauty pageant contestants, recruited from all over the world. Many of them had also signed modeling contracts requiring them to travel, wear the clothes of the world's top couturiers, and meet department store owners, successful businessmen, and the sons and fathers of prominent families.

Conscious of the reality that each year there would be a fresh new crop of beauty contestants waiting to replace them, many of these dinner hostesses relished the chance to meet the wealthy men and make the kind of arrangements that might preclude their returning to the far less glamorous homes from which they had tried so hard to escape.

* * *

EARLIER IN THE DAY, EACH OF THE BEAUTIFUL HOSTESSES HAD BEEN instructed in ways to engage her dinner companion in conversation. Given the opportunity, she would ask questions about his life, his work, or his special interests. Only if there was a lull in the conversation was she to talk about her own life or tell stories, real or imagined, about her world of beauty contests, modeling, and moviemaking.

The night would technically end after dinner and the screening of Manuel's latest movie. Arrangements for further entertainment, though strictly optional, were encouraged.

Three hours after everyone had arrived, the meticulously planned seven-course dinner was drawing to a close. As the waitstaff milled about picking up the dessert dishes, the hostesses took turns walking over to Manuel's Cognac bar, selecting a bell-shaped crystal snifter, and filling it with a generous portion of their host's best vintage Napoleon Cognac. Each woman would then proceed to hold the filled snifter over the flame of a candle, slowly rotating it until the glass and its contents were properly warmed, before handing it to her dinner partner.

The Cognac served, the hostess would retrieve one of the elegantly carved wooden humidors. Each was filled with a fine collection of Cuban cigars. Opening it, she would present the contents to her guest for inspection. The guest would carefully study the assortment, make his selection, and then test its aroma with a sniff, before raising it to his ear and rotating it between his thumb and forefinger, listening for signs of proper age and curing. When he'd made his selection, his hostess would skillfully clip off the end of the cigar, gently lick the outside surface, place it in her mouth, and, with the aid of a very long wooden match, proceed to light it before handing it to her host . . .

When the last cigars were lit, Manuel asked his guests to join him in the screening room. The men and their companions obligingly filed out of the dining area, down an elegant hall, and into their host's luxurious home theater, where a wide screen was suspended from the room's lofty ceiling. As they settled into the comfort of the large, overstuffed chairs, the men, each with a young beauty seated beside him, were enjoying themselves. Their good mood permeated the room.

In just a few minutes, they would finally see Manuel's latest, soon-to-be-released movie, the one they had generously invested in on their previous visit. Even better, this one featured the gorgeous Mercedes Cardona Velasquez, who now sat in their midst.

As they watched the first scenes of the film, the men struggled to make the connection between the elegantly dressed feline beauty seated near them and the sprightly, casual young woman on the screen. Dressed in the briefest of shorts and a thin cotton blouse, the movie version of Mercedes could be seen straining to lift herself out of the sea and into a small fishing boat. The laughter and snide comments clearly indicated the male members of the audience were enjoying what they were witnessing. Their enjoyment was not shared by the disappointed and embarrassed main attraction of the evening, however.

Once the screen flashed white, each of the dinner hostesses began to pass out the anticipated envelopes, two per guest. Meanwhile, Manuel stepped up in front of the glowing screen to announce, "My friends, I sincerely hope you enjoyed our latest work. Without your generous contributions, the making of this film would not have been possible."

A single clap triggered light applause, which grew in intensity when he motioned toward Mercedes and added, "You are all invited to remain. Talk to your hostess, talk to Mercedes, or listen to more mariachi music and take advantage of the open bar."

Few took him up on the offer. One by one, the executives thanked their three hosts—Manuel, Jordan, and Mercedes—for an extraordinary 3 days and, with feigned yawns, asked to be excused.

As each guest entered the portico holding the arm of his dinner hostess, he signaled to the valet: one finger indicated that only the limousine would be needed; two fingers indicated he would need a taxi to return his hostess to her home.

* * *

As the party began to thin out, Mercedes found herself sitting at a small table near the bar. She was accompanied by Manuel and Jordan. She was not impressed. Midway through the evening, she was beginning to comprehend the true meaning of what Manuel had really been proposing when he offered her the opportunity to become a serious dramatic actress. Clearly, any opportunity to appear before the camera had turned into the cheapening exploitation of her physical beauty. *So this is what is truly meant to be under contract to Arena Studios. Is spending the rest of the evening with the great lawyer from Wall Street also expected of me?*

Manuel kept getting pulled away—by departing guests, by house staff, or by vendors politely seeking payment. Jordan didn't waste any time in capitalizing on his absences. Leaning in close to Mercedes, he attempted to capture her attention by sharing some of the most impressive details about a few of the more fascinating people he'd met along the way.

His tactic was working. Mercedes found herself becoming captivated by his stories.

* * *

Her anger at Manuel was beginning to fade. Clearly, she was impressed by Jordan's worldliness and his attempt to fill in the details of his dealings with world leaders, powerful bankers, and corporate magnates. The more he spoke, the more approachable he made these luminaries seem. He was humanizing people she only knew from accounts in the newspapers and the weekly "Movietone" newsreels. Fascinated by the unusual nature of his stories, she began to ask a steady stream of questions.

Jordan was similarly impressed. He was beginning to see past her beauty to recognize the sensitive, inquisitive, intelligent, and kind young woman who lay behind her outer shield of glamour.

Each time Manuel reappeared at the table, Jordan stopped talking, leaned back in his chair, crossed his arms, and, not so convincingly, attempted to mask his annoyance at the interruption.

Unaware of what had been happening during his absence, Manuel's mind was clearly focused on accessing the success of the evening. "What do you think?" he asked. "Did everyone enjoy themselves? What do we have to do next?"

"Not much," Jordan said, his tone clipped. "I'd say your work is done, and my work is just beginning. To a man, they approved our plan. They funded our war chest, and everyone left feeling more closely bonded together in a common effort."

Manuel smiled as he finished the last of his snifter. *To a man, they approved our plan. They funded our war chest, and everyone left feeling an even greater sense of personal bonding. How could things have gone any better?*

Secretly, he was smiling at the thought of how much more compromising the film shot that night might become once it was safely stored in his secret safe. Rising from his chair, Manuel said, "Jordan, Mercedes, if you'll excuse me, there still are some duties requiring my attention."

Mercedes was suddenly conscious of being left alone with Jordan. Her attention was only half-focused on Jordan's telling of his next interesting stories. The other half was busy analyzing her different options. *Ole girl, this isn't the first tight spot you have found yourself. It might be a good idea if you think carefully about what you should do next. Whatever you decide could change your life!*

Oh, what the hell. This is not the first time or probably the last time you'll find yourself in this position. Why not wait one day, before making what could be a life-altering decision?

Having made up her mind, she gradually began to relax and refocus her complete attention on the nice-looking and handsome man in a refined sort of way. *Behind his gusto and sense of self-importance, he seems to be a sensitive, thoughtful, and a very lonely man.*

CHAPTER 5

Mary Wheeler Clarke

On the following day, at 7:00 p.m. sharp, the bell rang in Cecelia and Mike's thirteenth-floor Upper Eastside cooperative apartment. They stepped into the hallway just outside their residence in anticipation of greeting the highly regarded former OSS administrator. Moments later, the elevator doors opened and out stepped a tall, trim, middle-aged woman with short, curly, graying brown hair and large brown eyes. She had the tall and lithe body of a dancer somewhat softened with age. Dressed in a tailored tweed business suit of earth tones, she projected the image of a smart, professional woman whom you would feel comfortable talking to as if she was an old friend or older sister.

Her eyes twinkled as she extended her hand. "Thank you for your timely invitation. I've been looking forward to seeing you ever since I returned to New York." Handing them a gift-wrapped bottle, she continued, "Here is a small token of my appreciation."

"It's a pleasure to see you again, Mary," Cecelia said as she stepped forward to shake her hand. "Ever since Jacques explained what you have encountered, you can't imagine how excited we are to see our old friend from Switzerland."

Mike, momentarily, chose to stand back and watch as these two remarkably smart and strong willed ladies, with well earned respect for each other, silently accessed each other. The last time they had met, it had been under entirely different circumstances. That was a social occasion; tonight would be devoted to a deadly serious situation.

After waiting for the ladies to finish, Mike stepped forward, and, spreading his arms, engulfed the lady spy in a friendly hug. After disengaging, he said, "Mary, Claudine has described you as a bit of a storyteller. While we appreciate the purpose of the evening must be devoted to talking about serious problems, I hope we will take some time to learn more about your wartime experiences in Bern. How often do you think we have had an opportunity to spend time with someone who had such an interesting window to view the circumstances that led to the start, the conduct, and the conclusion of the war in Europe?"

* * *

AFTER ENTERING THE APARTMENT, MIKE STARTED TO UNWRAP MARY'S gift. "Cecelia, look at this bottle of wine Mary has brought us. It's a 1938 vintage Joseph Drouhin Gevrey-Chambertin, one of France's finest wines from its Bordeaux wine-making appellation. There has only been one other occasion when I have enjoyed the pleasure of this particular wine!"

* * *

MARY AND MIKE WERE SEATED NEAR THE BIG FIREPLACE WHEN Cecelia returned from the kitchen holding a polished silver antique tray that held three generously filled martini glasses. She extended the tray toward Mary.

Mike carefully lifted a second glass from the tray, before offering to take it from Cecelia so she could help herself to the third well frosted glass. As soon as they were all seated in front of the burning fire, in the well screened big fireplace, Mike asked the first question. "How are you finding life in New York?"

"It's funny you would ask," Mary replied. "There's no way the life of a part-time college lecturer and aspiring author can compare with the kind of work or office atmosphere the OSS director and I had grown accustomed to in wartime Bern. Though of late, it seems—with all the calls I have been receiving from some of my old friends—life in New York appears to becoming a bit more interesting."

Mike seized the opportunity to come right to the point. "Why have you chosen to bring what you have been telling Henri to our attention?"

"Well, first and foremost, it's important that you realize I've seen what I suspect may be happening in America take place before. Don't forget I had a ringside seat from which I could watch the German people, in their excitement of witnessing the arrival of the 'new man on horseback,' who never challenged his desire to create an 'Arsenal for Peace.'

"Later, as it became apparent that Hitler was transforming his 'Arsenal for Peace' to an 'Arsenal for War,' I found it particularly interesting when nobody questioned his motives. Even more confusing was the failure of people to question why the historical conservative hierarchy of Germany would choose to support a new reform party of questionable repute.

* * *

"REPORTS DESCRIBING THE INVESTMENT AGREEMENTS BETWEEN automakers, oil and chemical companies, aluminum and steelmakers, shipbuilders, commercial banks, investment banks, and others were constantly crossing my desk. I couldn't believe it as I watched hundreds of military appropriation contracts being offered on a noncompetitively bid basis to the same companies owned by those who had financially supported Hitler and his National Socialist Workers Party rise to power. The German citizens, impressed by the improvement in their economy, never questioned his rhetoric of fear. He was never asked to substantiate his claim that Germany was at risk from France in the West and Russia from the East."

Mike knew the story, but he listened intently, curious to learn more from her perspective. Finally, he asked, "When Hitler's armies invaded the Saar and the Rhineland in 1938, why didn't the French and the British take advantage of their military superiority to dissuade Hitler when they had the opportunity?"

* * *

"GOOD QUESTION. WHO REALLY KNOWS, BUT IF I HAD TO GUESS, IT was in their governments' best interest not to disrupt the economic growth of the transatlantic German cartel arrangements that included substantial

American, British, and French investment sources. Enormous sources of private pressure were being applied to search for peaceful means to resolve the 'German Situation.'

* * *

"WHEN PEOPLE SUCH AS YOURSELVES BEGAN TO QUESTION WHAT was really happening behind the scenes, no one of influence was willing to listen. Even your warnings about the possibility the German industrialists were leading the world to war failed to gain the motivated cooperation of responsible leaders. Now, 8 years later, you and your Sentinel friends have succeeded in opposing two serious threats to the public. You might ask yourselves, who else can we approach that might be capable of opposing what this enormously powerful coalition of prime military-industrial contractors may be planning? I worry we may be watching the self-serving influence of the American military-industrial complex penetrate ever more deeply into the American government. Should they be allowed to accomplish their objective, what do you think their ultimate objective might be?"

Mike and Cecelia sat in silence, awed by the gravity of this sweet, harmless-looking lady's worst fears. "There's certainly ample precedent for what you are suggesting," Mike said. "But as much as we'd like to take advantage of this information you're bringing us, we don't want to put *you* in danger. We don't want to be the cause of destroying confidences your friends have placed in you."

"Not a problem. Not only is most of this data publicly available—if you know where to look—but more importantly, I wouldn't hand over information if I didn't have their permission to share it. It's important for you to understand the sources of this information are, for the most part, distinguished former military leaders who share an uncommon love for their country. It's their concern over the growing influence of the military-industrial complex taking place inside our government that has caused them to come forward."

* * *

OUT OF RESPECT FOR CECELIA'S FINE DINNER, PERFECTLY complemented by Mary's bottle of wine, they talked about everything *but* business. An hour later, the trio pushed back from the table, relaxed, well sated, and anxious to resume their discussion. As the three of them retired to the comforts of the living room and the warming fire, Mike, ever the consummate host, asked, "And, what would you be your choice for an after-dinner drink?"

As Mike busied himself searching through his liquor cabinet, selecting the right kind of glasses and pouring the drinks, Cecelia asked Mary, "Why don't we take advantage of Mike's absence and you tell me more about your personal experiences in Bern. Surviving with two young children, a demanding job, and a tough boss couldn't have been so easy."

"The view from Bern couldn't have been more exciting. By the time I arrived in Bern in 1938," she said, "the city had become one of the few places where agents, military officers, concerned private citizens, and diplomats from friendly and hostile foreign countries could regularly congregate. It was cosmopolitan, it was politically neutral, and it was rapidly becoming a center for European intelligence.

"Almost daily, the director's and my work brought us into contact with an amazing combination of high-ranking Allied military officers, government officials, and case operatives vitally concerned about daily events that appeared to be leading to inevitable military conflict."

"Given the size of your workload at the OSS," Cecelia said, "how did you find time to create and maintain so many interesting relationships? From my own experiences, I've always found these people to be high-powered, high energy, extremely demanding, very skeptical, and terribly overloaded. How was it that they were willing to make the time to talk to you?"

"You're right about the daily press of our workload. I applied myself as best I could. I wanted to become regarded as a timely and accurate research administrator. In no time, I found myself fulfilling the role of the go-to person. Rather than wait for my written reports to make their way through channels, certain higher-level commanders and case officers started dropping by my office to get copies right off the press. These same men would use the opportunity to ask me about any useful information that I might *not* have included in my final report. It didn't take long before interdependent personal bonds of friendship began to develop.

"These same friends who are working in the relative obscurity of highly confidential work environments began to learn of some new secret plan being developed to restore defense spending. Believing the plan was some secret plan that applied only to their company, my friends reported their surprise when they discovered the same subject was being discussed by some of their other friends who worked for other defense companies.

"If it were only one or two projects, they might have written it off as nothing to be concerned about. But after hearing of so many different incidents occurring from so many places, virtually overnight, they were inclined to believe some new master plan must be in the works to accelerate the rearming of the American military."

Mike, his brow furrowed, asked, "If what you suspect is really being planned, documentable information of the actual plan must be well hidden and carefully guarded. Obtaining confirmation might be difficult.

* * *

"WHY DON'T YOU GIVE US A COUPLE WEEKS TO POKE AROUND TO SEE what we can learn? It's getting late. Why don't we plan to reconvene as soon as we have learned something?"

CHAPTER 6

Marco's Notes

To his wife, Anna, Marco Tancredi looked more relaxed than he had in years. He had learned the value of hard work from his Sicilian immigrant parents at a very young age. A proud product of the tough New York City streets, without the benefit of a college education, he had spent much of his life working two jobs: one to help support his father's family and one to support his.

On this particular morning, Marco and Anna were quietly sitting in the sunlit breakfast nook of their new West Side eighth-floor apartment. More than 3 months had passed since escrow had closed on the sale of Marco's owners' garbage collection company, and he had received his very large six-figure management bonus. After a lifetime of living in the brownstone flat in their old family neighborhood that had once been the proud center of Italian heritage, he had decided to purchase a cooperative apartment in a newly completed building bordering the Hudson River.

Always a prolific reader, he was studying the *Wall Street Journal* and enjoying a second cup of coffee when the red phone, the phone that everyone else knew not to answer, started ringing. Setting down his newspaper, he said, "I'll take it in the other room."

The walk to the rear of the apartment gave Marco time to think. He suspected his lines were still tapped, and he hoped whoever was calling knew to be careful about what they said.

A familiar voice said, "Marco, would you mind meeting me for lunch at the same restaurant where we ate at last week, at the same time? We need to talk."

The familiar voice was that of his young partner, the son of an old friend, Armando Camarillo. He was the oldest son of one of the men he first met when they arrived in America. They shared a small one-bedroom apartment, they worked as waiters in the same restaurant, on Sundays they attended church together, and they spent what little spare time they had talking of their dreams of living in America. Two years ago, Marco had innocently asked Armando how his new business was progressing.

Seeing the look of fear, Marco had immediately said, "If it's money you need, I can lend it to you."

"Uncle Marco, it's not a question of money. The business has been profitable almost from the start. When I offered to pay back my 'hard-money' lenders, they said they were entitled to 25 percent ownership in my business! If it were only a question of ownership, I might have agreed to their new request, but there was no way I wanted them as partners, even silent partners."

* * *

THE INTIMIDATING ANTICS OF THAT PARTICULAR LENDER WERE WELL known to Marco and many of the older members of the tight-knit neighborhood. When the lender tried to take advantage of the young, inexperienced, recent college graduate, they had crossed the line of accepted street code conduct.

It hadn't taken the streetwise "Uncle Marco" long to understand what had happened. "Armando, why don't you take that pretty young wife of yours on a vacation and give me a few days to see what I can do about your problem?"

One of the more carefully kept secrets was the arrangement Marco made with Armando's lender. By the time Armando returned, Marco was ready to make him an offer he couldn't refuse. In exchange for his putting up all the money required to pay off the lenders and operate the business, Marco had requested a 50 percent interest in the now debt-free business.

When his friends would ask him why he was willing to use his hard-earned savings to help a friend salvage his business, Marco would answer, "Garbage collection, trash removal . . . What's the difference? They are just different forms of waste management!"

At that time, Marco, still employed full time by the garbage company, was limited to offering his new, young partner the benefit of his experience in the business, introductions to influential people, and, on occasion, morsels of sage advice.

Quickly, building owners and office tenants began to take notice of the new company. New orders flooded in, not just from buildings and tenants in New York City but from other northeastern cities. In a remarkably short time, Marco and Armando were serving the building maintenance needs of tenant and building owners up and down the Northeastern Corridor.

* * *

Marco arrived at the designated restaurant a few minutes early and made his way to his regular table situated in the rear of the restaurant. Sitting with his back to the wall, he was able to watch anyone who entered the restaurant. At exactly on the agreed time of arrival, an obviously excited Armando came striding through the front entrance, a long cardboard tube tucked under his arm.

Marco hardly glanced up as the jet-black curly haired young man walked up to the bartender, engaged him in small talk, and then disappeared into the men's room for the prescribed 5 minutes. If anyone had been following Armando or paying any unusual interest in his arrival, Marco, the bartender, and the men staked out across the street would have had an opportunity to take notice and push the button, activating the yellow warning light.

Watching his young partner emerge from the men's room, Marco was reminded of how much he disliked asking his friends to observe his extraordinary security precautions. He knew, under normal circumstances, as only someone weaned on the streets of New York knew, you couldn't refuse to give the *"men on the arm"* their customary take and hope to survive. Although, the *"Dons"* who were responsible for maintaining peace among the *"connected family businesses"* were aware and supportive of Marco's plan to clean up and sell the borough's family-owned garbage business he had been asked to run, he never understood how far their protection reached.

Armando was speaking as he sat down at Marco's table. "Marco, I have something you need to see." Reaching into the side pocket of his jacket, he pulled out a thick packet of papers and set them on the table. They measured

4-by-6 inches and were embossed with a corporate logo, the name of the company, the name of the executive, and his title. Each of the executive memos was covered with difficult-to-decipher handwriting, some on both sides. Some of the notes had been folded, others crumpled. On each, the name of the caller and the date of the call had been carefully written.

After surveying some of the notes Armando had placed before him, Marco shrugged. "I don't understand. To me, these notes look like so much discarded trash."

Armando smiled. "Do you remember when I told you members of our maintenance crews are in the habit of extracting the discarded executive notes? My guys are always looking for anything they might regard interesting or unusual. During their midnight lunch breaks, for their entertainment, they take turns reading their interpretation of what they regard as some of the more interesting notes. Once read, they are thrown into the incinerator and forgotten.

"Some time ago, they started to collect any of the notes that referred to something called 'Manuel's Club.' Unable to cipher what they were suggesting, they brought the notes to me asking for an interpretation."

"Armando, just what do you think all this trash is telling you?"

Flashing his most mischievous smile, Armando said, "Watch what happens next." After he pulled out the tightly wound roll of butcher paper from the long cardboard tube, he spread it over the unobstructed white linen tablecloth covering the adjacent table. First, he started to explain the grid he had drawn with a blue ink pen. Pointing to the names written across the top of the chart, Armando explained, "Each is the name of the person who received a call. The names written down the left side of the chart are the people who initiated the call. Where the vertical column intersects with the horizontal row, I took the liberty of arranging the notes in chronological order and adding my interpretation of what they were discussing."

"I still don't get it," said Marco. "What is it I'm not seeing?"

"Well, first of all, you must realize these are very powerful executives. Once you analyze all these different conversations, you start to see a lot of crossover and get a picture of what they're doing. They're all part of something called Manuel's Club, and the big topic of conversation is the secret meeting they recently had in Mexico and the Mexican political war chest they helped fund. According to my analysis of the separate pieces of information, I concluded they are hoping to use the funds to finance some kind of a program that will cause the American government to accelerate the rearming of the American military and restore military contracting."

With the benefit of Armando's explanation, Marco leafed through the notes a second time. Finally, he said, "Now, I guess I am beginning to understand. It would appear these notes are describing some kind of multicorporate plan to compromise the authority of the United States government for their own selfish benefit. Do you think anybody but the two of us understands what we have discovered?

"Armando, even if you're only half right, I think we need to call my good friend, Don Cerreta. Don works in the federal prosecutor's office. You have heard me talk of him. He was the man who helped his friends expose some very interesting 'Oil Club' fraudulent business practices. If anybody will understand the implications of your information, it will be Don. He'll know what we should do."

CHAPTER 7

The Mighty Warrior

Life in the Stone household was becoming complicated. For the first time, considerations of health were preventing Mike's wife, Cecelia Chang Stone, from playing an active role in an OSS or Sentinel operation. The stress of the 109-day kidnapping, a 2-month tour of China, Indonesia, and Malaysia, a rare strain of amoebic dysentery, and the exertion required to prevent the Dutch recolonization of Indonesia had taken its toll. There was nothing physically wrong with her, but her nervous system could only tolerate a limited amount of pressure.

Ever since Mike began to suspect the Sentinels may become involved in opposing another effort to abuse the American system of free enterprise, he knew he needed to help his "Mighty Warrior from Hong Kong" to find a less demanding but meaningful role that would keep her challenged.

Mike was pleased when Cecelia enthusiastically approved of his suggestion they spend a week in Carmel, California. The last time they had made this trip together was in 1943. He remembered how concerned he had been over all her unexplained absences in San Francisco and all the late-night phone calls.

One night when they were walking along the beach, she had explained her previous work with the federal government's "Office of Special Services," OSS. She had played an instrumental role in assisting wealthy families remove their wealth in advance of the invasion by the Japanese. Her sharing what must have been highly confidential information with him had broken the growing tension and had helped him to understand how much she cared for him.

* * *

THE TOP WAS DOWN ON THE RENTED RED FORD CONVERTIBLE AS THEY sped south along Highway 101 toward Carmel. The brilliant sun illuminated the lush countryside. The orderly orchards, the long parallel rows of crops that appeared to meet in the distance, the rich, warm, recently tilled soil, the tall groves of eucalyptus trees, and the old red farm buildings, together, created a memorable scene.

It was late in the afternoon when they arrived in Carmel. Mike drove straight down to the foot of Ocean Avenue, parked the car, and beckoned for Cecelia to follow him toward the beach. Like Mike, she slipped off her shoes and hurried after him. Feeling the warmth of the sand on the bottoms of their feet and between their toes, they walked along the water, watching the sun slowly disappear like a big red ball falling into the Pacific Ocean.

When Mike noticed Cecelia was no longer following close behind him, he turned to look for her. She was wandering aimlessly, like someone lost in thought. Changing direction, he caught up to her, put his arms around her, engaging her in a warm, protective hug. He could feel her tiny body beginning to tremble, and the tears of her silent crying ran down his cheek. Concerned, he caressed her tenderly, and in the gathering darkness, he gently lowered her down on the still-warm sand. Content to sit quietly, holding her in his arms, he was experiencing a very unusual moment of intimacy. He patiently waited for her to explain.

* * *

THE COOL EVENING FOG WAS BEGINNING TO ROLL IN OFF THE OCEAN. Finally, he dropped his arms and pulled back from Cecelia before he said, "Wait here. Take my coat while I gather some driftwood and make a fire before I retrieve the blanket and the bottle of wine we left in the car."

The fire Mike built gave off waves of heat. The wine was having its soothing effect. Wrapped in a foglike shroud of quiet, totally separated from the rest of the world with its worries and pressures, they were enjoying the warmth and comfort of each other and the fire.

When the fire began to wane, Mike unwrapped himself from Cecelia. With all possible haste, he began to gather all of the driftwood he was able to spot in the failing light.

He was stacking his last load of wood within easy reach of where they would be sitting when Cecelia said, "I think I'm ready to discuss what's bothering me."

She waited for Mike to position himself back under the blanket, refill his glass, and then said, "If for one minute you expect me to stand aside and watch the rest of you work on the industrial-military complex problem, you don't know me as well as I thought. Knowing you and loving you as I do, it's important you understand I need to have my own project . . . call it my own kind of music to dance to, even if it's only a little dance!

"This will be the first time in more than 15 years when we have not been working together. I'm going to need your help, your support, and your love. Just knowing you understand will provide me with the confidence I'll need."

Having said what she wanted to say, she hugged him ever tighter, snuggled deeper under the heavy blanket, and whispered, "I am beginning to believe there other issues that require our undivided attention!"

* * *

Sitting in the warm sun on the open patio of the Cypress Inn, Mike and Cecelia were savoring the last of their late breakfast and discussing what they would enjoy doing most on their first full day of their vacation.

"I have an idea," Mike said. "I know how much you appreciate good sculpture. Gordon Newell, a longtime friend of my family, has a studio on the wharf in Cannery Row. He does very interesting work and has sold his sculpture to private collectors and museums all around the world. His studio is as fascinating as his work. It is located in part of an old, dilapidated sardine factory he bought and renovated without disturbing the outer character of the building. Who knows, maybe we'll find one of his smaller sculptures that will nicely fit into that lit, indented space in our front hall wall."

* * *

It was early that same afternoon when they arrived at the old, drab warehouse that housed Gordon's sculpture studio. Their knocking on the frame of the open door was drowned out by the loud, repetitive clink of a hammer hitting a chisel hitting a block of marble. Unsure whether to enter unannounced or wait for the racket to stop, Mike said, "Knowing Gordon, he could be at it for hours. Let's just walk in and let him know he has company."

Once their eyes adjusted to the dimness of the cavernous studio, they saw Gordon standing before a giant slab of upright marble with his back to them. For several moments they watched the absorbed artist as he worked, chip by chip, on the piece of marble that must have been 10 feet high, 6 feet wide, and 2 feet thick. With the removal of each little chip, the big sculpture was beginning to resemble an enlarged replication of the small maquette sitting on the adjacent workbench. Formed out of wax, the model was not more than 15 inches tall.

* * *

Gordon was startled when he turned to reach for a different sharpened chisel when he realized he had an audience. "What do we have here? Mike, who is this lovely creature? Have you brought me the female model I have been waiting all these years to sculpt?"

"Gordon, this woman is my wife. She is the infamous Cecelia Chang you've heard me talk so much about."

Before either Gordon or Mike could say another word, Cecelia had moved over to where she could see both the maquette and emerging shape of the sculpture. Fascinated by what she was seeing, she turned to Gordon and asked, "Would you mind explaining what you are hoping to accomplish?"

Pleased by her attention, her interest in his work, and her excellent question, the man behind the tools began to explain. "I have a longtime collector of some of my work who asked me to spend enough time with him to enable me to develop a sense of who he really might be. After I had time to think about what I observed, he suggested that I develop an idea for a sculpture that represents what I thought I had observed."

* * *

Shifting her gaze between the maquette and the massive block of granite, she asked, "I don't get it. What is there about such a large piece of granite with a variety of different grooves, or negative space, running from top to bottom that represents what you have noticed about your client?"

Fascinated by Cecelia's question, the admiring sculptor launched into small talk with Cecelia, and before Mike could object, Gordon took her by the arm and started to show her around his studio. When they paused to inspect each individual sculpture, the artist would explain what he was attempting to accomplish. How his sculpture reflected what he was attempting to portray. Next, he would describe some of the problems he had encountered along the way.

* * *

For the next hour, Mike quietly followed them as they toured the studio, slowly moving from piece to piece as Gordon explained the story behind each one.

Wholly consumed with Cecelia, listening to her questions and observing her reaction to his answers, Gordon not only showed her the work he had on display in his primary studio but insisted they go into the adjoining building where he stored his unfinished pieces.

When the casual tour ended, Gordon picked up one of the smaller sculptures, one that Cecelia had seemed particularly interested in, and handed it to her. Then he said, "Please accept this small token of our new friendship."

Unsure of what she should do with the offered gift, Cecelia turned to Mike in a silent plea for help. Without hesitating, he walked over to her, lifted the heavy sculpture out of her hands, and said, "I'll put it in the car before he changes his mind."

When Mike returned, the sculpture safely stowed in the trunk of the convertible, Cecelia and Gordon were locked into what appeared to be a serious conversation. He approached and put a hand on each of their shoulders and asked, "All right, you two, what kind of trouble are you planning?"

"Mike!" Cecelia exclaimed. "Gordon just invited us to join him now for a few drinks with his good friend John Steinbeck over at the Bear Flag. You *have* to be familiar with John Steinbeck; he wrote *Grapes of Wrath* and *Cannery Row*! Can you imagine how interesting it will be to meet a Pulitzer-winning author in the very same setting he described in his books? Oh, Mike, please say yes!"

* * *

Mike had seen some pretty remarkable people drink and tell stories, but it was nothing like what he and Cecelia were witnessing. For the next 2 hours, sitting next to Cecelia at a sturdy oak table in the sleepy little bar, it was becoming quite clear that as long as the steady procession of cocktails continued to arrive, the two raconteurs were not to be denied. In Mike and Cecelia, they had a new audience for their old stories—and someone to pay for the drinks.

Word of a possible "free drink" began to spread among the regulars of Cannery Row. Under the spell of the revelers, laughing generously, sharing stories of their own, Cecelia and Mike found themselves hosting a full-fledged Cannery Row party. By two o'clock in the morning, Mr. and Mrs. Stone had more than earned a place as honorary drinking members of the local clan.

* * *

Later the next morning, the bright sun shining against his eyelids awakened Mike. Momentarily uncertain where he was, he threw off the covers, climbed out of bed, and looked around. Slowly, the events of the previous night came back to him, along with the fact that he had somehow managed to navigate their way back to their second-story room at the Cypress Inn. The clock on the wall read eleven o'clock.

A small, motionless lump lay curled in the fetal position on the opposite side of the bed, jet-black hair splayed over the white pillow. Filled with panic, Mike wondered if she was all right. To make certain she was, he reached down and gently touched her neck.

Feeling his touch, Cecelia turned over, opened her eyes, stared around, and asked, "Did John and Gordon really ask us to join their club?"

* * *

Later that same afternoon, the Stones were prowling around the old town of Monterey when they discovered the Army Language School. Once Mike explained its purpose, Cecelia was having a difficult time comprehending why every branch of the armed services, from bases all over the world, would send personnel to learn so many different languages at one location.

The teachers, Mike explained, were foreign nationals recruited for their expertise in official written languages as well as their command of numerous local dialects.

As they stood debating what they should do next, a group of students streamed out of the language school. They were intent on making their way across the street and into an unremarkable-looking local tavern. Grabbing Mike as they streamed out, Cecelia said, "Let's follow them. I need to talk to them."

Never surprised by his wife's insatiable curiosity, he replied, "Why not," before he extended his arm and offered to lead her across the street. Inside, Mike settled onto a bar stool at the far end of the bar. He planned to spend the time mindlessly crunching on pretzels and sipping a cold beer.

Cecelia was truly in her element. She walked straight up to a kind-faced man and, in no time, she had been asked to join him and his friends for a friendly beer.

Mike smiled as he watched her begin to ask questions. When two of the students responded, she learned they would be assigned positions in two different provinces in China. Immediately, she began to speak in her privileged Hong Kong dialect. Responding, the two students began to speak flawless Chinese but in the dialects of the provinces where they would be assigned.

* * *

FLATTERED BY HER INTEREST IN THEM, THEY LISTENED AS SHE ASKED, "Where do you come from? Where have you attended college? What language are you here to study? Why are you interested in government work? Where are you hoping to be assigned? What are you planning to do when your service commitment is complete?"

* * *

MIKE WAS FINISHING THE LAST OF HIS SECOND BEER WHEN CECELIA walked up behind him and announced, "This Army Language School is one big melting pot of people from different backgrounds who have come together to study languages. Why couldn't the same concept be applied to the study of international political science and commerce—kind of an expanded version of the program we attended at Berkeley?"

Mike chuckled, amused by the earnestness of her question, and asked, "What are you planning to do, start a school for future Six Sentinels?"

Not taking Cecelia seriously had always been a serious mistake. One look at her standing defiantly in front of him, her hands firmly placed on her hips, the emerald-green eyes flashing, and the square set of her delicate facial features, Mike immediately realized he had just said the wrong thing.

Clearly upset by his careless statement, Cecelia, not above expressing how she felt, said, "Listen, Mr. Banker, there are two undeniable facts of life that even you would recognize. One, we aren't getting any younger, and two, these abuses of free enterprise are beginning to appear with alarming regularity. If we expect to perpetuate what we have started, please explain to me why you don't think it is necessary for us to create a new kind of school, one where students from all over the world could study our Power-Cycle concept? Who knows, we might hatch a new generation of Sentinels."

* * *

A FEW DAYS LATER AS THEY DROVE THE RENTED CONVERTIBLE BACK to the airport, Cecelia aroused herself from a long stretch of silent introspection before turning toward Mike. "How would you feel about continuing on to New York without me? The language school has given me an idea. I want to take advantage of my being on the West Coast to check out a few ideas."

Mike knew better than protest. To argue would be futile. *Could this be the start of the idea for Cecelia's special mission like we discussed on the beach?*

* * *

ARRIVING AT THE AIRPORT WAS TURNING INTO A STRANGE EXPERIENCE. Instead of returning the rental car and proceeding together to the gate, Mike arranged for its further use by Cecelia. Standing curbside at the busy airport, Cecelia and Mike were trying to decide how to say good-by. It seemed like a very strange thing for them to be doing. Finally, he reached out to her and with both arms, he drew her in to his warmest hug before whispering into her ear, "I've been thinking about your new idea. With all of us so busily focusing on the immediacy of the problem directly in front of us, none of us have had the time to think further ahead. I have to think the probability of what you are suggesting may be much bigger than any of us suspect. At the very minimum, we should at least attempt to discover if what you are suggesting is a realistic alternative.

"As much as I will miss you, I understand its importance. Take as much time as you need to find out whatever it is you need to learn, providing you call me every night."

CHAPTER **8**

Who Is Marco Tancredi?

NEW YORK, MAY 1948

Arriving home in New York to an empty house without Cecelia only served to make worse the feelings Mike had been experiencing on his long plane ride from San Francisco. *By this time, after all she has done on her own, I will never be able to forget how she looked when they carried her off the plane following her last trip to China and Southeast Asia.*

As he emptied his pockets on the captain's table near the front door he noticed a letter with the seal of the federal government embossed in the upper-left corner. He tore into it and found a handwritten note: *We need to meet privately. Don.*

It was late in the afternoon of the first day after he had returned to work. The office staff had departed. He was sitting in his office talking with one of his oldest and most trusted friends, Don Cerreta, a rising star in the U.S. Attorney General's office They were savoring the 12-year-old McCallan single malt Scotch whisky Mike faithfully stocked in his bar when he broke the silence. "Just before I left for California, I received a very strange call from Jacques. He has been hearing rumors that the American military-industrial complex may be cooking up some kind of scheme to resurrect military spending. During the conversation, he requested Cecelia and me to meet with an old friend, Mary Wheeler Clarke."

Interrupting, Don asked, "Are you talking about the woman who worked with the OSS office in Bern, Switzerland, during the war, the same woman who lives here in New York, the same woman who has been receiving phone calls from former postwar high-ranking military officers?"

Stunned by Don's unexpected comment, Mike asked, "Receiving phone calls from high-security clearance government employees? Have you been monitoring Mary's calls?"

"Listen, ole friend, no one with the kind of security clearances she enjoyed is ever allowed to retire from the OSS. They are placed on inactive status and allowed to pursue a private life, but they never leave our employ. As a precaution, for the next 3 years, we regularly monitor their communications. Until approximately 3 months ago, nothing of consequence appeared to be happening. It was after it was reported that she began to receive more than an occasional call from retired high-ranking military officers that we started to pay closer attention. Tapes recorded of those conversations only revealed they would be visiting New York and they were interested in visiting their old friend. We have no knowledge of what they talked about or why, so suddenly, so many of them wanted to talk to Mary."

"Don, I think I may be able to shed some light on what all those calls and invitations may have been about. Why don't I mix us another drink, before I tell you about what Mary told Cecelia and me over dinner in the privacy of our home."

After explaining the essence of what Mary had told them, Mike said, "Let's not forget she was considered a top-notch newspaper reporter, highly regarded for the accuracy of her stories. According to what she said, her military friends are anxious to learn if she can be of assistance in communicating their suspicions to people who will know what to do with their information. If she hadn't known of Cecelia's and my association with the Sentinels, I doubt if she would have called us."

"Mike, call it coincidence or whatever, but I think I may have stumbled onto a new angle that may help you solve Mary's problem. Over the years, you have heard me talk about my friend Marco Tancredi, or 'MT,' as he is called by his friends. Marco is the person who cleaned up and sold an old 'family-owned' New York garbage collection company to a publicly listed waste removal company. Prior to his retirement, MT used part of his personal savings to invest in a start-up building maintenance company. Today, it is responsible for cleaning the offices of some very large East Coast industrial companies.

"Last week, while you were in California, he called, seeking my advice. Apparently, he and his partner Armando were presented with a batch of executive notes retrieved from the waste baskets of certain senior executives of industrial companies that employ the services of his company. It appears they have deciphered the information on those notes, and it describes the same subject Mary wanted to discuss with you."

"Wait a minute, are you suggesting that scraps of notes removed from tons of office garbage are capable of describing a multicorporation scheme to manipulate the U.S. congressional appropriation process?"

"No, I'm dead serious. Armando deciphered all the notes, plotted them out, and cross-referenced them. He and Marco have reason to believe that proceeds secured from a Mexican political war chest have been contributed to the campaign funds of the same congressmen who serve on the House Un-American Activities Committee. It would appear fanning the public's fears of Communism is a major consideration supporting these hearings. According to their interpretation of the information contained in these notes, it's all part of a plan to accelerate the restoration of Defense appropriations. It sounds precisely like what you were just telling me about."

"And this Marco is a reliable source? A friend, you say?"

"Not just any friend—Marco is my oldest and best friend. He could very well be one of the most unusual people you will ever meet, and I trust him completely.

"Both of us are the firstborn of parents who emigrated from Sicily. We grew up together on the streets of one of New York's toughest Italian neighborhoods. For as long as I can remember, we were taught, *'If you expect to partici-pate in the American Dream, you can't afford to surrender to the temptations of the neighborhood.'* Every day, Marco and I had to make difficult choices. All through grade school and high school we were being hardened in the crucible of the streets. When we refused to participate in many of the activities of our *street friends,* we were constantly bullied, badgered, and criticized. If someone picked on one of us, they quickly learned they were picking on both of us. It was a rare day when we returned home without scratches, bruises, and new tears in our much-mended, washed, and pressed shirts.

"Once we graduated, I was off to college, but college was never an option for Marco. On the first Monday following graduation, he went to work for the local garbage company. The following Monday, he started his night job at the local fire department.

"Marco was always a hard worker. Following along behind those slow-moving big trucks, hoisting the heavily laden garbage cans up and over the high top of the sides of the moving truck was not so easy, but Marco never complained. The whole time he's hauling and lifting those big, heavy cans, he's keeping up a running conversation with the residents, street to street, block to block, neighborhood to neighborhood. Marco had a way of turning trash day into a neighborhood social event."

"So how'd he go from being the beloved trash man to becoming a senior executive of a garbage collection company?" Mike asked.

"Another thing about Marco, he has insatiable energy, curiosity, and imagination. He doesn't read newspapers—he *attacks* them. Maybe it's to compensate for his not going to college. It didn't take long before the owners recognized his personal skills, his work ethic, and his ability to be a quick learner. Hoping to develop him as a manager, they began to cycle him through assignments in each of the company's operating components.

"Progressing up the ladder was testing Marco's ability to resist the *temptations of the street*. You have to understand, in New York, the garbage companies in each of the boroughs are owned by different crime-connected families. The company Marco worked for was no exception. As his role in the company improved, a growing conflict between his new responsibilities and his personal values was beginning to surface.

"Concerned, he decided to talk to one of the owners. He needed to learn, if he respected their position, would they respect his. The owner told Marco they'd been aware of his misgivings for quite some time, and if his services weren't so valuable, they would've let him go a long time ago. He was assured they wouldn't ask him to do anything that violated his principles as long as he respected their need for confidentiality.

"All those conversations occurred prior to 3 years ago. Shortly thereafter, everything changed when the owners of the garbage company were arrested and charged with money laundering and extortion. That was when Marco was placed in charge of running the business on a day-to-day basis. Thanks in no small part to Marco's penchant for straight talk and his detailed experience in managing each part of the business, he was the only person who was acceptable to the federal administrators and the incarcerated owners.

"On Tuesdays, he'd meet with the federal officials. He was expected to explain the prior week's events, describe the coming week's agenda, and answer any questions they might ask. No matter how hard he tried to provide the federal administrators with complete and accurate answers, he could sense they were having a difficult time believing him. After all, how could they be expected to completely trust someone who grew up on the streets with so many well established members of one of New York's major crime families, and who'd spent all of his adult life working for a crime-connected company?

"On Wednesdays when he traveled to Sing Sing prison, the incarcerated owners suspected he was being asked about more than what the feds needed to know about his daily operations. It was becoming increasingly apparent they were having trouble trusting someone who regularly met with the feds.

"The burden of cleaning up and managing a company and being caught between two sets of supervisors, neither of which trusted him, or each other, was taking its toll on Marco. He was no longer the talkative, caring friend. He was becoming increasingly quiet and seemingly preoccupied by something other than what people were interested in discussing. He was missing Thursday night poker games and was not regularly attending church on Sunday. At the family dinners, he no longer occupied the center of attention. He would sit, pick at his favorite foods, and leave his glass of wine unfinished. Out of respect for his privacy, his family would watch as he sat quietly.

"His friends, his family, his owners, and the federal administration officials couldn't understand why he insisted on spending time trying to meet executives of large, publicly traded corporations. When he tried to explain that he was attempting to accomplish the same kind of exit strategy he had been reading about in the *Wall Street Journal,* they failed to understand the brilliance of his plan.

"On the rare occasion when he had a late-night dinner with his best and oldest friend, Don Cerreta, Marco frequently used the opportunity to explain his plan. When Don would question why publicly listed New York Stock Exchange companies would be interested in acquiring a *family*-owned, low-status garbage company, Marco would customarily say, 'Don, for a college boy, I would have thought you would understand that I'm creating a cleanly run, growth-oriented operating company with unlimited growth potential!'

"For the next couple of years, we all watched as he began to prepare the company for being sold. First, he reduced operating expenses by eliminating the bribes the owners had historically paid to the *'guys on the arm.'* That was when Marco hired his first bodyguard and started sitting with his back to the wall.

"He either fired or replaced family members who were not *'pulling their weight.'* He replaced the aging moving vehicles with larger, more efficient units. He retooled his processing equipment with more modern, high-capacity machines.

"At the same time, he started to expand his customer base—and by reaching out to potential customers in the other boroughs, he was poaching on another family's territory. It was considered to be a very dangerous business practice.

"Not surprisingly, Marco's actions caught the attention of the crime lords who oversaw all the different *'family-operated businesses'* in the New York boroughs. The family leaders were both alarmed and curious. Normally, they strictly enforced their rule that no borough-oriented business of theirs was to be allowed to poach on a neighboring business.

"Technically, Marco had never enjoyed an ownership position in a family-run company; he was expected to observe the *'rules of the street.'* While he understood the unspoken laws of the neighborhood, Marco reasoned that any rule could be changed if he had a good enough reason. I still remember the day when he explained why, if he was allowed to complete his plan, the sale of the company would open the door to *big money* for all the other family garbage companies.

"Everyone stopped questioning his judgment on the day he showed them the acquisition offer he had received from a big publicly traded company. They became even more curious about how the government might react, when on Tuesday he showed the offer to the administrators at the Federal Building. At first, they refused to consider approving the consummation of a transaction that would enable convicted felons still serving their sentence from prospering while their business was under control of a federal receiver.

"Marco was prepared for the question. 'For the sake of conversation, let's suppose the same business was not owned by a convicted felon. What objection or possible jurisdiction would the government have?'

"They were confused by the question. Marco continued, 'Here in my hand, I have a contract that calls for my acquisition of the company on the same terms and conditions listed in the third-party offer I have been presented.'

"Ten minutes later, Marco, signed agreement in hand, was headed for what he presumed would be his last visit to Sing Sing. That was the same day when MT had solved his problem, achieved a clean exit, and earned a substantial six-figure bonus. Marco 'MT' Tancredi had avoided the temptations of the neighborhood and participated in the American Dream."

Fascinated by Don's description of his old friend, Mike said, "I'd love to meet him. From where I sit, he seems like the kind of man who might appreciate what we are trying to do."

CHAPTER 9

Natalie Cummins

BERKELEY, JUNE 1948

Half an hour before midnight on a balmy Thursday, Natalie Cummins and David Marcus, live-in companions, were driving eastward, across the upper level of the San Francisco Bay Bridge. They were returning home after attending a charity benefit hosted by one of San Francisco's more socially prominent families. With the top of their convertible lowered into the down position, they were enjoying the warm summer night and the sight of the orange-tinted full moon rising in the east above the Berkeley Hills.

The presence of Natalie Cummins, the retired but still celebrated star of both London and New York musical stages, had ensured their hosts' event would be well attended, and had indeed been a rousing success. Natalie, always pleased to perform for her friends, had been in great voice.

As the guests were departing, they made certain they graciously thanked their hosts for a fine evening, handed them a sealed envelope, and expressed their confidence that the charitable function would be long described as one San Francisco's more spectacular charitable events of the year.

* * *

D AVID, WHO HAD CONSUMED MORE THAN ONE GLASS OF CHAMPAGNE, was concentrating on his driving. Natalie sat in irritated silence. He had learned the hard way that questioning her when she was in one of these moods usually made things much worse.

As they were passing through the Yerba Buena Tunnel, his curiosity and concern for her prevailed over his better judgment. Hesitantly, he asked, "What happened tonight to upset you? I thought the evening and your performance were a great success!"

Natalie sighed. "Just once, I would like to feel like I was an invited friend who had been asked to perform and assist some worthy cause. But tonight, I felt like I was the *dancing bear* invited to perform so our hosts could squeeze more money out of their friends.

"When I wasn't performing, I sensed that I was expected to mingle with the guests. All they wanted to do was ask me questions about other actors, producers, and composers with whom I've worked. Not once did anyone express any curiosity about *my* personal interests, *my* teaching, or *my* life away from the theater, the person behind the mask."

Slowing for the tollbooth on the east side of the bridge, David carefully ventured an observation. "Natalie, after all this time, you must have learned how intimidated people can become when they first meet a famous actress. You and I are familiar with what happens when people have made the effort to become aware of the real you—not just the image they've imagined."

Natalie, somewhat mollified, treated him to a small smile.

They had turned off the Bayshore Freeway and were beginning their slower trek up the winding streets that led past the University of California, up into the Berkeley Hills, when David said, "This might not be the proper time for me to bring this up, but on two different occasions tonight, two different men approached me to inquire if you would be willing to audition for the new musical films they are planning to produce. I have their cards if you want to call them."

"Why would I want to complicate our lives by going back to work?" Natalie asked.

Amused by the question, David said, "I have always believed, deep in every girl's heart, is a secret wish to become a movie star. I have always assumed the day would come when you decided to return to the stage."

"David, don't you understand how much I care about you and want to become a supporting member of your exciting life? In the last year, since I retired from the stage, I have traveled around the world to help you sell those energy bonds. I have agreed to live with you while you complete your Visiting Fellow teaching assignment at the university, and I've even agreed to teach History of the American Musical Stage to undergraduate students. What else do I have to say to convince you this last year has been the most enjoyable time of my life?"

They had pulled to a stop in their slanted driveway that led from the street downhill to the garage. After turning off the motor, setting the handbrake, and putting the gear shift in reverse, it was a very serious David who turned toward her. "Natalie, I want you to listen very carefully to what I am about to tell you. Ever since I asked you to live with me, I have been prepared to support you in whatever you choose to pursue. I might not like having to share you with your life on the stage, but I would prefer that to losing you."

Natalie could tell by his strained tone of voice that he was keeping something back, something he was refusing to share. *What is he trying to tell me? Is he encouraging me to make those calls, or is he telling me how upset he would become if I went back to work?*

* * *

FOR SOME TIME, WHENEVER DAVID PICKED UP NATALIE AT THE TRAIN depot in Oakland, he would worry about who would be stepping from the train. *Would it be my Natalie, the woman whose constant companionship, adulation, and affection I have become so dependent on, or will it be Natalie the star?*

* * *

DAVID WAS STANDING ON THE PLATFORM WATCHING THE INCOMING train slow to a steam-hissing stop. Three cars down the platform, he spotted her among the other passengers exiting the train. Even at that distance, he knew, with one look, that something terrible must have happened to her in Los Angeles. Her head drooped, she wasn't smiling, and she was moving very slowly.

As soon as they reached each other, he wrapped his strong arms around what felt like an uncharacteristically frail body of someone who was emotionally disturbed. He could feel the strength of her tight hug and then the wetness of her tears on his neck. He continued to hold her and refrained from moving until her sobbing began to ebb. He then led her into the small coffee shop inside the train station, sat her down in a vacant booth, called the waitress over, and ordered two cups of coffee and one two-scoop vanilla ice-cream cone. Gathering his thoughts, David finally ventured, "Tell me, my dear, what problem can't be solved with an ice-cream cone and a long talk with your old pal?"

The waitress soon returned, and Natalie readily accepted the cone. With each lick, she seemed to regain more of her composure. Finally, when she looked up with her tearstained cheeks, she said, "David, do you have any idea of what those *sons of bitches* were expecting me to do?"

Her statement startled him. It was the first time he had ever heard her swear.

"They didn't want me for my talent and commercial success. They just wanted me as a replacement for some very talented actresses whose names have appeared on the Hollywood Blacklist.

"As interesting as it might be to star in a big-budget Hollywood musical, I'll be damned if I am going to be associated with their game or be responsible for putting qualified actresses out of work! Can you believe it? Nearly the names of 300 writers, actors, and directors have been put on the blacklist. Overnight, these people have been put out of work, *and* they are being prohibited from finding new work in the only industry they know.

"It's all part of this Communist inquisition stuff being conducted by the House Un-American Activities Committee. They are attacking Hollywood actors, writers, and directors suspected of having some prior affiliation with the Communist Party. If these people are not willing to sign affidavits incriminating themselves and their friends, they are served subpoenas and are expected to appear before the House Un-American Activities Committee (HUAC) for questioning."

"Natalie, apparently, you have not been reading the newspapers. It just gets worse. This legally constituted congressional committee is questioning anyone who refuses to sign those affidavits or an employment-related loyalty oath. I'm having a difficult time understanding how the fear of Communism can cause the American government to violate the personal liberties of its citizens who are presumably protected by the Bill of Rights."

After carefully composing what he was about to say, he reached over, put both arms around her, and whispered in her ear, "To me, the whole thing seems like a big publicity stunt designed to scare the hell out of the American public. The question we should be asking is . . . 'What are they trying to accomplish?'"

As they walked from the car to their front door, Natalie suddenly stopped, looked directly into David's eyes, and asked, "You're a smart guy. What do you think it might be? What are your friends telling you? What would HUAC stand to gain by using its hearings to scare citizens over the threat of Communism?"

CHAPTER 10

Attacking Mr. Bill

WASHINGTON, D.C., JUNE 1948

Throughout the spring of 1948, the Hollywood Blacklist had grown in size and public recognition. Just as J. Jordan McWilliams and Congressman Richard Allen Bailey had predicted, no one, not even the most hardworking, serious, and talented people in Hollywood, were free from scrutiny. Those who refused to sign incriminating affidavits were subpoenaed and scheduled to appear before the committee.

Skillful public relations campaigns continued to amplify the threat of the atomic attack at every opportunity. Any incident that suggested possible aggressive behavior on the part of the Russians was played up in the press. The publicity was being carefully managed to expose a country exhausted from fighting the last Great War to fear the possibility of a whole new threat. Political candidates found it useful to accuse their opponents of being "soft on Communism."

Frightened citizens built bomb shelters in their backyards. Schools regularly conducted air raid drills during which boys and girls were taught how to seek shelter under their desks. Street signs were erected to point the way to the closest public shelter. At movie theaters, weekly newsreels featured the Distant Early Warning Line, the radar surveillance system being constructed in Alaska.

Screenwriters were a favorite target of the anti-Communist zealots. The investigation arm of the HUAC had identified a promising new target: William

W. Weyl, or "Mr. Bill," as he was known to his friends. A best-selling author, a celebrated New York playwright, and a prolific screenwriter, Mr. Bill was one of Hollywood's most respected personalities. During the war, he had been one of the first members of the film industry to enlist in the navy. He was a member of one of the early classes to earn their wings at the navy's flight school at Pensacola, Florida. Following graduation, he was sent to a secret airbase in Western Nevada, known as "Area 51," for special training.

In early 1942, Mr. Bill was one of the first newly graduated pilots to be assigned to a carrier group in the South Pacific. Flying missions off the carrier and land-based airstrips, Lt. William W. Weyl was one of the first American pilots to become a decorated ace pilot. He was being promoted as one of the early authentic heroes to emerge from the early chaotic war America was unsuccessfully waging in the South Pacific. Articles describing Lieutenant Weyl's accomplishments frequently appeared in the American newspapers and weekly magazines. Newscasts often reported on his latest "kills." While the war raged on, he had been asked on two different occasions to return to the United States to tour assembly plants and help the government sell war bonds. Mr. Bill was becoming a familiar name in American homes, offices, factories, and on school playgrounds.

Now, only a few years following Captain Bill's separation from the navy, the FBI had placed his name on their list of possible subversives. They had honed in on his prewar literary work, *Spain: Road Test for Fascism*. Set largely in the trench warfare of the Spanish Civil War, his book told the story of loyal, brave, Spanish patriots who valiantly fought alongside local Communist forces. They were engaged in an unsuccessful attempt to defeat national armies under the command of Fascist General Franco, whose armies were trained and equipped to test Nazi Germany's recently developed air and ground equipment and weaponry.

Mr. Bill, a serious and decorated defender of America, never considered his subpoena as a confrontational threat. When he refused to sign what he considered to be an inaccurate affidavit, he never considered the possibility that a writer of novels and screenplays, and a decorated war veteran, would be suspected of Communist subversion. Choosing to appear without the benefit of counsel, he would do whatever he could to be helpful and leave as quickly as possible.

Congressman Bailey and the rest of the committee were pleased. The appearance of a known war hero would help them to convince the American public the spread of Communist influence could be found anywhere. What better way could the committee demonstrate the pervasiveness of spreading Communism than to expose a decorated war hero as a Communist sympathizer?

* * *

MOST OF THOSE IN THE ROOM FOR THE HEARING WERE NOT AWARE that the witness, Mr. Bill, and Richard Allen Bailey had both attended the University of Southern California at the same time. Although they were members of different fraternities, the social world of fraternities and sororities was small and relatively close. Their paths had frequently crossed. Every time Bill thought back to those days, he remembered the former football hero as being braggadocios, craving to be the center of attention, and a seeker of approval. He remembered why the nickname "Slick" suited him so well. Ten years had passed since he had last seen the *"campus hero"* but his recollections of Dick's ball handling skills, his ability to bed rich women, and his ability to talk his way out of trouble still remained clearly etched in his mind.

As the hearing was called to order and he was sworn in as a witness, Mr. Bill watched Bailey, now older but still displaying his signature arrogant air, began his questioning of him and his book. Almost from the asking of the first question he doubted Bailey had ever read his book.

In the first round of questions, Mr. Bill answered Bailey's questions with "yes" and "no" answers. Or at most, with very few words. As they moved deeper into the hearing, the questions began to take on a more sinister tinge. It was difficult for Mr. Bill not to perceive the committee regarded his book *Spain: Road Test for Fascism* was being written out of some deep conviction on his part that Communism was a noble and worthwhile enterprise.

Several questions later, when he began to realize he was being regarded as a Communist sympathizer, he concluded that he needed to start thinking about how best to protect himself. Two questions later, he responded, "Excuse me, Congressman, if I correctly understand your question, it pertains to the hero, or protagonist of the book, and begs the question, 'Was he a secret member of the Communist Party, trained in Moscow by the Russians?' Since I don't recall including any information describing what you have just finished asking me, may I inquire if you, personally, have read my book?"

Unprepared for the challenge, Bailey attempted to regain the high ground. "Did you attend a party at the home of Mr. and Mrs. Cyril Adams on May 17, 1937?"

"Most likely; that was years ago. I can't verify the precise date. But, yes, I regularly attended social functions at their home around that time."

"And were you aware that Mr. Adams and several of his guests were active members of the Communist Party?"

"Yes, sir, I recall participating in several conversations where people were comparing the then-current economic consequences of Democratic Free Enterprise with those of socialist economics."

Believing the witness had finished answering his question, Congressman Bailey was beginning to pose his next question when Mr. Bill continued his testimony. "Might I inquire what law was broken? Was it against the law to be a member of the Communist Party in 1937? Did we break the law by discussing the comparative advantages between Democratic Free Enterprise and socialist economics? Am I mistaken in my belief American citizens are granted the right to be a member of whatever political party they choose, they are free to assemble with people of their choosing, they are free to discuss whatever they wish, and as an author, I am free to write about whatever I choose, and in any manner I choose, provided I don't violate any laws pertaining to libel and slander?"

"Not so fast, Mr. Weyl. It's only fair that I advise you that unless you cooperate and answer the questions of this committee, regardless of your desire to invoke your First or Fifth Amendment rights, you can be found in contempt of Congress. Do you understand?"

Glaring at the congressman, Mr. Bill said, "I'll tell you what I believe. In appearing here today, I expected to be asked routine questions about anything I might know about Communist influence I may have witnessed as a citizen, a former military officer, or a working member of the Southern California motion picture industry. I now believe, by answering any more of your questions, I could implicate myself, or even worse, someone else."

Congressman Bailey, challenged by the response but not wishing to test the legal validity of a witness invoking his First and Fifth Amendment rights, snatched up a sheet of paper, strode up to where the accused sat, and slapped it on the table in front of him. In his most intimidating tone, he commanded, "Mr. Weyl, I want you to carefully study the names on this sheet. When you are finished, I will be asking you some questions."

When the witness raised his head after reading the names on the list, Bailey asked his first question. "Do you recognize any of the names on that list?"

"Yes," said Mr. Bill. "Several are friends of mine. I have worked with some of the others professionally, and some I only know by reputation. All of them are highly respected, hardworking members of Southern California's motion picture industry."

"Very well, Mr. Weyl. Now, will you please tell the committee which of these people you know to be members of the Communist Party, have attended Communist cell meetings, or you have observed discussing Communist activities?"

The next morning, a shocking headline appeared in many of the nation's largest newspapers.

"Indicted for Contempt of Congress"
Written by Walt Matthews

Refusing to answer questions of the House Un-American Activities Committee regarding his friends' involvement with the Communist Party, Mr. William W. Weyl, a decorated naval aviator and celebrated screenwriter and novelist, was charged with contempt of Congress. If convicted, he can expect to spend 6 months to 2 years in a minimum-security prison.

In a private interview with Mr. Weyl, this reporter has learned that he has been terminated by his employer and that his name has been added to the Hollywood Blacklist. If convicted of contempt of Congress, he will forfeit his military and Social Security benefits in addition to doing jail time in a minimum-security prison.

After witnessing this civil rights debacle, this reporter feels compelled to ask, "If a law-abiding, highly decorated war hero, a distinguished writer of plays and movies, can be terminated by his employer and stripped of his protection under due process of law, how can we, with our more limited knowledge of the law and limited financial resources, be expected to defend ourselves against the tyranny of our own government?"

* * *

THAT SAME MORNING, SITTING AROUND THEIR CONFERENCE TABLE, members of the House Un-American Activities Committee were discussing the events of the prior day's hearing.

"Well, Dick," said the chairman, "I guess the bad news is that we didn't obtain all the information we sought. On the positive side, we certainly received a lot of publicity. One thing for certain, any future witnesses will understand what can happened if they expect to protect themselves with the First or Fifth Amendments. On balance, I would say we had a pretty good day."

CHAPTER 11

Natalie's New Mission

LOS ANGELES, SEPTEMBER 1948

Revolted by the content of the newspaper article written by Matthews, anybody in Hollywood who wasn't already aware of the committee's attack was on high alert. In this environment, news of Natalie's refusing two coveted roles rapidly spread throughout the motion picture industry. When asked about her decision, she was quoted to have said, "I regard Hollywood's use of inquisition tactics as a corrupt and overreaching attempt to unnecessarily scare the American people about an unproven threat of Communist influence."

Almost immediately, she started receiving calls and letters from people who wanted to compliment her on her courageous stand. Appreciative of their comments, Natalie made the time to write notes that expressed her appreciation of their support.

When she started to receive invitations requesting David and her to attend small dinner parties in private homes of some of the more prominent members of Southern California's entertainment industry, they made an effort to accept as many as possible, so David and Natalie rearranged their busy schedules. They would depart from the Oakland train station on Thursday nights and wake up in Los Angeles on Friday mornings.

Over enjoyable meals and expensive wines served in the luxury of private homes, David and Natalie would discuss the latest developments with the seriously concerned luminaries of the film industry. The more they listened, the more they learned about how the lives of many of the more liberal personalities who might have been attracted to the politics and economics of socialist Communism were being threatened by Hollywood's studio system and the House Un-American Activities Committee.

* * *

Back at the University of California, Berkeley, Natalie was becoming aware of her students' interest in her weekend trips to Southern California. They were curious to learn more about what was going on behind the scenes. The suggestion that personal liberties were being attacked, copies of the blacklisted personalities were being circulated, and people were losing their jobs represented big news in the university's liberal student environment.

One day after class, a small group of her more proactive students asked Natalie to join for an after-class cup of coffee at their small, off-campus local hangout. The growing companionship reminded her of her early life in London when she, together with her aspiring actor friends, would gather for a small cup of coffee and a lot of shop talk. There was one big difference, however. Her students were in the habit of asking highly intelligent and very penetrating questions.

Over the course of several weeks, their conversation was dominated by her students asking questions and her struggling to provide worthwhile answers. Then one day, one of her students asked, "How difficult could it be to determine if these out-of-work, established actors might find work in England's motion picture industry?"

The comment reminded her of the same question she had previously asked David one night over dinner. His lack of response had confused her. She wondered if he did not have an opinion, or if he regarded her possible interest as a threat to their lifestyle.

Intrigued by the question, Natalie responded by asking the group for their opinion on what they thought she should do. Everyone had ideas. When she felt an idea had merit, she would attempt to focus the group's attention on that particular idea. What had started as casual conversation quickly turned into a Socratic debate. Not wanting to forget any of the constructive questions and answers, Natalie removed a pen and notepad from her briefcase.

Concentrating on writing notes, she would frequently interrupt to ask questions of clarification.

When her students began to excuse themselves, Natalie remained behind, ordered another cup of coffee, and began to study her notes. Only halfway through, a different kind of thought occurred to her. *What was happening? Were we discussing all the different ways David and I might be able to solve the blacklisting problem, or were my students conducting a very interesting method of teaching and learning?*

* * *

Had Natalie not been so excited to tell David about what had happened, she might have noticed the ever-tightening expression on his face. Sitting at the dinner table, he dabbled at his food and was unresponsive. After a time, Natalie couldn't help but notice his lack of interest or the absence of any insightful questions. Afraid she might say something she might regret, she excused herself and began to clear away the dinner dishes.

Bent over the kitchen sink, scrubbing the last of the pots, she began to think, *Why shouldn't he be interested in my new ideas? I certainly have demonstrated my interest and support for his.*

When the last of the dinner dishes had been dried and put away, she started to leave the kitchen to join David for their nightly cup of tea. Some instinct told her, *Why don't you remain in the kitchen a little bit longer and think through what kind of conversation you are planning to have with David?*

Pretending to sharpen the kitchen knives, she was free to let her mind run, think about things she had seen but not taken conscious notice of when they were conducting his tour of the British Commonwealth Banks. When she replayed the different meetings, she could remember the more complex questions directed toward her, the kind of questions designed to expose her more limited knowledge of the oil industry. *I can still recall seeing the looks of surprise when I answered their questions, and then asked a question of my own. If I have gone to all the trouble to be properly prepared, give up my career on the stage to travel and support a man I love, why is it so wrong to assume he should be willing to at least take an interest in what I am doing?*

In the next moment, she would recall the conversation they had during their ride over the bridge. *In one breath, he talked about how much he depended*

*upon my constant companionship, and in the next, he talked about being sup-
portive of anything I wanted do. What was I supposed to have believed? Have I
allowed our relationship to deteriorate? Why hasn't David said anything?*

For the first time, Natalie was beginning to feel twinges of guilt over the
time and energy she had been devoting to the Hollywood problem. *Hopefully,
things can remain on hold until I finish launching Natalie's Bridge.*

* * *

NATALIE WAS RAPIDLY BECOMING A FAMILIAR AND POPULAR FIGURE IN
the City of Angels. Within a month, she had opened a small office near the corner of Wilshire Avenue and Rodeo Drive in West Los Angeles. The combination
of the heavy foot traffic and the temporary sign announcing her pending opening brought much traffic, agents, and friends from the trade, who were making
an effort to walk around and over the debris to talk to the famous actress.

* * *

BEFORE THE EMERGENCE OF NATALIE'S BRIDGE, NATALIE AND DAVID
had been in the habit of reserving their weekends for each other. They would
spend their private, quality time enjoying each other. There were no people from
the entertainment industry, no curious fans, and no investment managers to distract them or interfere with exploring the many wonders of Northern California.

Moored at the Berkeley Marina was their heavy wood-planked construc-
tion, a wide-beamed boat powered by two dependable diesel engines. The
sturdy seaworthy craft represented their vehicle of escape. Friday nights would
be spent on board, safely moored in ship's home birth. Friday afternoons were
spent unloading and carefully storing the bounty of their afternoon spent
purchasing all the supplies they would need for their next 2 days at sea. Well
established habits called for Natalie to unload and store their newly purchased
favorite foods and wines, clean the highly polished mahogany walls, the
teak-floored galley, and the master stateroom. When she finished, she would
arrange all the dinner accoutrements on the small dining table in preparation for their first dinner on board. Her work complete, she would unpack
their clothes, check their bedding, and make certain everything was properly
arranged in the bathroom.

Knowing how David liked to tinker in the engine room, she would open a bottle of her favorite wine, place a long-playing record on their phonograph, and proceed to her favorite on-deck chair. After she had collapsed in its comfort, she would begin to enjoy the wine, watch the sun set beyond the Golden Gate Bridge, and think about tomorrow's start of their 2-day cruise.

Preparing the boat for their weekend cruise was one of David's responsibilities. After opening the hatch to the engine room, he would disappear for what seemed to Natalie to be a very long time. First, he would unload his purchases from the marine store, then check each item against his list. He would then proceed to check the bilge, making certain nothing strange or unusual had leaked in the space below the powerful diesel engines and bottom of the hull. With the aid of the ever-present red shop rags, he would carefully wipe down the surface of both engines, the generator, the fuel pumps, and fuel lines. Next, he would carefully inspect the rubber motor belts, the electrical connections, and the capacities of the cooling system, oil reserves, and the fuel tanks. Pronouncing the boat seaworthy, he would proceed to replace or repair each of the items he had carefully recorded in his log book upon his last postcruise inspection.

* * *

Returning above deck, he would pour himself a glass of wine and turn the record over before joining Natalie on deck. No matter how many times he had repeated the same sequence, he always stopped to study Natalie dressed in her white dungarees, blue canvas tennis shoes, and her red and white checkered shirt neatly tied around her slim waist. When he carefully studied her, he could still see the signs of her lightly muscled body tone developed from her many years of dancing.

Studying her face as he climbed the few steps from the galley to the aft deck, he still saw the short, curly, light brown hair and her green eyes that had excited musical theater audiences in New York and London. Then there was always that moment when he had to pause and reassure himself that all this was real, not some part of a dream.

After refilling her glass, he always asked, "Well, my dear, what will it be? Would you like to sail around the bay, stopping at our favorite pier-side restaurants? Or, weather permitting, we can sail outside the bay and argue if we should turn left or right. Or, if you prefer, we can sail into the mouth of the delta and proceed along either the Sacramento or the San Joaquin rivers."

Questioning her about her choice of destination was a game they always played over dinner. Her predictable response would always be, "What do you prefer?"

He would then respond by suggesting they visit someplace he knew she wouldn't want to go. Smiling inwardly, he would patiently wait for her predictable response.

"Didn't we visit there last month? Unless your mind is set on going there, why don't we take advantage of the weather and sail north to Bodega Bay? We could moor, walk around the village, and see if they are serving sand dabs, or abalone at the small little restaurant that enjoys such a lovely cliff-side view? I think a very cold, very dry martini, and a couple of servings of fresh oysters might be a very appropriate way to start our first night at sea!"

* * *

ONE BRIGHT, SUNNY MORNING, NATALIE WAS WORKING IN HER NEW office in Los Angeles when the front door creaked open to reveal a nice-looking older lady dressed in a simple smock and chalk-white tennis shoes. The woman greeted Natalie kindly and introduced herself as Gloria Adams.

"Pleased to meet you," said Natalie as the name registered in her brain. "Are you *the* Mrs. Cyril Adams who hosted all those parties Bill Weyl was being questioned about by the House Un-American Committee?"

"The one and only," Gloria said with a knowing smile.

Not more than a few minutes of casual chatter was required before Natalie realized this was a woman with whom she wanted to become better acquainted. Asking Gloria to join her for a cup of coffee, she soon learned that this sunny woman had once been considered one of Hollywood's most beautiful starlets, and many years ago, she had starred in a number of low-budget films. A recent widow of one of Hollywood's more successful writers, she had remained an active participant in many of the entertainment community's social and charitable causes.

Despite their age difference, Natalie and Gloria soon discovered they had a lot in common and shared many of the same values. From that day forward, they became fast friends—to the pleasure and the benefit of both, as they would soon discover.

Sensitive to Natalie's busy schedule, Gloria would wait and drop by her office late in the afternoon to inquire whether Natalie had a few minutes to join her at the nearby neighborhood tavern for a glass of wine. On one such afternoon, Natalie and Gloria sat facing each other in a small booth near the far end of the bar, two glasses of chilled chardonnay sitting between them. Uncharacteristically, Gloria, the sunny woman, was agitated. Her normal, unshakable positive demeanor was giving way to something of grave concern.

After a long pause, Gloria said, "Many of these blacklisted people are friends of mine. I can no longer stand aside and watch what is happening to them. Isn't there something I can do to be of assistance?"

CHAPTER 12

Dinner Is Served

NEW YORK, NOVEMBER 1949

When Cecelia announced dinner was being served, the Sentinels knew they were expected to stop talking, take their seats at the table, and prepare to enjoy the special meal that she had undoubtedly spent the day preparing.

After waiting for Mike to finish filling the last glass from the well-chilled, napkin-covered bottle of white wine, Jacques prepared to address his Sentinel colleagues. Taking his time, he allowed his gaze to shift from one face to another. With the exception of David Marcus, who, for some unknown reason, appeared to be upset and preoccupied, everyone else seemed to be eager to start the real business of the evening.

Mike suggested, "Why don't we ask Natalie and Tony to tell us what they have been doing. Word has it that they have busy doing some very interesting things.

"Before I ask Tony to bring us up to date on the latest developments at Sentinel Vineyards, I think it might be helpful if I filled the new members in on how we came to invest $25 million in such an ambitious national premium wine experiment.

"Several years ago, in 1944, as an integral part of our plan to prevent the German industrialists from using part of their $2½ billion profits of war to finance the organization of a future Reich, we were required to do a number of things. We convinced them that the best way for them to smuggle $2 billion of gold out of Germany was to convert their wealth into more easily transported gold bearer bonds. Their adoption of our idea was contingent upon our obtaining Western World Bank approval of such a large issue to assist a sworn enemy of war. Had we failed to convince the participating banks the transfer of wealth into the Western banking system was preferable to allowing Hitler to use their money to secure the loans he needed to finance his war effort, I seriously doubt we would have received their support.

* * *

"Once the actual gold-bearer bonds were printed, we executed the second part of our plan. Thanks to Mr. Sean Meyer, the dapper-looking English gentleman seated to my left, and Claudine Demaureux, my future wife, and the creative and highly regarded Swiss banker, we succeeded in duplicating the $100 million of the issued but un-cashed gold bearer bonds. Once we succeeded in cashing a nominal sum of our duplicate bonds, we determined bank authenticators were not able to distinguish between our forged bonds and the authentic bonds cashed by the German owners, we were ready to proceed with the third phase of our plan.

"The third part of our plan called for us to smuggle the hundred million dollars of duplicate gold-bearer bonds in $10 million increments, into 10 different Western bank centers, and present them for cashing. We were counting upon the fact that it would only be a question of time before banks, confused by the presence of identical bonds, would refuse to cash any additional bonds of that particular series. When that occurred, we would have achieved our original objective of preventing the German industrialists from using their 'fortunes of war' to finance the organization of a future Reich.

"One of the things we needed to avoid was creating a money trail that could be traced back to us. Fortunately, Tony presented us with an opportunity to literally bury $425 million in the ground. Tony, how long has it been since we bought the 5,000 acres and planted our first grapes? Five years?"

The people sitting around the table turned their attention to the tall, handsome, deeply tanned and well-muscled Italian winemaker. Despite being a soft-spoken man of few words, Tony Garibaldi loved the opportunity to talk about grapes, wines, and the Napa Valley. The subject made him come alive.

Unaccustomed to being impressed with men she met along the way, Natalie couldn't help but notice Tony's youthful vigor, his Mediterranean handsomeness, and how excited he seemed to be when he was talking about grapes and wines. *Clearly, he is a fellow dreamer who is devoted to chasing challenging goals!* She was paying the same kind of attention to Tony giving his report as she would to a writer of a new play as he read aloud from his manuscript.

Had she not been paying such close attention to Tony, she might have noticed David's reaction to her interest in Tony. Always threatened by attention Natalie constantly attracted from other men, David had developed the habit of watching for any signs that she might be attracted to some other man. Her rapt interest in Tony was unmistakable.

Natalie was forced to snap out of her trance just moments after Tony finished giving his report. She heard Jacques asking her if she wished to talk about her new project. "From what we have been hearing, the preliminary reports appear to be indicating your early efforts are starting to shake things up a bit on both sides of the Atlantic. Would you mind sharing?"

Not willing to risk glancing at David, she began, "Thank you, Jacques." Flashing her famous smile, Natalie nodded before saying, "You have no idea what is happening to your colleagues in Southern California. Hollywood personalities are being threatened by a modern version of the Spanish Inquisition, only this time, they are calling it Hollywood Black Listing, which required the movie studios to prevent the employment of anyone who is expected to have had some previous affiliation with the Communist Party. Talented people are prevented from seeking employment in the only industry they have known. Natalie's Bridge is a transatlantic casting company designed to employ out-of-work Hollywood personalities in London's moviemaking industry. Interestingly enough, the spark of the new idea was produced by one of my students.

"The simplicity of her idea is astounding. One afternoon, when over a cup of coffee, she casually asked why I haven't taken advantage of my experiences on the English stage to find employment for Hollywood's disenfranchised but commercially proven personalities. Putting one foot in front of the other, we have unquestionably discovered there is a strong base of interest on this side of the Atlantic in seeking employment in the British filmmaking industry. Once we complete our documentation of interested job seekers, their qualifications, and their experience, my next step will require me to visit the London moviemaking industry and assess the depth of their interest."

Observing this intelligent and self-assured woman describe her next project was producing a strange effect on Tony. Seldom had he witnessed such a convincing presentation from a man, much less a woman. He had always regarded her as a very beautiful and talented star on the musical stage, somebody whose lifestyle and interests placed her in a world well beyond anything he would be comfortable discussing. Watching her talk about her new life was creating an entirely different impression, however. *Something must have changed. Why would such a successful star, in the prime of her career, retire from the stage, teach musical theater at the University of California, move in with someone like David, and put her varied talents to work to helping Southern California movie people find work in England? What have I missed? Maybe I should make more of an effort to become better acquainted.*

* * *

ONCE THE DINNER DISHES HAD BEEN CLEARED, MIKE DIRECTED THE conversation back to the central matter at hand. "Each of you have already received a copy of the memorandum I sent you describing the detailed information contained in Mary and Marco's reports. The more I think about this situation, the more I am convinced the problem is much more complicated than just focusing our attention on the prudence of accelerated defense spending. Jacques and I both agree the real problem requiring our attention is that of our opposing the ever-deepening penetration of the military-industrial complex. Controlling government spending will just be the way we keep score!"

After nodding her assent, Cecelia asked, "What can we do about these congressional hearings? As things stand, without the benefit of any well prepared opposition, Dick Bailey and his pack of jackals are using threats, intimidations, and false accusations to intimidate and scare helpless witnesses. The government, with its unlimited resources and superior knowledge of the law, has taken advantage of the unpreparedness of witnesses, the absence of qualified counsel, and the fear of incarceration to create and enhance concerns over the potential threat of Communism.

"Why aren't these bullies susceptible, like any other bullies, to some of their own medicine? How do you think they might react if someone was able to develop effective responses to their unfounded accusations and intimidating tactics? What do you suppose might happen if we found someone who, if properly prepared, could effectively resist their challenges and put up a real fight?"

"I may have already met the right person," Natalie said. "Her name is Gloria Adams. Some of you might know her as Mrs. Cyril Adams, the hostess of the cocktail party made famous in the William Weyl hearings. She was an actress before the war, and is still entrenched in the Hollywood community and has several friends who've been targeted by Bailey's committee. She's angry, and she doesn't have much to lose at this point. I think she'll be eager to cooperate. Getting her before the committee could prove to be the more difficult problem."

The room grew eerily silent. Everyone was lost in thought. No one was particularly surprised. They were busy trying to think of an appropriate response when the characteristically quiet Tony said, "Cecelia makes an excellent point. In Italy, before the last war, my family and their friends were generally aware of what Mussolini and his fascist colleagues were doing, but they didn't make the effort to oppose him until it was too late. Look at our own efforts to warn the world of Hitler's wartime ambitions for worldwide rule. Without a voice capable of reaching our *influential* friends, we had no way to oppose the German industrialists, who, left unattended, could threaten the world.

"I may be speaking out of school. Given the fast-changing nature of the American musical stage and its ability to raise the consciousness of its audience regarding current social issues, why shouldn't we take advantage of Gloria's and Natalie's public identification? What could be more important than developing our own means for communicating directly with the public?"

Before anyone could say anything, the other members around the table were caught by surprise when David suddenly leaped to his feet. "I can see where this is heading! Before anyone says anything, I want to make it perfectly clear, don't count on me or Natalie to do anything more than what she is already doing with her Natalie's Bridge project. Our personal life is already in shambles. The last thing we need is another project for Natalie!"

Embarrassed by his compulsive behavior, and sensing the strained and silent reaction from his fellow Sentinels, David excused himself from the table, made his way to the front door, and left without offering any explanation. Natalie, sitting quietly at the table, did not rise from her seat and/or choose to follow him.

CHAPTER 13

Call Gloria

LOS ANGELES, NOVEMBER 1948
One of the first things Natalie did upon her return to Los Angeles was to call Gloria Adams. Curious to learn what had transpired in New York, Gloria eagerly agreed to meet her the next day at their favorite neighborhood bistro.

As Natalie entered the dimly lit restaurant 15 minutes before the appointed time, she was surprised to see Gloria, wearing a big smile, already sitting in their favorite booth.

"Thank God you're finally here!" the older woman teased. "I've been so excited to learn what happened in New York, I arrived half an hour early."

They were well into their second cup of coffee by the time Natalie finished outlining the three parts of their plan. "My colleagues are convinced, given a thorough examination of the law and the careful preparation of a strong willed witness, we can reverse the effect their pulpit of public opinion is having on the public. We think you might be that strong willed witness."

Gloria, showing her delight, clasped both her hands in front of her, before saying, "You can count on me. There is nothing that would give me greater pleasure than preventing those jackals from attacking my friends!"

* * *

AFTER MIKE, DON CERRETA, AND THEIR INDEPENDENT LEGAL research consultants interviewed Gloria, they all agreed she possessed the prerequisite intelligence, energy, and tenacity to endure the hearing. The only remaining question concerned her ability to grasp the essence of the legal case they were planning to prepare. When asked, Gloria responded, "All you are asking me to do is to learn how to respond to the committee's questions in the legal vernacular this role will require."

* * *

SATISFIED WITH HER ANSWER, THE VENUE OF THEIR WORK WAS shifted to New York. Mike and Don went to work organizing a group of highly respected constitutional lawyers to research the problem. Each week, they would meet with the lawyers to ask questions and evaluate their work. Copies were also sent to top constitutional lawyers in New York and Washington. Suggestions were welcomed. Changes were made. By the end of the process, Mike and Don were convinced they had something that, if properly presented, would be convincing, and, more importantly, catch Dick Bailey and the rest of his committee by surprise—and unprepared.

Mike couldn't help but speculate, "I wonder how the 'Hounds' will react when the unsuspecting 'Fox' turns on them and delivers some of their own medicine?"

* * *

WITH THEIR PREPARATION COMPLETE, THE GROUP DECIDED TO HOLD a "moot court hearing" as the final test of their work. Highly regarded and recently retired federal judges would be in attendance. Gloria would play the part of the witness, while Mike was selected to be the presiding judge. Don Cerreta was selected to play the role of the committee's chief interrogator, Dick Bailey.

* * *

THE RESULTS OF THE "MOOT COURT" PERFORMANCE WERE interesting. Gloria, the retired actress, was in full possession of the memorization and delivery techniques she had worked so hard to develop in an earlier time. Mike, Natalie, Don, and the other members of the legal team were pleasantly surprised by the energetic intelligence and retentive skills Gloria was able to insert into her new role. Gloria had mastered the ability to answer questions in a brief and confident manner without appearing arrogant or disrespectful.

CALL GLORIA

* * *

In Washington, public demonstrations outside the halls of Congress had become a regular occurrence. Friends and colleagues of the blacklisted Hollywood Ten, activists concerned about the encroachment of American civil liberties, and people who were opposed to the government employing their resources to attack its own citizens were gathering to peacefully express their indignation. Many of the marchers carried signs printed with the slogan "Free the Hollywood Ten."

* * *

With all the interest being stirred up, it was only natural that Walt's editor urged him to dig ever-deeper in his reporting. He would say, "Sometimes, I think we're covering this story exactly the way we're expected to. Due process of the law is taking a hell of a beating, and I think the public deserves to know why. We are talking about the U.S. Congress, not some religious inquisition. Why don't we try to understand what is really going on, and report the *real* story?"

* * *

"Trust me," Walt assured him, "nothing would give me greater satisfaction than to get down to D.C. and help people learn what the real story behind the story really is."

* * *

Walt had been covering the demonstrations outside the Capitol for 3 days when he recognized the slim, sweet-countenanced older lady in chalk-white tennis shoes, wearing a well-tailored, somewhat plain smock. She was quietly walking through the crowd holding a sign that read "Hollywood Ten + Me."

Smelling a story, he started walking toward her, pulling out his notepad, and retrieving his pen from his breast pocket.

* * *

Two days later, Walt Matthews's article describing the former actress's indignation at the hearings and capturing some of Gloria's more colorful insults of Richard Bailey and the rest of the committee began to appear in the *New York Times* and its 32 syndicated newspapers. Each article ended with the reporter challenging the committee to call her as a witness. This little old lady who dared to challenge the authority of the House Un-American Activities Committee was becoming a symbol of the growing concern over the abuse of civil rights.

* * *

"Call Gloria" was becoming a chant of the assembled crowds. It was printed on signs hoisted above the growing crowds. On a near-daily basis, editorial sections of newspapers featured letters from readers supporting Gloria. Careful observers noted that the public was becoming more interested in the conduct of these hearings than in their content. Reports of alleged subversive activities were giving way to the questioning of the government's possible violations of civil rights and the badgering of witnesses.

* * *

Drawing upon her careful coaching, Gloria gave reporters skillfully crafted answers organized to subtly support the legal position they planned on exposing should she appear before the committee. Interviews with the charismatic actress regularly were appearing in the national press. The feisty old lady in chalk-white tennis shoes was fast becoming a symbol, with whom the American public was able to identify.

* * *

In their closed sessions, the committee nervously discussed the wave of controversy rising around Gloria. The chairman was asking, "Do you think we need to pay attention to all the commotion she is creating? Should we request her appearance? After all, how much damage can one washed-up old actress cause?"

CHAPTER 14

Going Their
Separate Ways

BERKELEY, CALIFORNIA, MAY 1949

Neither Natalie nor David trusted themselves to discuss what had happened in New York. Hopefully, with the passage of time, the tension between them would die down and their relationship would survive. David returned to San Francisco by plane. Natalie took the train. After returning home, they managed to avoid talking about their feelings. The demands for Natalie's time in Los Angeles didn't stop. Claiming conflict in schedules, David stopped accompanying her to Los Angeles. He was also keenly aware that her absences were interfering with their weekend sailing adventures.

Caught up in the excitement of launching the transatlantic casting bridge, Natalie was not conscious of how far the deterioration of her midweek relationship with David had progressed. One night after a particularly challenging day, when she returned to an empty hotel room, she was reminded of the many lonely nights she had been forced to endure after exhausting performances. Recalling how she used to feel, *Here I am, after working so hard to make good things happen, returning to an empty room, without anyone to talk to or share my experiences. Who enjoys going to a movie by themselves? Why is it so difficult to live an active life and have someone to share it with? Somehow,*

I need to find a way to patch things up with David before things really get out of control.

Starting to experience twinges of guilt from the lack of attention she was paying David, she asked herself, "Have I unconsciously substituted the challenge of making my new venture work with my previous career in the theater? Maybe, if I can find a way to reduce my trips to Southern California to every other weekend and spend more time with David in the middle of the week, he will take notice I really care about him and I am making an effort to preserve our relationship."

* * *

TONIGHT WOULD BE HER FIRST NIGHT HOME. WANTING TO DEVOTE more attention to David, she had planned something different. As soon as her last class was over, she left school. No more coffee with the girls. Stopping at the neighborhood market, she selected whatever she would need to prepare one of David's favorite dinners, Roast Beef and Yorkshire pudding. Having made her selections, she wandered over to the liquor section looking for a bottle of his favorite red French and white Italian wines.

Walking the length of a block to her parked car, she was passing their favorite record shop when she spotted the long-playing album of Puccini's last opera, *Turandot*, in the new release section. *Who knows, in addition to appreciating my gift, he might associate the familiar plot, "iron maiden's melting under the kiss of the secret prince," with what I am trying to do.*

Arriving home well before David normally was expected to appear, Natalie set the table, peeled the potatoes, thoroughly washed and chopped the salad vegetables, decanted the red wine and put the white on ice. Next she set about to carefully prepare what she hoped would be the highlight dish of the evening, the Yorkshire pudding. From years of experience gained from cooking the delicate and difficult to prepare old English recipe for her family on the Sussex farm, she carefully measured out each of the ingredients, placed them in small bowls, and arranged them in order she would be using them. From her mother, she had learned the secret of a great "Yorkshire" lay in the preparation of the properly greased pan. Before leaving the kitchen, she placed the roast and the potatoes in the pre-heated oven.

GOING THEIR SEPARATE WAYS

* * *

Before disappearing upstairs to change into something more appropriate for the evening she had planned, Natalie placed the long-playing record on the phonograph, retrieved the aromatic candles from the hall closet, and took special care to set the table the way David had long preferred.

David was not only late returning home, but appeared preoccupied when he came through the front door. Without saying a word, he passed by the anxiously awaiting Natalie, proceeded over to the telephone, and asked the operator to make a transatlantic call to Riyadh, Saudi Arabia.

Shocked and disappointed by David's impersonal behavior, his failure to notice the carefully set table, or smell the aromas coming from the kitchen, there was nothing she could do but try to understand his strange behavior. When she recognized the number he had given the operators as the same number of the Prince of Saud's private residence number, she began to relax. *Something of extreme importance must be on David's mind. Relax, ole girl, as soon as he completes his call to the Prince, he will recognize your efforts. Why don't I pour me a glass of wine, walk out on the rear porch, sit down in my favorite chair, watch the sun set over the Golden Gate Bridge, and wait for David to join me?*

* * *

He was just completing his call when she re-entered the house. Still hoping to salvage the evening, she poured two glasses of wine, walked over to where he was standing, set down the two glasses on the nearby table, and engulfed him in her warmest hug, kissed him, and whispered, "I've prepared your favorite dinner, brought home two of your favorite wines, but it is my personal brand of dessert that I hope you will enjoy the most."

Using both hands to gently remove her arms, he disengaged himself, retreated to the front hall, retrieved his hat and coat, and exited out the front door without a word.

Caught completely by surprise, she now knew she had a serious problem on her hands. When she returned to the porch, she was carrying the bottle of wine *and* both glasses.

* * *

She was sipping the last of the wine when she began to wonder, *This is the second time the threat of my career or personal interests has destroyed an important relationship. What am I supposed to have learned? Could it be that I can have a career or a good relationship with an exciting man, but I can't have both at the same time?*

When David failed to return, she finished the last of the wine. A very disappointed Natalie concluded, *I guess there is nothing to prevent my spending the summer in London, assembling the other half of my bridge!*

CHAPTER 15

Stacking the Deck

EL FUERTE, MEXICO, NOVEMBER 1948
The need to supplement the funds in the Mexican war chest couldn't have come at a better time. On almost an everyday basis, the newspapers were reporting the latest developments involved in the committee's questioning of another high-profile witness. Magazines, published weekly, were featuring stories written by former war correspondents, recounts of the testimony of called witnesses, capsulated summaries of their independent research, and their speculations of the possible consequences of the "Red Menace," the spreading influence of Communism. Television, in its infancy, was transmitting visual images and recorded testimony directly into private homes of the American public. Discussions of yesterday's committee events were becoming a regular part of daily conversations.

Signs directing citizens to the nearest air raid shelters were beginning to appear on high-traffic streets. In the schools, air raid survival procedures were being taught and rehearsed with increasing frequency. Showings of *Movietone* weekly news reports were being played in the local movie theaters. Pictures of the Distant Early Warning radar structure being constructed in Alaska were shown to the children during the Saturday matinees and their parents in the evenings.

Families were constructing bomb shelters in their backyards, and parents and children would carefully stock these shelters with food, water, fuel, bedding, and extra clothing. On the weekend, families would practice taking sanctuary in the shelters.

At the same time they were being fed a steady diet of the approaching threat of Communism, the younger people were getting married, taking advantage of the "GI Bill of Rights" to extend their education, having children, looking for work, and seeking ways to spend their pent-up war savings.

Following a series of private discussions, it was decided that another of Señor Arena's old friends, Tom Jenkins, should be asked to invite "Manuel's Club" to his dove hunting ranch for the November 1st opening of Dove Season. Located next to Lake Hidalgo in the province of Sonora, approximately 25 miles east of El Fuerte on the western slope of the Sierra Madre Mountains, it boasted of some of Mexico's finest dove hunting and bass fishing. Its remoteness insulated guests from any unwanted attention.

The nature of the invitation indicated the 2-day stay would be entirely devoted to business, hunting, and fishing, well punctuated by the marvelous cuisine of Tom's kitchen staff and his collection of prewar Pinot Noir wines made from grapes grown in France's Bourgogne region.

Under normal circumstances, the much-coveted invitations to hunt White-winged and Mourning doves would have provided sufficient incentive for these busy executives to take time out of their busy schedules. The prospect of world-class dove hunting and bass fishing made the need for taking care of pending serious business even more appealing.

It had been 8 months since they had last met in Acapulco. There was a growing mountain of evidence that what had been presented as a theoretical plan was rapidly taking shape as a well implemented program. The growing fear of Communism was occurring at an astonishing rate. Public discussions regarding rearming were becoming more common. Stories describing even the remotest of Communist-related occurrences were being disseminated by the press. A new crop of Republican congressional candidates, possessing impressive credentials, supported financially from some new and unknown source of campaign financing, were favored to win election.

Descent to the dirt strip, carved out of the sage brush terrain near El Fuerte, required two extra passes. The first pass was needed to inspect for any livestock that may be standing on the strip or grazing alongside. The second pass was needed to herd any cattle, horses, pigs, or chickens away from the strip. A strange assortment of vehicles were parked alongside the deserted strip.

The aged, well-worn, much-dented vehicles with cracked windows showing signs of rust contrasted with the sleek, well polished black limousines that had awaited them on their prior arrival in Acapulco. Had anybody been observing the arrival of the smaller private aircraft, they would have concluded the disembarking men were American sportsmen who Tom typically invited to hunt and fish.

What was left of the afternoon was devoted to transporting the arriving guests to their accommodations in the lodge, unpacking, naps, and refreshing showers. Having changed into their tropical hunting clothes, they no longer resembled the high-powered executives that had departed their point of origin earlier that same morning. Similar to their other visits, when they appeared at the carefully planned cocktail party, they were pleased to see their old well respected friends with whom they were engaged in the serious business of reviving government military contracting.

Following the congenial cocktail party, discussions over dinner and after dinner were limited to taking care of business. Starting at five o'clock the next morning, their time had been reserved for hunting, a buffet lunch served in the field, and an afternoon of bass fishing.

The cocktail hour was devoted to Jordan's reporting on the disturbing progress that was being accomplished with all three of the separate strategies he had described in Acapulco. His presentation was concise and succinct, only interrupted by questions for clarification. Anxious to move the discussion to the new crop of *committed congressional candidates* that were smoothly making their way through the nomination and electoral process, he reported, "After completing my tour and meeting all the prospective candidates each of you or your regional political representatives suggested I interview, I felt the need to make a solitary decision. In my judgment, there were so many qualified candidates, rather than be forced to deny the candidacy of a promising young politician, in accordance with the limitations of our budgeted stipulations, I decided we should support the election of the larger number of qualified candidates. I made this decision out of the conviction our interests would be better served if we committed both our nominating and final election budgets to assisting the larger number of outstanding candidates to become nominated. Once we have diagnostic proof of their electability and we are assured of their future loyalty, I plan to return to you and obtain the additional financial support we need to finance their final election campaigns."

The Detroit automaker, wishing to reinforce Jordan's decision in a positive and supporting manner, asked, "Is there some magic number of committed loyal votes we will need to assure passage of our agenda items?"

"Excellent question! As I attempted to explain in Acapulco, we can never be confident of how accurately we can predict how the traditional voting congressmen will vote for or against any particular bill of importance. The question we have been attempting to resolve is how many committed, loyal votes will be needed to be added to our predictable voting base to assure passage. For the most part, they are under the influence of the National Party. While each of you are entitled to make your own enquiries, it's important that Manuel's Club remains anonymous and refrains from conducting any form of direct communications. Not confident that we will ever know what a foolproof 60 percent majority will require, I concluded we should support the largest possible number of qualified candidates and remain prepared to take advantage of each election cycle to add more qualified members to this first crop."

Someone sitting near the rear of the room announced, "Jordan, now that's what I call skillful leadership. Already, I have been hearing stories describing this new, hot group of candidates making their way toward Washington. Not only do my friends appear to be impressed by the size and the talent of this new wave, but they are wondering where all the money has been coming from required to fund so many 'high-octane' campaigns. I hope I speak for everyone in this room when I say, 'Good job!' Thank you. Without further ado, why don't you pass the envelopes? Isn't it surprising to learn how quickly the cost of making movies can increase?"

"Not so fast!" From the right side of the room, the high-pitched voice of the chemical producer from Delaware asked, "Jordan, in arriving at the total amount of additional funding you will need, have you included any extra funding you may need to complete your publicity campaign and put the finishing touches on your Washington lobbyist program?"

Smiling before he answered, Jordan said, "The magnitude of the free publicity, generated from our congressional hearing campaign, has been so prolific, we have not been required to commit more than half of what we originally allocated for publicity purposes. Although I can't be certain, I have assumed the remaining funds should provide us with adequate reserves to deal with any unanticipated contingencies."

From the left side of the room, the deep booming voice of the steelmaker from Pittsburgh could be clearly heard. "Gentlemen, as you understand, I am not known for my frivolous tendencies. When I think of all the fine progress Jordan and his team have accomplished, the relative magnitude of what we stand to gain, and the difficulty and risk involved in organizing another meeting, I would like to suggest we double the number contained in the enveloped we are about to receive."

No one was quite certain whether the standing ovation was meant to approve the suggestion or demonstrate their appreciation of Jordan's actions, but nobody really cared. The jubilant environment erased any restraint over enjoying after-dinner cocktails, conducting congenial conversations, or learning of recent developments in their friends' businesses. Old friends and valued colleagues were enjoying themselves. They were taking satisfaction in what they had helped to create. They were imagining when their factories would be fully devoted to producing needed goods for the American military. Unfortunately, any thoughts of rising at five o'clock to go hunting the next morning were conveniently ignored or entirely forgotten.

CHAPTER 16

Gloria's Finest Performance

WASHINGTON, D.C., FEBRUARY 1949

Within a few days, the committee had assembled its list of questions for Gloria Adams. The subpoena was issued and served. Richard Allen Bailey was chosen by his colleagues to lead the questioning.

When the day arrived for her hearing, Gloria took her place. She was sitting at the witness table exhibiting a serene sense of self-confidence. She was dressed in what had become her trademarked grandmotherly smock and chalk-white tennis shoes. Her Sentinel-supplied attorney was seated next to her. Don Cerreta was sitting at the far end of the table. Natalie, Walt Matthews, and Mike, some of the last to arrive, were sitting unobserved near the rear of the hearing room.

If Gloria couldn't respond with her customary one-word answer, she would look confused and ask Bailey for further clarification.

The opening questions addressed to Gloria were simple in nature and were being offered in a pleasant, nonconfrontational manner. Gloria answered each of the questions with yes and no answers. After the first hour, the environment in the hearing room began to change. The questions were becoming more complex and open-ended. They were the kind of questions that were difficult to answer with yes and no responses. Gloria, as planned, responded with short, concise answers. If she couldn't answer in the manner that had been agreed to, she politely inquired for further information or questioned the accuracy of the foundation of the question. Upset by her unwillingness to answer in a more complete fashion, the frustrated committee chairman slammed down his gavel before he announced in a loud threatening tone, "Miss Adams, I think we deserve more complete answers."

The well prepared actress responded despite the outburst with supreme calm. "Excuse me, Mr. Chairman, how can I be expected to respond if I don't understand the question or believe the premise for the question doesn't conform with what I believe to be true? Perhaps if Mr. Bailey would explain the basis of his questions in a clearer fashion and refrain from basing them on value judgments and incorrect assumptions, I could respond more readily."

"You are out of order! Don't for one second believe you can *play cute* and refuse to answer our questions. Do you understand that the committee can hold you in contempt of Congress?"

"Excuse me, Mr. Chairman, may I interrupt?" asked Don Cerreta who had been quietly sitting at the far end of the witness table. All heads turned toward the respected federal prosecutor as he slowly rose before asking the court reporter if she would be kind enough to read back the transcript of the prior question and Miss Adams's answer. "Mr. Chairman, once she reads back the transcript, I think we should be able to determine if the witness refused to answer any question or simply asked for clarification."

The chairman placed his hand over his microphone, turned to Bailey and the other committeemen seated nearby, and asked, "What should we do? How can we deny a request from a federal prosecutor?"

Bailey and the others only shrugged.

With a deepened frown, the chairman turned back toward the front of the room to ask, "Would the stenotype operator please read back the last question and answer."

Once she had read aloud the exchange between Gloria and Bailey, Cerreta immediately stated, "I think the transcript clearly states the witness was asking for clarification. The law clearly states that a witness is not required to answer any question not deemed relevant to the case at hand. If she doesn't understand the question, how can she be expected to respond?"

The room came to life with excited murmuring. For the first time, someone had challenged the committee. Its leaders seemed genuinely confused.

The eyes of the spectators shifted between the chairman and Bailey, watching as they struggled to respond.

Without warning, Don Cerreta continued his line of questioning. "Mr. Bailey, do my notes accurately reflect the circumstances under which the subpoena was issued?"

"I've scanned the case," Bailey hesitantly answered.

"Very well. In that case, I'm sure you won't mind telling us which law you believe Miss Adams is suspected of violating."

* * *

SILENCE WAS THE ONLY REPLY.

"What law did Miss Adams, or any of the guests who attended her party in October of 1937, succeed in breaking? Was the fact that some of the guests were known to be members of some Socialistic or Communistic political party? Oh, by the way, would you remind us if being a member of the Communist Party was against the law in 1937?"

Spontaneous laughter from the spectators and the press brought another angry banging of the gavel.

"Very well," Cerreta coolly suggested, "let us return to the circumstances of the hearing. What law did Miss Adams break by inviting friends to her house? Does the record suggest that they were planning the overthrow of the United States government?"

Clearly, the atmosphere in the committee room had changed. Counsel for the witness was asking the questions, and committee members were unsure or not prepared to respond. The chairman, looking to his fellow committeemen for assistance, found only perplexed looks. Unsure how to respond, he called for a 10-minute recess.

During the break, the elevated excitement in the room grew stronger. Complete strangers were excitedly talking to the person standing next to them. They were expressing their surprise how quickly the role of the inquisitor and those who were being interrogated had been reversed. The animated conversations, occurring all throughout the room, were only interrupted by the banging the chairman's gavel signaling the resumption of the hearing. He then proceeded to announce, "I believe this entire matter can be cleared up if the witness would agree to answer one final question." He gestured toward Bailey.

Gloria listened closely as Bailey read the question. Once he had finished, she said, "I respectfully decline to answer. I prefer to invoke my rights under the Fifth Amendment."

The shocked silence in the room was complete. The brave lady had just put the Fifth Amendment defense into play and challenged the very foundation of the committee's assumed authority.

"Miss Adams, are you aware that we regard your refusal to answer an act of contempt of Congress?"

Rising from her seat, Gloria stood erect before the committee before speaking. "I have been advised by counsel if there is a possibility that I might incriminate myself, I have to assume that it is being inferred that I have broken the law. Accordingly, I enjoy the same protections as provided under the Fifth Amendment."

"Miss Adams, I don't know from whom you're getting your legal advice, but I must remind you that you are appearing before this committee to answer questions. No, you have not been charged with a crime. Therefore, your protections under the First and Fifth Amendments do not apply. I must advise you that unless you answer the question, you will be found in contempt of Congress."

Don Cerreta slowly rose. His deliberate movement attracted the attention of the committee, members of the audience, and the entire press corps. There was something about the impression he was sending that indicated a matter of extreme importance was about to be discussed.

The federal prosecutor, after handing a copy of the brief to each member of the committee, the opposing lead counsel, and the court reporter, began his remarks. "The U.S. Attorney General's office, knowing this question might arise, has developed its own brief. With your permission, I would like to enter it into the transcript of this hearing. You may wish to review it before we proceed or you consider charging Miss Adams with contempt of Congress!

"In essence, this brief concludes that if the committee's questioning of Miss Adams infers that a crime has been committed, the witness is entitled to use her rights as prescribed by the First and Fifth Amendments in exactly the same fashion as she would if she had been charged with a crime."

The chairman immediately flipped through the pages, his face reddening. After a full 2 minutes of silence, he announced, "The witness is excused."

The spectators went wild, laughing, whistling, and clapping as the press busied itself with making notes. The committee, its lawyers, and its staff filed out of the room in embarrassed silence.

Once the noise had receded somewhat, Gloria, her attorney, and Don proceeded toward the rear doors of the hearing room. Anyone who had been seated rose to join in a standing ovation. Gloria Adams had just given her finest performance. With the assistance of the Sentinels, she had leveled the legal playing field of the House Un-American Activities Committee.

* * *

SEVERAL DAYS LATER, EXHAUSTED FROM HER LONG COAST-TO-COAST flight, Gloria entered her darkened house. When she flipped on her hallway light switch, she took a step back in shock: all her closest friends, along with Natalie and David, stood waiting for her in the living room. "Surprise!" they all shouted together.

Gloria was at a loss for words. Never in her wildest dreams had she imagined going to Washington to join a political protest, or that she would earn the appreciation of so many of her friends and acquaintances. Quickly regaining her composure, she reached over to her desk, picked up a yellow pad, and said to the gathered friends, "Now that all of you are here, I was wondering if you would mind writing your names down on this pad and indicating if you are or ever have been a member of the Communist Party. There are some people in Washington who are depending upon me to furnish them with the information."

Gloria got her laugh. The tension was broken, and the party began. The first round of champagne bottles had been popped and the hors d'oeuvres had been served. Myron Goldman, the well-known CEO of one of Hollywood's largest studios, after clinking a fork against his champagne flute, said, "Excuse me, everyone!"

When the jovial chaos of the party died down, he continued. "All of us in the industry wish to express our gratitude for all you have done. You, Miss Adams, and all your Sentinel friends, have improved the lives of so many people. Hopefully, you have provided our country with an important lesson in how fragile our civil liberties can be and how diligent we need to remain if we are to protect what is uniquely ours. We will forever be in your debt. Nice job, thank you!"

The guests cheered and raised their glasses.

Making her way to the piano, Natalie could feel everyone's eyes following her. She thought, *They must be wondering what is planned next.* After looking around at all the faces, she asked, "How many of you remember before Gloria became the beautiful star in all those earlier movies, she was originally recruited for her singing and dancing skills?

"Gloria, before I ask you to join me in a song, I have something I would like to give you. I am holding in my hand four serious inquiries of employment from London. It appears that news of the 'Heroine of Hollywood' has crossed the Atlantic! Your presence appears to be requested. On behalf of all your friends, I would like to congratulate you on once again being a working member of our industry!"

As the applause died down, Gloria walked up and hugged Natalie. The older actress then turned to the guests, and after extending her arms, she started to talk. "For some time, I have begun to feel my active life, as I have known it, was drawing to a close. Isn't it interesting to learn what can happen when one *pissed-off* old broad decides to get mad and do something about it?"

Some of those who were standing and applauding were having a difficult time comprehending the reaction of others. Close, longtime friends of Gloria's appeared to genuinely appreciate all of the positive reinforcement she was receiving. Those who were attending to extend their gratitude were some of the most demonstrative. Then there were the others who were still engulfed in the inquisitional tyranny. Not certain of what would happen next, they chose to stand quietly and allow their presence to speak for their appreciation.

When the mixed applause started to settle down, Natalie motioned to the accompanist to take his place at the piano and motioned for Gloria to join her. When things had quieted, Natalie turned to her new-old friend and asked, "And what would a 'Pissed-Off Old Broad' care to sing?"

CHAPTER 17

Playing of the Year

MEXICO CITY, NOVEMBER 1948

Following the conclusion of hosting "Manuel's Movie Night," Señor Arena had been receiving periodic calls from his uncharacteristically effusive friend, J. Jordan McWilliams. He wanted to thank his friend for arranging his evening with Miss Mercedes Velasquez and expressing his desire to meet her again. Manuel took this endorsement seriously. In his mind, it helped confirm his opinion of Mercedes as someone who understood the game and could be counted on to play her part with his other rich and influential Mexico City friends.

Over the following months, Mercedes found herself enrolled in acting classes, working with a voice coach, and taking ballet lessons. Almost every week she was asked to study new scripts and prepare for screen tests or auditions. To her delight, she discovered the roles she was testing for demanded serious dramatic talent.

Her wardrobe, her makeup, and her jewelry and accessories now reflected top-of-the-line Mexico's finest shops that customarily lent to the studio. Señor Arena personally supervised the selection of every item. Everything seemed so different . . . nothing like the halfhearted effort the studio had put into preparing her for the embarrassingly small role in Manuel's previous film.

The rest of the studio crew began to realize that Mercedes was being set up to be Señor Arena's most recent "Plaything of the Year." When they talked among themselves, they would say, "Manuel should award us for our performance on the set!"

On the days reserved for screen tests, Manuel could be seen standing behind the camera, holding a copy of the script. One moment he would be studying the pages; in the next, he would be inspecting the camera settings, checking the lighting, and making suggestions to the director.

Almost every night, Manuel requested that Mercedes accompany him to what seemed like an endless stream of private parties, gallery openings, and political receptions. On the evenings when they attended the symphony, ballet, or opera, the exquisitely styled starlet could be seen sitting next to Manuel in his private box. The ever-present press was always nearby, taking pictures and asking questions.

After several weeks, word began to circulate that a serious new role was being prepared for Mercedes. Manuel had selected her for the lead in an exciting new movie and introduced her to the renowned director assigned to the film.

On the set, the cast and crew treated her with courtesy and respect. Her drama coach and script assistant were constantly by her side. Even the director, known for his impatience and harsh temper, was quick to compliment her when he approved of her work. When she failed to please him, he patiently showed her what he wanted.

On the weekends, it was not unusual for Mercedes to receive invitations to accompany one of Manuel's friends she had met at the constant receptions they had been attending. The big wealth of Mexico was held by a surprisingly small number of older families. The financial titans she met owned spectacular homes in any one of several coastal cities, near small villages, or on large family-owned haciendas.

Separate rooms were always provided. There were closets well stocked with a broad selection of bathing suits, casual lounging clothes, and high-fashion evening and cocktail dresses, all carefully chosen to fit her. Velvet-covered boxes containing gifts of expensive jewelry were to be found sitting on top of her bedside table, together with a short welcoming note from her weekend benefactor.

Sometimes, her host would request she join him on his elegant yacht. Once she was on board, she never knew whether the ship would remain in port or venture out of the bay and turn north or south. On the shorter trips, they would sail up to Zihuatanejo, while the longer trips usually ended at Puerto Vallarta.

Mercedes particularly enjoyed the longer cruises. Once they had arrived at their destination, onboard cranes would gently lift the highly polished, wood-planked Chris Craft powerboat from its cradle and carefully place it in the water. During the day, the powerboat was used to pull water skiers or inspect the more interesting caves that were to be found at the base of the shoreline cliffs. At night, the same boats would serve as their ship-to-shore taxi.

Some of the eloquent dinner parties were hosted by one of her host's friends. To Mercedes, she looked forward to meeting his male friends, the same men she had often read about in the Mexico City newspapers. As she became more accustomed to the elegance of the dinner parties and the presence of what appeared to be some of Mexico's most important men, it hadn't taken very long before Mercedes began to notice that none of the other women were married to their evening's escort. They all shared the advantages of youth and beauty. Some of them were talented musicians, recognizable actresses, and models. And some were secretaries and personal assistants. At first, she was somewhat surprised by the effort their host-dates made to introduce their companions to each of the other men.

It was until she had witnessed this *"tribal ceremony"* for the third time when it occurred to her that she was part of another unspoken competition between the male guests to determine which one of them would be accompanied by the most beautiful and desirable woman.

Mercedes, an experienced beauty contestant, was amused by the extraordinary attention she was receiving. She learned to insist that she be escorted to the beach club that existed in every port they visited. The lively action of the beach clubs would customary not begin until 1:00 a.m., about the same time that Mexico's custom of late-night dining would be completed. Housed in a large, cone-shaped, open-air building, complete with a large, circular bar and a high thatched ceiling, the clubs were the source of local excitement. Dominated by the loud mariachi music being played on the raised stage behind the circular bar, the two large cocktail areas, each furnished with small tables and wicker chairs, were separated by two very large dance floors. The club was always filled with Mexican men who loved to dance. The lively patrons, invigorated by generous amounts of rum or tequila, would perform their favorite Latin steps with a variety of the attractive single women who regularly frequented the club.

Mercedes loved the mixed fruit juice and rum drinks, the music, the conversations with intelligent men, the constant laughter, and the intoxicating atmosphere of the club. Sometimes, she and her partner joined the congested movement on the dance floor, and sometimes, she accepted another man's invitation, and sometimes she danced alone. Her beauty and her growing celebrity status always caught the attention of the people sitting in the cocktail areas, the other dancers, and the ever-present press. The budding starlet was learning to enjoy the admiration of the approving crowd.

Later, back on the yacht, a still exhilarated Mercedes understood she would have to decide whether to accept the inevitable lovemaking invitation from her generous host. Clearly, she believed it was the lady's choice. If her host had been rude, less than charming, inattentive, less generous with his gifts of jewelry and clothing, or not physically appealing, Mercedes could politely excuse herself and retire to her separate stateroom.

* * *

MERCEDES NEVER DISCUSSED HER LATE-NIGHT ADVENTURES WITH Manuel. She had no way of knowing that each of these trips had been approved, in advance, by him, and that he only gave his consent when he received a significant favor from, or owed a debt to, one of his friends. They did, however, become a topic of frequent conversation among Señor Arena's wealthy, influential Mexico City friends. Those who had succeeded in spending the entire evening with the actress received their approval. Unwittingly, she found herself involved in a very sick game, a game played each year by the wealthy and powerful.

CHAPTER 18

Plan

The news of Gloria's appearance before the committee had immediately caught the attention of J. Jordan McWilliams and the other members of Manuel's Club. Independently, they were able to confirm what they were hearing from people who witnessed her performance. To a person, they all agreed, *"The days of the committee's bullying tactics were drawing to a close. No longer would their more important witnesses appear unprepared or without the benefit of qualified counsel."*

Unaccustomed to defeat, J. Jordan McWilliams felt in the pit of his stomach impending doom. He barricaded himself in his office. He did not return phone calls or answer his correspondence. He asked his secretary to cancel all his meetings, decline requests for future meetings, and keep his calendar clear. He needed time to think and prepare.

Jordan had studied Don Cerreta's brief. After several readings, he knew from experience he was looking at a highly sophisticated, thoroughly researched, and exceedingly well written, precedent-setting example of legal craftsmanship. After sitting back and thinking about what he had just finished studying, the wily veteran was forced to conclude, *It takes an extraordinary amount of time, legal expertise, and expense to put together a landmark legal brief of this quality. This brief is well beyond the scope of what the government is capable of accomplishing. Someone else had to be responsible. Who is capable, who possesses that kind of money? Who is so determined to oppose us? What are they trying to accomplish? Groups like this just don't happen!*

* * *

THE MORE HE THOUGHT ABOUT HIS PROBLEM, THE MORE CONVINCED he became he needed assistance. *Who can I trust? Who stands to gain by stopping us? Could it be one of Manuel's Club members? Could it be Manuel? There is a lot of our money in his safe. Could it be some branch of the government, or could it be Manuel's Cuban investment partners?*

Do I need to have a chat with some of my security company friends? Maybe they could discover what is going on, who is behind this, and suggest a course of remedial action.

* * *

AS THE DAYS WORE ON, HIS DEPRESSION DIDN'T SUBSIDE. QUITE THE opposite; it continued to deepen. There had never been a time in his life for headaches, emotional distractions, or wasted time. He knew he had no choice. *We can't continue to carry out this plan and not risk exposure until we learn who is behind the opposition and deal with the problem.*

* * *

EACH MORNING WHEN HE AROSE, HE COMPLETED HIS FLOOR EX-ERCISES, dressed for the day, and went to his car. He no longer insisted on reading the morning papers and dictating any new thoughts. His cherished routines no longer held any joy for him.

Long walks in Battery Park, boat rides to the Statue of Liberty, and dinners alone at Sweets, his favorite seafood restaurant near the Fulton Fish Market, helped relieve some of his anxiety, but not all. No matter how hard he tried, he sensed the growing doom that his world was about to collapse.

* * *

ON THE NIGHTS WHEN HE DID RETURN HOME, HE WOULD ATTEMPT to explain to his wife over their nightly Old Fashioned what was happening.

When he tried to express his fears, his wife seemed unconcerned. Disappointed by her seeming lack of interest, he would have to listen to her as she said, "I am sure you will find a solution; you always have. Everything will appear better tomorrow after a fine dinner, a bottle of your favorite wine, and a good night's sleep."

Wishing to limit the dinner conversation to nonthreatening small talk, he would listen quietly to his wife describe her charitable endeavors, the daily activities of their children, and any new gossip she had heard from the "girls."

When he again tried to tell her that the problems were serious, her inability to relate to his problems was rapidly shifting his opinion of her. He felt she was becoming one of his enemies.

* * *

ONCE HE GOT TO BED, HE WOULD LIE AWAKE, WORRYING ABOUT HIS problems, becoming increasingly upset. No matter how hard he tried, dropping off into a deep sleep was becoming more difficult. On one such sleepless night, Jordan finally gave in to his restlessness and stepped out of bed. He padded downstairs, poured himself a drink of his favorite Cognac, quietly made a fire in the library fireplace, lit one of his favorite cigars, and eased into his deep, comfortable chair.

As he watched the flames dance through the sides of his amber-filled snifter, he found himself momentarily at peace. For the first time in 4 days, he could sense his mind clearing, not unlike the temporary lifting of a thick fog. He was starting to see glimpses of new alternatives, ways to overcome his recent defeat. Anything has to be better than sitting here and stewing in his own juices.

It was during one of these nightly sessions when the idea that there was nothing to prohibit him from discussing his concerns with attorneys who represented the majority of the companies operated by the members of Manuel's Club when the thick fog that had been clouding his mind started to rise. *These were no ordinary lawyers; they were men experienced in dealing with disturbing news, using their analytical minds to search for new solutions, and working cohesively together to execute new plans of action. They obviously had risen to the pinnacle of their profession and earned their positions of trust and respect the hard way. There were valid reasons why they served as confidants to their powerful employers. Individually and collectively, they represented some of the nation's more brilliant minds.*

Late in the afternoon of the following day, Jordan and the six attorneys were gathered in the privacy of his office at Southwick & Cornforth. The day staff had departed. Other than the building maintenance staff, there was no one present, no one who could report their meeting.

To a man, each of the lawyers was deeply concerned about the future of Jordan. By the end of the first hour, it had become clear that they only had two choices: shut down their operation and abandon the rearmament goals or find an alternate solution.

Ben Holt, a bear of a man with a keen mind and considerable curiosity, a former Harvard classmate of Jordan's, was attempting to summarize. "I think there's something going on here that we don't fully understand. Take that legal brief, for example. Whoever provided that work has to be well funded and motivated to oppose what we are attempting. Their presence raises two questions . . . Who are they, and why are they so determined."

Pete Scott, the Houston attorney, immediately said, "It has been reported that Mike Stone and Natalie Cummins were seen sitting together in the back of the hearing room when Gloria Adams appeared before the committee. I know from personal experience that Mike Stone is the same Mike Stone of Stone City Bank and one of the original Sentinels. He and his friends were deeply involved in their effort to diversify the oil industry. They are no strangers to our kind of problem and deserve to be respected. If they are involved, and judging by the growing number of Hollywood personalities that are appearing in the audience of the committee hearings, I would think this problem is not going away."

Alarmed by this revelation, Jordan said, "That means trouble! Several of my German clients tell me these Sentinels, prior to the conclusion of the last war, managed to prevent them from using their 'fortunes of war' to finance the organization of a future Fourth Reich."

Bert Damner, the Seattle aircraft lawyer, said, "I am not aware of any connection between the musical stage and Hollywood movie production. How do we not know whoever is behind this is primarily interested in the civil rights issues that may be involved, not our rearmament plan?"

Dale Pennington, the Los Angeles lawyer, immediately answered, "It's no secret. Natalie Cummins has recently announced her intention of starting a transatlantic entertainment industry casting company. According to reports, she appears to be intent on taking advantage of her theatrical associations in London to find employment for out-of-work commercially successful Hollywood movie actors, writers, and directors. It would appear she has become most upset with the inquisitional Communist tyranny the Hollywood studios are attempting to impose on members of their industry. If she was accompanied by Mike Stone, could it be she has managed to enlist the assistance of the Sentinels?"

Ken Hoffman, a bespectacled Pittsburgh attorney known for his caution and dedication, spoke next. "Jordan, knowing we have someone as resourceful as the Sentinels on our trail scares the hell out of me. I question whether the Sentinels would become involved unless they believed the problems they are hearing are part of a more elaborate plan. I don't think we should discount that possibility. Should the sources and recipients of our fund become public information, breaking a few election laws could become the least of our worries.

"Fortunately, our Mexican war chest has recently been replenished with twice the amount of money you originally requested. Under current conditions, knowing we have access to the extra funds gives me some comfort. At least we know we have plenty of money available to fight back, should it become necessary. In the meantime, I strongly recommend we shut down the Acapulco operation, repatriate the balance of our money, and destroy any records Manuel may be keeping as soon as possible."

"Fine, fine," said Burt Damner, a long-recognized supporter for moving the appropriation bills through Congress as quickly as possible. "My clients have been telling me these new planes they have on their drawing boards should render obsolete every frontline aircraft currently in use by the Americans or the Russians. Final preparations are being undertaken to advance their development from the design stage to the prototype manufacturing stage. The prototypes are needed for final testing. They believe the prototype stage is the most critical phase of new product development and must be carefully protected. Until this stage has been successfully committed, the consummation of the really big contracts cannot be completed."

* * *

BREAKING INTO THE CONVERSATION, PETE SCOTT ASKED, "BURT, ARE you suggesting we are to ignore the risk our clients will be exposed to should we proceed with our present plan?"

"No, I am about to suggest we approach the problem from a different direction. What do you think might happen if we approached the National Committees of both the Republican and the Democratic parties to inquire how supportive they might become of our particular agenda in exchange for us individually and collectively making significant financial contributions, with the prospect of more to follow?

"In my haste to introduce fresh thinking, I may have failed to mention other steps that have to be part of any plan. If you will allow me to explain, I think I might convince you why this new plan can be made to work.

"In Texas, we have a group of wealthy and powerful businessmen who regularly meet in Suite F of Houston's Shamrock Hilton Hotel. They assemble for the purpose of assessing the political electability and philosophy of aspirants seeking election to offices throughout Texas. Prior to contributing to their individual campaigns, we have to be assured they are prepared to support the political agenda of both the state and the Central Republican Committees. By the time they have progressed up our political ladder, we have assured ourselves they can be depended upon. Interestingly enough, I have been reliably informed the Democratic Party follows a similar procedure.

"By contributing to both the state and national political committees of both the Republican and Democratic parties, we should be able to control who gets nominated. From that point forward, we can relax. Independent of who wins the general election, our interests and agendas will be well represented."

Thinking ahead, Jordan asked, "How many seats do we have to control before we can create a majority in a close vote on *sensitive* legislation?"

"Not as many as you might think. You would be surprised to learn how frequently senators and congressmen habitually vote along traditional party lines. If we were to assume those votes will be somewhat evenly split over issues of concern, we will only need to control enough votes, when added to the regular vote, to provide a majority. If I had to guess, we would need to control less than 10 seats in the Senate and maybe 40 seats in the House."

Hoffman, who had been making some notes, asked, "How much will it cost to support the election of 55 members to Congress? I am not up to date on what the current cost of a campaign at each of the different political levels is, but when you multiply any reasonable estimate by 55, you are talking about a lot of money."

Expecting the question, Pete was ready with his answer. "Maybe not as much as you might think. When you factor into consideration we will only be willing to support candidates who have provided evidence of their campaign fund, raising our contribution should represent less than 50 percent of their total campaign costs to support one-third, or 17 candidates, every 2 years. As a consequence, the annual cost becomes much more manageable, well within the collective contributions Manuel's members are accustomed to making each year. The only difference is we would have to develop some means for coordinating our individual contributions to national political parties."

Thinking out loud, Jordan asked, "Should we be ready to abandon one of our original concepts. Wouldn't it be more practical to limit our support of new candidates to compensate for our failure to attract the cooperation of a suitable number of incumbent candidates?"

* * *

AN OBVIOUSLY AGITATED BERT DAMNER WAS ON HIS FEET. "JORDAN, I agree with you. While there is little doubt that given enough time, the new programs we have just finished outlining should provide us with the desired control, how does that program address our more immediate problem? Before we abandon our present program, don't we need to focus our efforts on what will be required to introduce and pass our pending legislation?"

* * *

HEARING ONLY COMMENTS OF ASSENT AND NOTICING THE NODDING heads of approval, the rejuvenated and much relieved *"Lawyer from Wall Street"* said, "Gentlemen, I would like to congratulate you! It would appear that not only have we succeeded in turning a very nasty problem into an even better potential opportunity, but the implementation will require our clients to become more dependent upon our respective legal services. Maybe we should think of ourselves as the *Voices Beyond the Voices Behind the Curtain?* Why don't we plan on completing our research assignments and reconvening at the earliest possible opportunity?"

CHAPTER 19

Mercedes Exits Mexico

MEXICO CITY, JANUARY 1949

One night after attending an exhibition of Diego Rivera's most recent painting, Manuel invited Mercedes to accompany him back to his house for an after-dinner drink. Without thinking about the possible consequences, she automatically accepted his invitation. With everything seeming so exciting, she didn't think to question what was really happening. He had a lot to drink, and she wanted to make certain he safely returned home.

Mercedes must not have been paying attention when he said, "Let's do something different; I have something I want to show you."

They were comfortably sitting on one of the magnificent overstuffed white leather couches in his viewing room when he offered her one of his large, bell-shaped snifters generously filled with his favorite Cognac. She was surprised when he stood up, walked to the far wall, and punched a cleverly concealed button. A wall-size panel began to move, revealing a very large walk-in safe.

* * *

STANDING BEHIND HIM, SHE COULD SEE LARGE STACKS OF AMERICAN dollars, shelves of color-coded files, long narrow tubes that appeared to be filled with gold coins, and rows of large, one-inch thick cylindrical metal cans that presumably contained movie films all carefully labeled with titles she couldn't read. His attention seemed to be focused on the top-most row. Taking his time, he selected one of the thin cans, opened it, and withdrew the 16-millimeter movie reel before saying, "Here, this should prove entertaining."

The moving of another panel revealed a motion picture projector. A big screen dropped out of the ceiling. As they were sitting on his big deep couch, sipping Cognac, they watched one of his friends, a man who Mercedes had previously met, enjoying himself with one of the girls Mercedes knew from the studio. Without warning, Manuel pulled her over to him, pushed one of his hands down her front, and began fondling her while he watched the movie. Next, he grabbed her other free hand and stuck it down the front of his trousers. That was when Mercedes pulled back her hand, stood up, and walked out of the room.

Sitting in the back of the cab, she realized she needed to escape from Manuel's world and the unfortunate situation she had unwittingly allowed to occur.

* * *

AT ARENA STUDIOS, THE WHEELS OF MOVIE PRODUCTION HAD BEEN slowly turning. The producers of Mercedes's new film regarded her as a beautiful but unremarkable actress; reviewing the takes was not an immediate priority. The canisters containing the developed films of her latest takes had been stacked on the bottom shelf, along with the films of movies of lesser importance. Judging from their dust-laden appearance, they had been left unattended for quite some time. When the arrangements were finally made, only the cinematographer, the dialogue coach, and the assistant director were sitting in the room.

To their surprise, they were watching the captivating performance of a fine actress. She was delivering sensitive, well written dialogue with naturalness and professionalism normally associated with a veteran-accomplished actress. Her performance was electrifying, the on-screen chemistry she managed to develop with the handsome middle-aged male actor enlivened every scene. Realizing they had vastly underestimated her acting abilities, they replayed the rushes over and over. Finally, all three men agreed, there was something special about Mercedes's abilities, something they had not seen in a very long time. With renewed enthusiasm, they dragged the lead director and the executive producer into the small theater and asked the projectionist to rerun the rushes. Thirty minutes later, it was agreed; they would schedule the next shoot for the following Monday.

* * *

ON MONDAY MORNING, WHEN MERCEDES FAILED TO ARRIVE AT THE studio for her hair and makeup appointments, the impatient lead director and the crew waited for an hour. After another hour had elapsed and she had still not arrived, the concerned director sent his assistant to find her. Forty-five minutes later, he returned to the set and told the director, "She's not here; she's not in her apartment; nobody has seen her. Her driver reported when she failed to appear curbside, he knocked on her apartment door, and when he failed to receive a response, he contacted the apartment manager, who used his passkey and allowed me to enter her apartment. Everything was cleared out. All her clothes, her money, her jewelry—everything! Clearly, she has left and is not planning to return."

* * *

Unaware of what had occurred at Arena Studios, a hungover and depressed Manuel was sitting behind his desk, drinking coffee, and hoping nothing of importance would interfere with what was going to be a difficult day. The events of the previous Saturday night were still embedded in his wounded brain. *Mercedes isn't the first unappreciative actress who has stormed out of my home, and she's probably not the last.*

* * *

FOLLOWING A PERFUNCTORY KNOCK, THE DIRECTOR ENTERED ARENA'S office, then collapsed into the deep leather chair and announced, "Boss, it looks like we have a problem."

There was nothing Manuel could do but sit quietly, sip his coffee, and listen as he was told what had happened. He was not surprised by what he was hearing. Feeling no obligation to relate what had happen between Mercedes and himself, he was tapping his forehead with his index finger as he attempted to focus his foggy attention on the anxious director.

After a long pause, he said, "If what you are telling me about her performance is accurate, this is a movie we need to finish shooting. We've invested a great deal of our investors' money in this production, and the studio needs a hit! We can't afford to lose her. Somehow, we need to find out where she went and bring her back! Finding her may not be so difficult. Convincing her to return, positively motivated to complete the movie, may be more difficult."

* * *

A FEW DAYS LATER, A LARGE CARTON CONTAINING 24 PERFECT, LONG-stem red roses, a new contract, a very large check, and a personal apology from Manuel was delivered to Gloria's home in Brentwood. It was addressed to Mercedes Velasquez.

Mercedes was confused. Never in her wildest imagination had she assumed that Manuel would apologize and literally make her an offer that would be difficult to refuse. As tempted as she might have been to return to Mexico City and finish the film, she understood her returning to Mexico City would expose her to Manuel and his pack of jackal friends. In the next moment she thought of the reel of film Arena had stored in his safe. *Maybe I am being a bit hasty,* she thought.

CHAPTER 20

Target Manuel

NEW YORK, DECEMBER 1949

Word of Cecelia's remarkable discovery was quickly circulated among the other Sentinels and their colleagues. From all indications, it seemed apparent that Manuel Arena's indiscretions might be the weakest link in a very complex chain and vulnerable to attack. It was mutually decided it was time to attack on a second front. Should they manage to legally obtain possession of the Manuel's Club operating records, presumed to be in Manuel's private safe, they reasoned they might be able to publically expose the source of the contributions and the recipients. Voter reaction to the information would not only interfere with the designated candidates' quest for election or re-election, but severely hamper the identified lobbyists, the law firm, and the responsible donors' ability to directly support future candidates. Members of Manuel's Club would have to abandon their grand plan.

* * *

NEEDING TO FIND SOME WAY OF MAKING CONTACT WITH SEÑOR Manuel Arena, Mike asked Natalie to call Gloria Adams. Despite its size, he knew the film industry was a closed world—longtime members seemed to know, be aware of, or be familiar with everyone who was an active participant. Hopefully, Gloria might be able to establish some kind of contact with the filmmaker from Mexico City.

VOICES BEHIND THE CURTAIN

* * *

Natalie immediately arranged to meet the fast-rising, much-celebrated "Heroine of Hollywood" at their favorite tavern. After waiting for her eyes to adjust from the bright sunlight to the darker atmosphere of the small neighborhood tavern, Natalie was relieved to see Gloria sitting in their favorite booth.

"Wonderful to see you, Gloria!" said Natalie. The two women hugged in greeting. "It's been too long. Things are becoming so complicated, you'll have to excuse my not calling sooner!"

"Oh, with all the work you're doing with Natalie's Bridge, I'm not surprised. To what do I owe the honor of your call?"

"At our meeting in New York, the Sentinels decided to initiate the next element of their plan. Have you ever heard of a Mexico City movie producer named Manuel Arena? He and his files represent their next target. Mike Stone is in possession of information derived from two separate sources which indicates Señor Arena manages a Mexican financial war chest that provides the funds these military industrialists are using to finance their plan to accelerate the rearming of America. Some of those funds were used to finance the political campaigns of some of your old friends who are currently serving on the HUAC.

"We believe Arena has detailed records and a substantial amount of money stored in a private safe. If we can find some way of getting into his safe and obtaining possession of his files, Mike is convinced we might be able to prevent this secretive plan to escalate American defense spending."

"What does all this have to do with me? I would have thought after all that I have already done to help you, your need for any further assistance would have evaporated."

"Gloria, we are hoping you might help us by finding some way we can learn more about this mysterious figure."

"I am familiar with him, but in name only," Gloria said quickly. "I never met him, but I'm familiar with his reputation. Let's just say, he's not known for the *quality* of his studio's work." After a few beats of silence and another healthy sip of wine, Gloria laughed. "This sounds like a movie script! American industrialist conspiracies, records, and money hidden in Mexican safes . . . I realize, of course, you are being quite serious. What you have just described could be the plot for some new movie. Why don't you give me a few days to think about it? I've met so many people over the years I wouldn't be surprised if I know someone, or someone who knows someone, who knows all about your 'Mexican Moviemaker.' As soon as I come up with something, I'll contact you, either here or at your home up in Berkeley."

* * *

WITHIN A WEEK FOLLOWING HER RETURN TO HER HOME IN BERKELEY, Natalie received a note from Gloria. It read: *I think I've found the person you're seeking. Mercedes is a former tenant and dear friend who suddenly appeared on my doorstep a few days ago, needing a place to stay. She is an aspiring actress who was scheduled to play a leading role in one of Arena's next movies. Something must have really gone wrong. Overnight, she abandoned her role and suddenly returned to Los Angeles. All I know is that she was under contract to Arena Studios and refuses to discuss what happened. The only thing she would tell me is she is deeply disappointed in herself and would like to get even with Señor Arena.*

After I explained your situation, she has consented to talk you. Why don't you call me, and I will set up a meeting where we can meet in the privacy of my home in Brentwood.

Obviously pleased with Gloria's timely response, Natalie phoned her and made arrangements to take the first available train back to Los Angeles. Refreshed by a good night's sleep on the gently swaying motion of her drawing room bunk, an excited Natalie disembarked in the Los Angeles Union Train Station, then walked down the long platform to the main depot. Without stopping, she made her way to the place where available taxicabs would be waiting.

Within 30 minutes, she emerged from the cab, paid the driver, and immediately made her way up the small hedge-lined entryway to a very charming, older, but immaculately maintained, white-plaster, blue-shuttered, red-tiled roof Southern California home. It was typical of others homes she had noticed in the immediate neighborhood that were long preferred by former and retired members of Hollywood's theatrical community.

The minute Natalie entered Gloria's living room, her attention was drawn to one of the most beautiful Hispanic women she had ever seen. When she rose from the couch, Natalie became even more aware of the woman's height, full figure, and remarkable facial beauty. As she moved across the room in her graceful feline way, Natalie instantly became aware of the sensuous aura she radiated. Even before they were introduced, the veteran musical actress couldn't help but wonder, *If her presence produces that kind of effect on me, another woman, I can only imagine what kind of affect she must have on men!*

Gloria, pleased to make the introductions, said, "Mercedes, I would like you to meet a very special friend of mine. Ms. Natalie Cummins is the woman I've been telling you about. It would be difficult to name anyone else who is trying any harder to slow down anti-Communist tyranny we are being forced to endure here in Hollywood! Working in Mexico may have its problems, but you have to believe me when I say, they pale by comparison to what is taking place in Hollywood!"

"Natalie," Gloria continued, "I would like you to meet a friend of mine, Ms. Mercedes Velasquez. You may recognize her—she is the former Miss Universe, from Toledo, Spain. She has just returned from Mexico. I think you will be very interested to hear what she has to say about Señor Manuel Arena."

Rather than move forward to shake hands or embrace, they stood motionless, studying each other. Any awkwardness that may have existed dissolved when, with a nervous Gloria's urging, they stepped forward and shook hands.

After gesturing to them to sit on the couch and chairs surrounding her coffee table, Gloria started the conversation. "Natalie, let me first explain how Mercedes and I became friends. Prior to her moving to Mexico City, she needed a place to live, and I needed a renter. Living under the same roof, it didn't take long for Mercedes and me to become good friends. She had seen some of my old movies and was constantly asking me questions about my early career. Naturally, I was interested to learn how a doctor's daughter from Toledo became Miss Universe, a successful model, and an aspiring movie actress. We have spent many a night talking. She was anxious to learn everything she could about the circumstances that allowed me to make my way from performing in the background as a member of song-and-dance corps to being considered for female lead roles.

"Although she never was willing to share some of the not-so-pretty details of what she has been forced to endure, I couldn't help but sense she is being challenged by many of the same problems you and I were forced to overcome."

Nervous about the direction of the previous comments, Mercedes interrupted. "Miss Cummins, before Gloria goes any further, I'd like to share a few things you need to understand about me. The rest of my story is not very pretty, but it's not the entire story. I don't know what disturbs me more—my naiveté or my current embarrassment over some of the things I've done. I'm still having a difficult time understanding how a serious, hardworking premed student and devout Catholic girl from Toledo, Spain, can end up an unsuccessful actress and seriously compromised woman!"

Not quite certain how to explain, Mercedes paused before deciding to begin by describing her early life. "I was no particular beauty as a young girl; I was gangly, tall, and shapeless. The relatively innocent and traditional life of a proper daughter of two hardworking Spanish doctors was suddenly interrupted when Spain's Fascist national forces bombed the hospital where my parents were working and where they were killed. Homeless, with no money, like so many others, I was forced to survive in the streets of a war-torn city.

"Fortunately, my grandparents found me and took me into their home in Madrid. Old-fashioned, strict, and devout Catholics, I was expected to earn my keep by performing what I considered, an excessive amount of daily household chores, attend school, attend church, and use any available time for studying. I had no personal life.

"About the time I turned 17, I started to mature. The boys at school were beginning to take notice. Older men were offering me gifts. I found myself starting to pay more attention to how I dressed, how I applied my makeup, and how I did my hair.

"One day, more as a joke than anything else, I let my girlfriends talk me into entering the Miss Madrid beauty contest. Thinking back, I must have considered the possibility of successfully competing in beauty contests might represent a possible route out of the life I was being forced to endure. One thing led to another, and before I knew it, I had won the title of Miss Spain and was on my way to the United States to compete in the Miss Universe contest.

"For the first time in my life, I was allowed to live the role of the playful, young woman who had remained so deeply buried inside me. Just after I was crowned, I received a modeling contract from I. Magnin's in Los Angeles. I was expected to travel to each of their big-city stores, model their new high-fashion lines, and make myself available to their more important customers, friends of the owners, and managers of their smaller affiliated department stores. The job paid well, the work was easy, and I was having fun for the first time in my life."

* * *

Natalie was having no difficulty relating to the woman's story. It wasn't much different from what she had experienced when she escaped the family farm in Sussex and made her way to London. Any young, attractive, and generously endowed woman was required to immediately differentiate between sincere offers of assistance and those associated with not-so-cleverly-hidden agendas of conquest. Raised on a farm with three older brothers and strict but loving parents, she was totally unprepared for the predatory practices she had been forced to encounter.

If a woman expected to survive with her dignity intact, she needed to quickly learn how to protect herself. Forever etched in her mind was how the thrill of her first invitation to audition for a supporting role in a new show had turned into a clumsy attempt to first bed her as part of the "qualification" process.

With her savings running low and the diminishing probability of the prospects of auditioning for a legitimate role that would present itself in time, the resourceful, prideful, and stubborn farm girl from Sussex began to look for part-time work.

It took a while but she learned how to schedule three part-time jobs to earn enough money to cover her meager living expenses and have enough time and money to pay for acting, singing, and dancing lessons.

In London's theatrical district, auditions were scheduled in the late mornings and rehearsals in the afternoons. A quick learner, Natalie scheduled her dog-walking duties in the early morning and late afternoons. Her food and beverage waitstaff jobs were scheduled for the dinner trade. And, by ten o'clock, she was always present to drive the unpopular graveyard shift for one of the local taxi companies.

"Had I stopped to think about what was happening, I might have realized, low on money, I was trying to generate a sufficient income to provide me with the *staying power* to survive and chase my dreams in the theater."

After pausing to make sure the wounded woman had understood she was offering constructive advice, not criticism, Natalie continued. "Then there was the second problem.

"Watching my new friends progress through the labyrinth required of aspiring actors, it became obvious to me that being cast in a role that properly showcased your special talent made any real progress even more difficult."

Natalie's last comments really hit home. Mercedes immediately started to think, *If I had placed more emphasis on my modeling career, I might have been able to create the kind of independence and objectivity Natalie is talking about. Hopefully, it's not too late to learn from my mistakes.*

Natalie, feeling the growing spirit of camaraderie developing between them, continued to explain. "Mercedes, I've been out of show business for more than 2 years, but I can tell you being cast in leading roles didn't solve my problem. In some ways, it made it worse. Becoming a recognized star makes you an ever more *highly treasured target of conquest*. I still have nightmares about being the object of trophy-hunting males, men who regarded me as some kind of trophy to be shown off in public and pummeled in private.

"For someone who regarded the learning of her craft as a serious matter requiring long periods of study and hard work, I was always conscious of how hard I worked to absorb and portray the scripts, the choreography, and the musical scores. As an actress, I am sure you understand how important audiences' reactions to your performance become. No matter how many years, how many performances, every night felt like opening night. Recognition of my efforts has always been a source of personal pride and probably my Achilles' heel.

"Not to be taken seriously, when it came to discussions or considerations of important matters outside the theater, was always a painful experience. It seemed the more successful I became on the stage, the less interested people became to learn about the person behind the mask."

Mercedes, no longer intimidated by the natural and friendly and famous actress, began to think, *Is it possible this woman really cares about me? At last, there is someone who understands my problem, someone whom I can trust! Whatever they have planned for me, I hope, by helping them, I will be able to work on my own problem.*

* * *

Gloria decided it was time to break into the conversation. "I've made reservations at a nearby French restaurant. Maybe you have heard of it, Le Centrale, it's a locals' favorite French restaurant. Don Cerreta has agreed to meet us there. He is the federal prosecutor who orchestrated my legal defense at the congressional hearing. He has developed some new ideas for preventing these industrialists from executing their plan and has expressed his interest in discussing them with you. Apparently, your association with Señor Arena represents an important part of his plan. Why don't we find out what Don has on his mind?"

CHAPTER 21

New News

Following a quick rap on the door, Mike Stone was excited to see Marco Tancredi and Armando Camarillo. After closing the file he had been reading, he motioned to his secretary to usher the two men into his office. Within seconds, she was back, followed by the streetwise executive and his Cuban partner.

"Marco, to what do I owe this pleasant surprise?"

Familiar with Mike's preference to come right to the point, Marco said, "Armando has continued to analyze more of the notes his people have been collecting. Yesterday, he brought me some new notes that appear to contain some very interesting new information. Armando, why don't you explain what you think you might have discovered."

The younger man spread a rolled-up sheet of paper across Mike's immaculate desk. Affixed to the paper organized in a gridlike pattern were more than a dozen of the executive's discarded notes.

"It's actually several new developments," said Armando. "First, it looks like McWilliams and company are planning to shut down their Mexican operation. They have concluded if someone is prepared to go to all the trouble and expense required to prepare the brief Don Cerreta presented in that hearing, they need to concern themselves about the risk of discovery.

"According to these notes, I think we have to assume they have decided to pursue a different plan.

"Knowing someone is aware of their plan and is committed to opposing their efforts, you and Miss Cummins were spotted leaving the congressional hearing room. Knowing your association with the Sentinels, they suspect you and the others might be involved. Apparently, at least three of the lawyers are aware of the Sentinels and their efforts to solve other problems. Mr. McWilliams has been authorized to hire some kind of a special security company to identify who is attempting to oppose them and eliminate their source of resistance."

Leaning back in his big chair, Mike said, "They picked up our scent faster than I expected. The original Six Sentinels are no strangers to private security companies. They know where to find us. We need to alert the others. In the meantime, we need to start thinking about developing our own source of protection. Asking the White House for assistance from the Secret Service may not be an option. Until we know, for certain, how deep the military-industrial influence has penetrated into the government, I suggest we consider other alternatives."

Responding to the question, Marco piped up, "I don't know anything about the Secret Service or other governmental law enforcement agencies, but there have been times when I felt it was important that I develop my own means of protection. From time to time, some of my '*old neighborhood friends*' have been very helpful. How would you feel if I were to explain our situation and determine if they would be willing to provide us with the protection we may need?"

Astonishment would be the word that best described Mike's reaction. Proceeding cautiously, Marco said, "Mr. Stone, before you say no, let me explain. If, for a moment, you could disregard the unsavory nature of how some of my friends have chosen to earn a living, you might appreciate the fact they think of themselves as proud and loyal Americans, just as devoted to preserving their way of life as we are! Believe me when I say, I seriously believe how upset they will become when they learn a coalition of corporate executives is abusing the privilege of 'Democratic Free Enterprise' in their pursuit of self-serving agendas. Why should they regard those efforts any different than what occurs in their '*street world*' when someone else is attempting to trespass on their territory?

"As Don may have told you, in the past, when I found it necessary to approach the people who are responsible for controlling possible conflicts between members of connected families, I have found it necessary to approach them, explain my particular situation, and seek their understanding and cooperation. On occasion, I have been pleasantly surprised by their response. They may be guilty of adhering to a strange code of justice, but it has been my experience they are smart businessmen and don't have a lot of tolerance for situations that conflict with their best interests or those whom they care about. If you knew where to check, I think you would be impressed by some of the things they helped arrange in Italy during the last war. I have been told about their efforts to help the OSS establish the cooperation of the Italian underground resistance. Your friend Mary Wheeler Clarke will explain their role in negotiating the Italian surrender and their effort to broker a deal with the German generals had their assassination attempt on Hitler not failed. With your permission, I would like to explain our situation to my friends. When they understand how these corporations are attempting to compromise the authority of our government, it is possible that they may feel as threatened as we do. Should that be the case, they could become very motivated to help us."

* * *

Mike had been involved in some strange conversations, but nothing like this one. *Never in my wildest imagination have I ever considered the idea of seeking the assistance of "organized crime" to protect me and my friends in our own government!*

Unsure or not knowing how to react to Marco's question, Mike Stone chose to stare straight-ahead and remain silent.

Observing Mike's reaction, Marco sensed he had received the only answer Mike was willing to give. He knew that meeting had concluded.

CHAPTER 22

A Quiet Evening with Cecelia

New York, April 1949

Each night after work, Mike looked forward to arriving home. No matter how difficult his day had been or how much evening work remained in his briefcase, Cecelia always made him feel appreciated and loved. From that first day when he met her on the Cal campus, almost 15 years ago, he had never ceased to be amazed by her fascinating presence. Her special way of greeting him, her exquisite dinners, her consistently insightful conversations, her unrestrained affection always represented the high point of his day.

The memory of his meeting with Don and Marco Tancredi still dominated his mind as he approached the front door of his apartment. *What is it that we don't understand about our Democratic Free Enterprise system that causes us to protect ourselves from our own government? Is it our pursuit of profit that causes so many complex problems, or is there some other unseen expectation that could be pushing us to such extremes?*

Just as he was reaching to insert his key in the front door, Cecelia pulled it open, as if she sensed his presence on the other side. The sight of the petite Asian woman with her fine figure dressed in traditional Chinese clothing always delighted him. Without a hair out of place, and with perfectly applied makeup, she leaned in for the kind of kiss most men only dreamed of. The two martinis, prepared to their liking and served in well-chilled long-stemmed crystal glasses, were sitting on the sideboard just inside the entrance, one for him and one for her.

Tonight was one of those balmy New York evenings, the kind that encouraged you to be outside. The couple carried their drinks out on the terrace overlooking the East River, the boroughs of Queens, Brooklyn, and the expanse of Long Island. Enjoying their nightly tradition of sitting on the balcony, sipping their drinks, enjoying the view, feeling the warm, soft breezes, telling each other about their day could take 15 minutes, and sometimes much longer.

Having recently returned from her extended stay on the West Coast, Cecelia was anxious to share what she had discovered. Clinking her frosted glass with Mike's, she asked, "What do the Army Language School, the Harvard Business School, Hastings Law School, and Dr. Tom's program all have in common?"

Mike knew he wasn't expected to answer her rhetorical question. From many years of experience, he was familiar with Cecelia's long-standing habit of answering her own question.

"One, they each have such outstanding academic programs, they are able to differentiate their curriculum and attract some of the finest young scholars from all over the world.

"Two, their autonomous character provides the schools with the flexibility to determine, generate, and adjust their course curriculum to reflect the most advanced academic progress, independent of the influence of donors, the government, or vested private interests.

"And three, their part-time employment structure allows them to recruit the most recognized and experienced teaching professors, many of which are simultaneously employed by other universities."

Visibly excited, Cecelia was like a sailing ship, sailing downwind, under full sail. Pausing only long enough to take another sip of her martini, Cecelia was using the planned interruption to study Mike over the rim of her glass. She needed to observe his reaction before proceeding.

* * *

HAVING ATTENDED CAL BERKELEY AND THE HARVARD BUSINESS School, Mike was thinking about his own experiences. *It's strange to remember what it was like in those days. Most of what I recall had something to do with my survival instincts. It seemed to me that our total being was dedicated to doing what was necessary to get from Monday through Saturday, just to start the process all over again the next week. At the time, I certainly don't remember giving much thought about the relative excellence of the case material, the history, and experience of my professors, or the privilege and advantages of being a member of a group that contained so many bright students who had been drawn together from such diversified backgrounds.*

"Cecelia, not only do I think you have come up with an exciting idea for a new school, but you also may have answered two other questions that, on occasion, have been creeping into my mind. If our recent observations about the continuous resurfacing of these Power-Cycle threats are accurate, we may be required to grow our own forces and begin to think about perpetuating our leadership."

It wasn't until they were halfway through dinner when Mike started to tell Cecelia about the distressing revelations Marco and Armando had disclosed to him. "If we allow that to continue, we will have a much more difficult time-proven political malfeasance. We could try to fight them in the courts and in the press, but I seriously doubt we could do much to stop them. On the other hand, if there was some way we could get our hands on Manuel's files, we might have the information we would need to expose what is happening. The threat of properly supported exposure could become a very powerful weapon."

"I don't know anything about Arena," said Cecelia, "but I have to believe his volunteering to turn over his records is the *last* thing he would want to do."

"Maybe not so difficult," a smiling Mike said. "I checked. He maintains a variety of accounts at our bank right here in New York. Perhaps tomorrow I need to take advantage of my executive privileges and have a look at those accounts."

* * *

Arriving early at the bank, Mike used his bank credentials to gain entry to the private accounts' file room. There was a long list of credit memorandums pertaining to Señor Manuel Arena, Arena Productions, and its sister companies, Arena Motion Picture Distribution and Arena Properties.

The corresponding voluminous files contained carefully dated copies of all the different cash transfers that had been made from his motion picture theaters into a master Arena Studios account.

Unwilling to risk involving a subordinate, Mike decided to personally search through all of the files. Each day as he was preparing to leave the office, he checked out one or two files, placed them in his briefcase, and took them home to peruse and return the next day.

At home, after dinner, he and Cecelia would study the contents of each file and make notes. They were beginning to use every horizontal surface of their spacious apartment to place their notes. Hopefully, they might discover some pattern that would assist in their interpretation of what might be happening. After a couple of weeks, Mike and Cecelia had amassed quite a collection of notes. What had once been a fanatically cleaned and neatly arranged apartment had become a burgeoning garden of paper landscaping.

Each morning after he left for work, she would search among all the growing number of piles. Walking from room to room, she would pick up one set of papers and place it next to another. For 3 days, she continued her reorganizing and analyzing of what appeared to a growing sea of seemingly unrelated bits of information.

When Mike arrived home on the evening of the fourth day, he was confused and disappointed. She wasn't waiting to greet him—no hugs, no kisses, no martinis, and no help removing his coat was being offered. Confused, he entered their apartment. His dear wife, uncharacteristically clothed in her pajamas, wearing no makeup and her hair pulled back ponytail style, was sitting in the middle of what looked like a sea of small papers. She was holding a clipboard in her left hand. She was using her right hand to pick up, one at a time, the small notes scattered around her. After carefully returning the note to its original resting place and with her hand now free, she would write some kind of notation on the paper attached to the clipboard.

* * *

NOT UNAWARE OF HIS PRESENCE, SHE HELD UP HER FREE HAND BEFORE saying, "I think I almost have it. Can you wait for a moment? I think I'm on the brink of confirming a pattern I discovered late last night."

* * *

His attention focused on the making of two martinis. He was surprised when he heard his normally demure wife excitedly exclaim, "Mike! I broke the code! You have no idea what Señor Arena has been doing! I have checked and rechecked my notes. I am confident that I have discovered how he is skimming his own operation."

For the next 15 minutes, Cecelia walked Mike through her findings. When sorted on a chronological basis, the weekly transfers of funds from each city approximated the difference between the revenues that were reported for sales tax purposes and what had been recorded in the theater ledgers. Next, she showed him the difference was equal to the amount of money that was transferred, each week, into his personal account.

"He's skimming," Mike said aloud.

"And from some very dangerous people. While it appears no single transfer is large enough to be easily noticed, I'd bet when you add it all together, over a long period of time, the total represents a significant amount of money. Certainly enough to catch the attention of his Cuban investment partners."

Shaking his head in pleased disbelief, he said, "Cheating on your taxes is one thing, but it pales in comparison to what Arena's done—and to what might happen if his Cuban investors were to learn about it.

"But, we are not finished. Knowing what he has done is one thing; proving in court is quite different. Somehow, we need to find a way to match his deposits to the missing movie house revenues. Once we can present documentable courtroom evidence to him, Arena is going to have to make a choice. He can take his chance, one of surviving the attack from his Cuban investors, or he can provide us with the information we are seeking."

CHAPTER 23

Dr. Tom Burdick

The Sentinels' doctoral professor was looking forward to Mike's visit. Tom Burdick had been keeping close track of his former six most unusual students who had received their doctoral degrees 1 June of 1935, almost 15 years ago. Over the course of those years, rarely did he not spend time thinking about how talented and responsible they were, and all that they had accomplished . . . He would often think, *How often during a long teaching career do six students come along that redefine the study of history, develop a conceptual model for interpreting the future consequences of current events, and organize themselves into a proactive group to oppose those who abuse the privileges of "Democratic Free Enterprise"?*

* * *

THE STUDENT AND THE TEACHER WERE SITTING IN THE DINING ROOM of Tom's Berkeley Hills home. They were savoring a bottle of prewar French Bordeaux Tom had been saving for a special occasion.

Chuckling, Dr. Tom said, "I still remember that first day when we met in the basement of Larry Blake's Berkeley restaurant. Not before or ever since have I had the opportunity to observe six young people who emitted so much bright light needed to illuminate whatever path in life you might choose to follow. I still recall sitting back and watching the six of you peel the skin off the onion, distilling your own unique conclusions, and then searching for ways to fit them all together into a large mosaic. When you began to organize your thought processes in what eventually became your Power-Cycle concept, I think I knew, even then, that you were entering new intellectual territory.

"After you graduated, on my own, I would select some current issue, research it, and look at my work through your Power-Cycle prism. It was uncanny how accurate the conclusions I was able to draw about what future consequences that I was able to predict. I was so impressed, I designed some new research projects to be used for future cases. I used them to introduce your Power-Cycle concept in my classes. Consistently, over the last 4 years, the Power-Cycle course has been voted the most popular class in our doctoral program."

Fascinated, Mike asked, "If the subject matter was so popular, why didn't you expand the size of your classes? Why didn't you talk to us?"

"Partially because my reach still isn't what I'd like it to be. Although the Power-Cycle curriculum has become so popular, the total number of students we are reaching is still a very small number.

"Then there is the second problem. When it became clear that you failed to attract the cooperation of the people whose assistance you needed to prevent the German industrialists from starting the Second World War, I realized there was an important question that still remained to be asked and answered.

"Five years later, when the six of you came together to provide the proactive leadership and problem-solving skills required to prevent the Germans from using their 'fortunes of war' to start a future Fourth Reich, I realized the best information in the world, without the active participation from people who know how to make things happen, is just interesting information."

* * *

TOM WAS SURPRISED AS HE WATCHED A WORRIED LOOK APPEAR ON Mike's face. "Was it something I said?" he asked. "Did I upset you?"

"No, not upset me. Are you kidding? Something you said triggered another concern, something Cecelia has begun to worry about. She is beginning to question what we should do, if these 'Power Cycle' problems keep occurring. How are we going to perpetuate what we have started. It would be interesting to see how she might react to what you have just told me."

Tom was confused. "Why Cecelia? I would have thought that you and Jacques, as the group's unofficial leaders, would want to lead the discussion."

Finished listening to Mike explain why Cecelia had the time and the interest, Tom said, "I completely understand. Please have her call me. I'd be happy to talk to her. Now, if that is settled, why don't we take a break? It's a beautiful day. We can walk and talk at the same time."

* * *

THE TWO MEN BEGAN THEIR LEISURELY WALK UP SANTA BARBARA Road, turned left on Spruce Avenue, and headed up the inclined street toward the entrance to Tilden Park. Mike, preoccupied by explaining his purpose for calling on his old professor, wasn't paying any attention to the fast pace he was setting. They were barely halfway up Spruce when Tom stopped. Breathing hard, he asked, "What are you trying to do, kill off your old professor? Can we stop for a minute while I try to catch my breath?"

Finally, when he was able to talk without gasping, the thoughtful professor asked, "When I received your note, knowing what you wanted to discuss, I was able to find out some very interesting things regarding Señor Arena. Before I answer, I would appreciate it if you would answer a question for me.

"If what you have been suggesting regarding the effort by the military-industrial complex to resurrect military spending is true, why are you so concerned? Are you certain you want to place yourselves in a position where you and your friends are playing *judge and jury regarding the need for new military armaments*? Aren't there other people who are responsible and more qualified to make those kinds of decisions?"

* * *

"TOM. IT'S NOT THAT WE OBJECT TO THE IDEA OF REARMING THAT concerns us. It's the way these military prime contractors are attempting to use their wealth and influence to circumvent traditional governmental appropriation practices that we are questioning. Perhaps I need to explain."

After resuming their walk at a slower pace, the old professor asked, "When you and your Sentinel friends have placed what you have learned under your 'Power-Cycle' microscope, what have you discovered that has convinced you that you've stumbled on to the opening gambit of military industrialists attempting to exert their influence within our government for their own self-serving interests?"

"Tom, let me share with you what really has us bothered. We have convinced ourselves that a postwar military buildup in the United States could trigger a reciprocal response by the Russians. While we don't anticipate that aggressive rearmament programs might lead to another world shooting war, it could mean years of escalating military spending, weapon development, and heavy government spending. If these programs are not properly evaluated by the designated and qualified congressional committees, how do we not know that a very costly 'Cold War' has not been triggered by those who are intent on introducing agendas of self-interest? Our interest in Arena is directly connected to learning more about his relationship with J. Jordan McWilliams and those military-industrial executives."

* * *

THE TWO MEN HAD REACHED THE TOP OF SPRUCE AVENUE. THEY were able to enjoy the view of the eucalyptus forests and vegetated grandeur of Tilden Park dropping away to the east. Looking west, they were able to see San Francisco Bay, the ships passing beneath the Golden Gate and Bay bridges, and the skyline of San Francisco.

Retracing their way back down Spruce Avenue, both men were enjoying the westerly grand vista while they thought about Mike's explanation of the possible consequences of what could occur should the industrialists succeed. They had turned onto Santa Barbara Road when Tom suddenly announced, "Your hunch was right. Jordan's friend, Manuel Arena, is *one bad and very dangerous Mexico City business coyote*. I was successful in learning some things about his movie business that you may find interesting.

"According to my friend, Arena enjoys a controversial reputation in Mexico City. No one seems to know where he finds so much investment capital. If he's not buying and distributing high cost American produced independently produced motion pictures, he's busy buying second-tier movie houses in major U.S. markets. Some of my friends have lent him money to purchase independent films. In each instance, the loans carried high rates of interest and were paid off well ahead of schedule.

"Then, there are others who have invested in his real estate syndicates. The funds were used to build or acquire second-tier movie houses through which he shows his films. Each year they receive envelopes with generous cash payments and no reports. As long as the checks keep coming, no one questions what is happening."

"I don't understand," said Dr. Tom. "If everyone is having such positive experiences, why is he considered to be a business coyote?"

"Because there doesn't seem to be any rational explanation for the difference in the amount of money he generates in Mexico and the amount of money he invests in films and real estate. There are enormous unexplained discrepancies."

* * *

"IF YOU DON'T MIND SOME OLD MAN'S ADVICE, IF YOU PROCEED against Arena, I would be very careful. According to my reports, he is ruthless and very dangerous; many of his friends may be worse."

* * *

HALF AN HOUR LATER WHEN MIKE WAS PREPARING TO LEAVE, DR. Tom said, "Thanks for asking me to help, even if it was only a little part, and make sure you have Cecelia call me."

CHAPTER 24

Myron Goldman

Los Angeles, California, April 1949
As Mike drove through Hollywood toward the big motion picture studio, he found himself feeling slightly apprehensive. He was calling on the head of a major studio. At the same time, Natalie was making a well-publicized effort to help the people this studio and others like it had put out of work. *I hope this meeting doesn't turn out to be one of those uncomfortable times when everybody is polite and nothing of any value is accomplished.*

Locating the studio was not so difficult. Entering and locating the president's office was proving more difficult. Forced to wait at the guarded entrance for what seemed like a very long time, he was finally given vague directions to a rear parking lot, bordered by what would appear to be a very nondescript row of offices. As Mike cruised the parking lot outside the studio, he was surprised to find a spot near the front entrance marked with a bright orange cone and a sign that read "Reserved for Mike Stone."

As soon as Mike entered through the large, hand carved wooden door, he was surprised by the ornate, large-room architecture of the interior executive suite. Designed to create an atmosphere well-suited for a rich and powerful executive, it created a remarkably different impression from the exterior appearance. Inside, to his amazement, the secretary stationed outside the head of studio seemed unusually pleased to see him. She beamed a smile at him and quickly walked around her desk to shake his hand.

"Good morning, Mr. Stone," she said, reaching him before he got half-way across the room. "Welcome to our studio. I believe this is the first time you've visited us. We've been reading about your friend, Miss Cummins, and all she has been doing to help so many of our friends. It's a great thing. I know Mr. Goldman is looking forward to meeting you and discussing her work."

Mike gave her a perplexed look as the big wooden door behind her opened, revealing a bald, rotund, and broadly smiling executive marching forward to shake his hand.

"You must be Mr. Stone," he said. "I'm Myron Goldman. My friends call me Myron. Let me start off by saying what a pleasure it is to meet the leader of such a talented group of people as the Sentinels. You and your Sentinel friends have been the subject of conversation between me and our mutual friend at America West, Pete Ferrari. Following what you and your friends have been accomplishing has become a personal hobby of mine. In an industry known for making great things happen in 120 minutes, you have no idea how refreshing it is to realize in real life there are people who are still prepared to attack threatening problems and make such important things happen. You are to be congratulated."

Whatever Mike had been expecting from the studio executive, his reception was a total surprise. He had been forewarned by Pete Ferrari of the fact that Goldman's studio had been one of the more aggressive supporters of Hollywood's Blacklisting program. Confused by Goldman's complimentary comments, Mike asked, "I am having difficulty with why you aren't critical of Natalie's and the Sentinels' efforts to provide witnesses with protection under the First and Fifth Amendments of the Constitution and reduce HUAC's ability to badger innocent witnesses."

"Relax, Mike—can I call you Mike? Secretly, we respect what she is attempting and look forward to the day when we can dispense with all this 'Fear of Communism' crap. In case you are wondering, I have devoted my working life to producing profitable movies. How do you think I feel when I am prohibited from employing many of our most proven, loyal, and talented people?

"Unfortunately, I am being forced to implement these crippling procedures from the money interests who fund the operations of the studio. I don't know how long it will take for them to realize it, but overnight, we may have made it possible for our competitors across the pond to take advantage of the situation.

"I don't know about possible conspiracies, but I do know how much money it's costing us every month when we are not making the movies the public is expecting. If the decision had been left up to me and some of my fellow executives, we would never have allowed this problem to get started.

"If our London counterparts are on their toes, they will perceive the opportunity we have provided to employ these out-of-work people to make the same kind of commercially successful movies we would have preferred to make.

"If Miss Cummins succeeds, her work will hasten the day when we can terminate all these blacklisting problems. That will be the day when our conservative financial *experts* will learn how much more it will cost them to attract their former employees. There is absolutely no question in my mind their agents will succeed in creating competitive bidding between foreign filmmakers and Hollywood's studio system."

* * *

AFTER LISTENING INTENTLY TO MYRON'S EXPLANATION, MIKE realized he and the other Sentinels had badly misjudged the actions of the studios. *The studios aren't the enemy; they are simply acting as the voice for their "behind the curtain" investors and lenders.* Confident he had an ally in Myron, Mike proceeded, "As I told you over the phone, we are trying to learn more about Señor Manuel Arena and his role in supporting America's military complex to restore Defense Department spending.

"We have reason to believe that Señor Manuel Rodriguez Arena may be controlling a sizable political war chest. The funds were contributed by a group of very large American military prime contractors. The proceeds from their Mexican war chest will be used to support several different programs organized to restore military appropriations."

* * *

"MOVIEMAKER FROM MEXICO!" THE STUDIO HEAD SAID WITH A hearty laugh. "Is that what that little macho asshole calls himself? He's lucky if he makes one bad picture a year. What nobody seems to understand is where he's finding the money he needs to outbid the major studios for so many independent films made each year in the United States. After he purchases them, he limits their first-run distribution to his second-rate movie houses. He and whoever is behind him must be making money from the first-run showing of the movies, their redistribution, the concession stands, and the real estate.

"Curious, we went to the trouble of having some of our counters check the revenues of his movie houses against the sales receipts he reports to the state tax authorities. The counter is just like the person restaurants employ to sit at a bar and count the drinks a bartender serves. You take the counter's tally and compare it to the money in the till at the end of the night. It's the proprietor's way of checking the honesty of his bartenders.

"So we performed a similar procedure at several of Arena's movie houses. Sure enough, our estimates of his gross ticket revenues exceeded the revenues he reported to the state tax authorities."

"Myron, are you suggesting Manuel Arena is skimming his own operation?"

"Without bank deposit records and cash transfer receipts . . . something with his name on it, there is no way we can prove he is the person doing the skimming."

Mike was excited. "Could I have a copy of those records? I might know of a way to prove what you are describing. Naturally, I would be willing to share anything we might unearth."

"For your group, of course." Goldman rolled his desk chair back, unlocked the bottom drawer on the right-hand side of his mammoth desk, pulled open a drawer, and removed a thick folder which he extended toward Mike.

"I can't tell you how much help you've been," Mike said, standing. "From a completely independent source, it has been suggested that not only is he suspected of skimming his own operation, but on several different occasions, he has been observed gambling large sums of money in Havana casinos in the company of known crime syndicate bosses."

As Mike was preparing to leave, Goldman said, almost under his breath, "All I can say is, God help Manuel Arena if anyone can prove that he's stealing Cuban syndicate money!"

* * *

TWELVE HOURS LATER, CECELIA BOARDED THE FIRST AVAILABLE FLIGHT to Los Angeles, armed with all her notes she and Mike had extracted from the bank records. She was excited by the prospect she might be able to help her Sentinel colleagues, even if it was only a "little dance."

CHAPTER 25

Don Meets Mercedes

Gloria and her two companions were greeted effusively by her old friend and maître d', Walter Taylor. Even though Walter was attempting to escort them as discreetly as possible to a corner table in the rear of the restaurant, patrons recognized at lcast one of the three famous women. Their entrance was creating quite a stir.

Don Cerreta, having arrived early, rose from his seat at the table in anticipation of greeting his two friends and meeting Mercedes. As they approached the table, despite his knowing Mercedes had been a former Miss Universe queen, he was unprepared for her uncommon beauty, her size, and the sensuous aura she projected. Aware of how critical her cooperation with his plan would be, as difficult as it might be, he knew it was important that he focus his attention on the person and what she had to say.

Ignoring generally accepted Southern California restaurant protocol, well-wishers, fans, and casual acquaintances ventured over to their table, introducing themselves and asking some very strange questions. Well accustomed, despite the unwelcome interruption, experience had taught the women to graciously greet each of the people, answer their questions, thank them for their interest, and shift their attention to the next waiting person. Thirty minutes later, their wine and appetizers untouched, they were able to settle down and start the process of introducing Don to Mercedes and explaining how valuable his contributions had been to recent Sentinel operations.

While Don was struggling to keep his attention on matters at hand, Mercedes was carefully listening to what this polite, mild mannered, and most attractive man was saying. Almost immediately, her thoughts changed from trying to determine if he was a friend or a potential perpetrator to admiring an attractive, intelligent, and experienced solver of difficult problems. Only superficially listening to what Don was saying, Mercedes was thinking, *I can understand how he was able to make life so miserable for the oil companies and turn the tables on the House Un-American Activities Committee. Assisting him might really be an interesting experience, certainly different than what I was forced to endure from Manuel, his friends, and the studio.*

* * *

THE 5-HOUR TRIP FROM LOS ANGELES TO MEXICO CITY WAS NOT AN ordinary flight well punctuated by food, drinks, and intermittent naps. Don insisted on using the time to carefully school his new pupil on the finer points of his plan. He and Mercedes were sitting next to each other in the first-class section. Knowing Mercedes needed to be convinced how important her services would be if they hoped to obtain Señor Arena's cooperation, he was describing, in detail, each phase of his plan and what they hoped to accomplish.

Although Mercedes was not able to follow everything she was being shown, she understood enough to appreciate the implications of Cecelia's work. She listened politely as Don began to explain the significance of the legal brief he was in the process of preparing. "Information collected, processed, and presented in this fashion will hopefully provide us with four options. If we fail to convince Señor Arena that cooperating with us and providing us with the information we are seeking doesn't represent his least bad alternative, we will be left with three other choices.

"With this kind of evidence, we shouldn't have any trouble convincing his Cuban investment partners of the fact that he has been skimming sizable amounts of money off the top of their movie receipts. I hesitate to think about how they might react to *that* news.

"Preliminary discussions with our friends at Treasury indicate they have suspected, for quite some time, Arena has been laundering money for organized crime and falsely reporting his taxable income. They would welcome the opportunity to pursue their case.

"Finally, Walt Matthews at the *New York Times* is not so patiently standing by to get his hands on this information. According to Walt, news of the skimming makes great copy, but he also wants to take advantage of circumstances surrounding the use of the money. He believes if he can authoritatively expose the identity of the contributors and the recipients, he could create a lot of disruption in their election objectives.

"Responsible members of the press live for the opportunity to take advantage of their presumed authority as the nation's 'Fourth Estate' to protect the interests of the people."

While Mercedes was having a difficult time comprehending all that was being discussed, she wasn't having any difficulty understanding the magnitude and the seriousness of the situation. Listening to Don, she began to realize how reassuring it was to listen to this kind and gentle man patiently explain the wisdom of his plan.

Don was not impervious to the incredible sense of presence this remarkably beautiful and attentive traveling companion generated. No matter how hard he tried to ignore what he was feeling and keep their conversation focused on the business at hand, he felt himself becoming increasingly aware of the rising tide of human chemistry passing between them. He'd been around attractive women, but never one so gorgeous, intelligent, and charming. It felt as if they were communicating on some kind of special frequency.

As the plane began its descent toward the Mexico City airport, the pilot came on the intercom to announce, "Today, we have a special celebrity traveling with us, who will be met by a delegation from the Mexico City mayor's office. After we come to a stop, please remain in your seats as they plan to briefly board and escort her off the plane."

Only half-listening to the announcement, annoyed by the pending delay, Mercedes settled back into her seat and stared out the window. As the plane bumped along the runway, she noticed a large cluster of people and cars assembled on the tarmac. The closer they got, the more detail she could see: white Chrysler convertibles filled with attractive young women, a host of newspaper reporters holding flashbulb cameras, a throng of what must be political officials, wealthy-looking men in business suits, and a mariachi band were all clustered together waiting for the plane to roll to a stop.

Once the landing stairwell had been pushed against the plane, the band started to play, and the remaining contingent moved forward. A thickset man dressed in a white linen suit and a big sash that supported what appeared to be an official government medallion climbed up the stairs and entered the plane.

Mercedes was still staring out the window. She had recognized two of the girls sitting on the flat surface behind the rear seat of one of the convertibles. One of them was the same friend she had recently talked to on the telephone. Only vaguely aware of the commotion that was being created as the mayor of Mexico City gradually made his way forward, Mercedes was surprised when he stopped at the row where she and Don were sitting. Suddenly, she realized *she* must be the celebrity, and this was Manuel's way of welcoming her back.

Surprised and still seated, there was nothing Mercedes could do but sit quietly, smile, and listen to the mayor. "It is my pleasure as the mayor to welcome our country's next great movie star to our humble city."

Passengers throughout the plane craned their necks to get a glimpse of the celebrity. A throng of waiting reporters pushed forward to interview the diva as she stepped from the last step onto the tarmac. The mariachi band was playing her favorite song. Manuel emerged from the crowd. Raising both of his hands above his head with a clapping motion, he signaled for the band to stop playing. After entwining the unsuspecting Mercedes in a welcoming bear hug and kissing her on both cheeks, he turned toward the crowd before announcing, "It is my pleasure to announce, now that the star of Arena Studios has returned, we will resume filming of *Mexico*. It's a story of a young progressive president and his brilliant and strong willed wife as they proceed to modernize our government."

The crowd cheered heartily. Only in her dreams had Mercedes ever believed she would receive this kind of reception. By instinct, she instantly transposed herself into her new role. She began to greet the waiting reporters one at a time, treating each to her winsome smile and motioning for him to step forward. After waiting for him to identify himself, she would listen to his question, try to answer in her most thoughtful manner, and then pose for his accompanying photographer. For the next 30 minutes, she played the humble but gracious star.

When the press conference was over, before she allowed Señor Arena to steer her toward his long black limousine, she said, "I thought it appropriate to include Don in everything we do. You wouldn't mind if I ask him to join us?"

The forced smile on Manuel's face clearly indicated he was not expecting Mercedes to insist on bringing a lawyer, particularly one who would remain by her side.

Mercedes was surprised when the limousine pulled to a stop in front of Mexico City's famous El Matador restaurant. A well-lighted, red-carpeted entrance leading from the curbside to the front door had been arranged. Large crowds of expectant movie fans lined both sides. More reporters and photographers were waiting to interview Señor Arena and his beautiful new star. This time, Manuel and Mercedes were smiling. Don, the rising star of the Justice Department, relegated to the role of following behind at a discreet distance, was not smiling.

The bulbs flashed, and the reporters asked their questions. Mercedes slowly realized she was being asked to play her old role as Manuel's personal trophy and the rising star of his soon-to-be-produced movie. Knowing Manuel as well as she did, she was always impressed by his ability to spin half-truths and focus the press's attention on promoting his next production. Even so, she wondered how long it would take before he exposed his true agenda.

CHAPTER **26**

The Pieces Fit

LOS ANGELES, CALIFORNIA, APRIL 1949

Cecelia's limited role in the Sentinels' operation officially started when her plane departed New York in April 1949. Despite the fact she knew it was just a small part, she understood her work might become the critical cause that would enable her colleagues to gain access to Señor Arena's safe and its telltale contents. For 12 hours her plane would be chasing the sun and was scheduled to land in Los Angeles at 7:00 p.m. just as the sun would be setting over the Pacific Ocean.

* * *

ANTICIPATING SHE WOULD BE LEFT UNDISTURBED FOR SEVERAL HOURS, she had planned to use the opportunity to condense her voluminous notes into a week-by-week summary of Arena's deposits into his personal accounts. *Once I am given the counters' reports gathered by Goldman's people and the result of our own investigation, all I will have to do is compare the aggregated difference between his gross receipts less what he has reported for sales tax purposes with my deposit summary and I should be able to prove that he has been skimming his own operation. Now to determine if the pieces fit.*

* * *

Cecelia was sensing her excitement when she felt the plane begin its descent to the Los Angeles Airport. *I feel well rested and ready for a really great meal and a special bottle of wine. How lucky can a girl be to know Mike and Don will be waiting to greet me.*

Peering out the window as the plane slowly taxied to the gate in the growing darkness, Cecelia could see Mike and Don standing behind the cyclone fence near the unlocked and open gate. *They remind me of two Praetorian Guards waiting to greet the arrival of a returning warrior, even if it's only the "Mighty Warrior" from Hong Kong.*

Sensing their excitement about introducing her to one of the newer fine restaurants of Beverly Hills and waiting to celebrate her arrival, any thought of work was instantly forgotten. *How often does a little girl from Hong Kong get greeted by her husband and a trusted friend intent on taking advantage of the wonderful life-style of Beverly Hills?*

Spending a night with the boys was always an exciting event. Everything seemed so much more interesting when they could talk about "guy" stuff despite the 3-hour time change, the combination of being introduced to a new restaurant, and listening to Don and Mike discuss what could be done if they were able to get ahold of Arena's records. She had been involved with other Sentinels, when with their possession of the right information, they successfully opposed a combination of some big and powerful companies. *The idea of challenging the powerful American Military Complex seems like a very bold plan. When discussed over a great bottle of French wine and a superbly prepared and served fine dinner, the idea becomes even more exciting.*

* * *

It was eleven o'clock California time and two a.m. New York time when they arrived at the Bel-Air Hotel. Too tired to take notice of the magnificently landscaped garden bungalows that were the residence of choice for visiting celebrities and lead members of the East Coast entertainment community, Cecelia politely declined their offer of a final-final after-dinner drink at the hotel bar. Proceeding directly to their bungalow, Cecelia went to her and Mike's room, opened her suitcase, took out what she would need, changed her clothes, and collapsed into bed.

* * *

THE NEXT MORNING, ANXIOUS TO GET STARTED, THE WELL REFRESHED mighty warrior had finished her morning cup of coffee and started her inspection of their room, the outdoor patio, and the lush landscaping of their surroundings. The voluminous records Goldman had delivered were stacked on top of a long narrow table that had been placed next to a long wall in the adjacent room of their suite. Wanting to wait for Mike to order breakfast, she began unpacking the boxes and arranging them in chronological order before placing them in neat rows on the floor of the extra room. Engaged in unpacking, she was only vaguely aware of Mike when he woke up and was silently watching her unpack the files on a pile-by-pile basis as she converted the floor into her personal, horizontal, paper-landscaped filing system.

* * *

HOPING TO PREVENT CECELIA FROM NOTICING THE LIVING EVIDENCE of his and Don's partaking in many more than one final-final after-dinner drink, without saying a word, he made his way through the dressing room and into the bathroom. Twenty minutes later, showered, teeth well brushed, shaved, and dressed in his Beverly Hills' uniform, a refreshed Mike emerged from the dressing room. Looking up, Cecelia was confused by the unusual appearance of her conservative banker husband. Gone were the dark suit, well pressed white shirt, a conservative-appearing tie, and highly polished black shoes. The man stepping into the room was wearing well-tailored and pressed tan gabardine slacks, a hand tooled leather belt secure by an engraved silver buckle, a blue and white checkered, long sleeved sport shirt, highly polished Bass-Weejuns loafers, black socks well punctuated with pink spots, a red and white bandanna tied around his neck, and sporting a blue blazer.

* * *

CECELIA WAS NOT FOOLED. "SINCE WHEN DID YOU DEVELOP THE habit of coming in at two o'clock in the morning smelling like someone who had fallen into a tub filled with gin? And what's with the sporty clothes? You look like some predatory movie star preparing to impress someone in the hotel's lounge. While I'm getting dressed, why don't you order something special from room service and we can enjoy breakfast served on that sunlit patio gorgeously landscaped with flowers, bushes, and trees, some of which I have never seen before."

* * *

SITTING NEXT TO MIKE, ENJOYING THE SMALL TALK, ENJOYING HER favorite breakfast, freshly squeezed California orange juice, eggs Benedict, crisp bacon, and sourdough toast was so enjoyable, the reason for their being there seemed very far away. *How long has it been since Mike and I have been able to enjoy each other's company, study the newspapers, and savor such a fine breakfast, in such a beautiful, warm, and comfortable environment?*

* * *

AT 9:03 A.M., THEY MET DON IN ONE OF THE HOTEL'S SMALL conference rooms that had been reserved for their private meetings. Two hotel bellmen entered the room; each was pushing a dolly loaded with copies of government tax reporting records. After asking Cecelia how she wanted the file boxes to be arranged, they set them down on the long narrow tables organized by state and city.

* * *

THREE DAYS LATER, CECELIA ANNOUNCED SHE HAD IDENTIFIED A match between the discrepancy between the estimated and reported revenues of the theaters in each city and the deposits made to Arena's personal Stone City banking account from that city.

Don and Mike double- and triple-checked her work. Satisfied with the results of her work, each man spent the next 2 days making the kind of carefully constructed notes they would need before proceeding with the next step of their respective plans. Cecelia was kept busy during the day. The early reports from their counters were beginning to appear along with the recent reports from the taxing authorities. A second room was needed to store the additional materials. An old storage room, located in the far end of the central common facilities, partially filled with old hotel records, was finally located. On any given day, Cecelia might be found in their bungalow, the small conference room in the main facility, or in the remote storage room.

* * *

DON WAS THE FIRST TO CHECK OUT OF THE HOTEL. SUBJECT TO confirmation by the second examination, he had all the material he would need to start creating the legal brief required to seek the necessary approval before impaneling a grand jury to indict Manuel Arena for fraud and tax evasion.

Mike's problem was a bit different. Before he could approach his board of directors and demonstrate probable cause required before the bank was empowered to freeze all of Arena's accounts, he needed to produce confirming evidence from a second source indicating fraud and tax evasion had been identified.

To help speed things along, with extra time on his hands, it was only natural for him to offer Cecelia his assistance. "Not in a million years," she responded. "Do you really believe that I would allow you to screw up what it's taken me weeks to organize?"

* * *

HAVING FREE TIME WAS A NEW EXPERIENCE FOR MIKE STONE. TO FILL up his extra time, he decided to work on his golf game, something he had always wanted to do but never had enough collected time to pursue. With the assistance of an old friend and a current member of Los Angeles Country Club, he was able to make arrangements to take a golf lesson each morning, hit practice shots, and after lunch, take a playing lesson from the same teaching professional. Mike had always thought taking lessons and hitting balls was helpful, but it paled by comparison with the improvement he was able to achieve from playing a round of golf, under the intense supervision of the pro. When he missed a shot the pro would drop extra balls, insisting he get it right before proceeding.

Late in the afternoon when they were playing the seventh hole on the North Course, Mike and the pro's concentration was suddenly interrupted when a Los Angeles police squad car, with its red and blue lights flashing, was driving up the fairway toward them. Mike had previously experienced receiving an urgent note delivered by an assistant pro driving a golf cart. Watching the approaching squad car was a new experience. He could never recall an urgency requiring a police car to drive down the pristine fairways of the famous old course. *Someone must have been killed or was in real trouble.*

Without offering any explanation, the two police officers stepped out of their car and immediately approached Mike before they announced they had instructions to transport Mr. Mike Stone to protective custody of the local police precinct.

Sitting in the back of the patrol car, all Mike could think about was the possibility something must have happened to Cecelia. When the squad car headed in the opposite direction from the Bel-Air Hotel, Mike was confused. When neither officer responded to his questions, the normally controlled Sentinel and executive bank officer lost patience. When he began yelling loud obscenities, demanding they stop the car and release him, in an effort to calm him down, the officer sitting in the right-hand front seat turned toward Mike before saying, "Even before you registered at the hotel, we received a tip from a reliable source explaining who you are and warning us there could be trouble. The hotel advised the police and took it upon themselves to employ extra security agents dressed as landscape workers and painters. They have been stationed in the gardens around your bungalows and in the hallways leading to the conference rooms. Their commander has been stationed at the front desk.

"Twenty minutes ago, we received a report from the commander that several men, casually dressed, carrying heavily laden sports bags, were attempting to check into the hotel with no previous reservations. The commander working behind the desk asked the man who appeared to be the leader of the group if they would like a complimentary cup of coffee while he called the reservation department to check for room availability.

"Refusing the offer, each of the men drifted off in a different direction. They seemed more concerned about wandering around the hotel than waiting for a response. They appeared to be interested in the conference rooms, the private dining rooms, and the garden bungalows.

"As planned, the commander's supposed call to the reservation department was routed to the Beverly Hills Police Department and the local FBI field office. Two patrol cars, cruising the area in a nearby unmarked car, were immediately dispatched. After receiving instructions to refrain from attempting to approach any of the men wandering around the hotel to prevent any unnecessary altercation that could harm a hotel guest or employee, the two officers in the nearest patrol car approached the hotel through a rear entrance. They entered the hotel through the service entrance leading to the food preparation facilities. The second car blocked the main entrance to the hotel. No arriving guests were allowed to proceed, and all departing guests were asked for identification. The hotel housekeepers, the maintenance personnel, and the extra security staff received orders to instruct all hotel guests to remain in their rooms. Doors to the public restaurants were closed and locked. No one was allowed to enter or leave.

"We were directed to proceed with all possible haste to pick you up on the golf course and deliver you to the station. Under no circumstances are we to allow you to return to the hotel. Once we assure the FBI all three of you have been safely delivered to the station, they are planning to initiate the second phase of our plan.

"Arresting heavily armed professional operatives in a public place can quickly become very dangerous. Our best hope is that they will voluntarily vacate the premises when they fail to locate any of you. Once they are off the property, we have a task force of squad cars blocking both the east and west drives of Sunset Boulevard. The car blocking the main entrance will join one of the blockades. We want the departing operatives to be well removed from the hotel. Once the operatives make their turn out of the Bel Air entrance, they will move in. Depending upon which direction they turn, one group will stop them and the other group will approach them from the rear. If possible, we want to take them alive. There are members of the Justice Department and the FBI who are very interested in what these men have to say."

Relieved to learn Cecelia was safe, Mike started to analyze what must be happening. He could understand why the two of them would be considered to be threatening and had become active targets. *What I don't understand is why the local police department and the FBI chose to become involved. Could it be that they are protecting one of their own and didn't realize Don had checked out early that same morning? Even if the law enforcement agencies had received the tip from one of Marco's friends, how do you explain how they were so prepared to react on such short notice? Don has some explaining to do.*

CHAPTER 27

White Box, Red Ribbon

MEXICO CITY, MAY 1949

The seating arrangements in the El Matador, long recognized for its celebrity clientele, were organized either to provide the highest possible exposure or the most well-preserved privacy. The table reserved for Señor Arena was offered maximum exposure. It was situated on a raised pedestal located in the center of the restaurant in clear view of the other patrons.

Any thought of serious conversation or ordering anything other than cocktails and hors d'oeuvres had to be postponed until the last of Manuel's friends had visited his table, expressed their congratulations, and waited to be introduced to his new star.

Much later, after they had enjoyed an elegant quail basted in a red wine, red-current, lemon juice, and melted butter sauce, Manuel decided to switch the conversation from innocuous small talk to a more serious subject. Focusing his attention on Mercedes, he said, "I hope there are no hard feelings over what I thoughtlessly allowed to happen, at least none that can't be put aside. I want to express my sincerest apology.

"Not long after you left, the director brought me the rushes of your new film and insisted that I look at them very carefully. Both he and I agreed that we have a great opportunity to make a fine movie of international appeal, one that will be a credit to you and your career as a fine actress and will reflect positively on the studio."

Caught up in the eloquence of the day and the evening, listening to what he was saying, she was not immediately conscious of the pressure she was feeling as he, under the cover of the table, firmly placed his hand on her thigh.

Revolted, Mercedes turned toward him, flashed her most engaging smile, grabbed one of his fingers, and bent it backward into what had to be a very painful position. His effort to smile looked more like a grimace.

Satisfied that her message had been properly conveyed, Mercedes looked into Manuel's eyes and said, "It's time for us to come to an understanding. If you think for one minute I have returned to pick up where we left off, you are sadly mistaken. There are only two conditions under which I am prepared to proceed. Would you prefer to talk about them now or wait until tomorrow morning?"

Clearly understanding he had made a serious mistake, one that he needed to immediately correct, he said, "Fine. Why don't you explain what you have on your mind, and I will give you my answers tomorrow morning, after we have both had a good night's sleep."

Mercedes smiled and nodded in approval. "First, you need to explain exactly what kind of working relationship you expect to have with me. Once I have heard what you intend, depending on what you say, we can then proceed to deal with the second problem."

"A second *problem*?" Manuel asked. "Is there something in the contract that requires our attention? Since you have seen fit to be accompanied by your lawyer, I feel confident we can work it out. Why don't you explain what is bothering you, and I can have my attorney begin to work on it."

"Manuel, it's nothing in the contract. As a matter of fact, our review has suggested you are trying very hard to make certain there are no contractual issues that might interrupt our proceeding. We are going to have to find a solution to a far more serious problem!"

"I don't understand. A far more serious problem? Maybe you should come right out and explain what it is that is bothering you."

Mercedes and Don realized the moment of truth they had so carefully planned had just been placed on the table. After glancing at Don for confirmation, Mercedes decided to answer Manuel's question.

"I'm sure you will understand why I don't trust you and believe my best interests can be served by the terms and conditions of some contract as long as you have that film of Jordan and I stored in your safe.

"How can I feel confident that the day won't come when you threaten to expose our intimate conduct for your own selfish purposes? I'm sorry that I have to say this, but under the circumstances, unless you are willing to provide me with that film you were so anxious to show me, there is no way that I will consider working for you!"

It was past midnight when Manuel returned home. Despite his exhaustion, he went straight to his safe. He quickly found the canister of film in question; it was marked with a red star. Without a moment's hesitation, he slid the panel back into place, made his way to the screening room, and loaded the reel into the projector. *One last viewing won't hurt.*

Watching the film, he couldn't help but be impressed by what a superb example of sensuous female beauty he was watching. As he ran the reel a second time, he began to notice Jordan and his aroused animal instincts. *This is one reel I'm really going to regret giving up,* he thought. What fantastic entertainment! What a valuable piece of blackmail material! Reluctantly, he wrapped the canister in an old Christmas gift box, secured it with a red ribbon, and attached a personal note.

The next morning, Manuel, his attorney, Mercedes, and Don were sitting around the big table in Manuel's office when he handed Mercedes the large white box tied with a red ribbon. "I assure you," he said, "my only intention is to make a great movie. I hope this gift convinces you of my desire to demonstrate that we are starting a new chapter in our relationship, one in which each of us will treat the other with the trust and courtesy normally enjoyed by working professionals."

Encouraged by her smiling response, he handed her the revised contract. "To make certain you believe me regarding any matters pertaining to my personal conduct, I have taken the liberty of instructing my attorney to insert some additional clauses. You will note several draconian remedies have been included should you find it necessary for you to protect yourself from any of my disrespectful conduct.

"To make it easier for you and Mr. Cerreta to inspect the changes I have had inserted, I've taken the liberty of underlining and highlighting the new language. Why don't the two of you take your time reviewing them, and we can meet at my house early this evening over a cocktail and a superb dinner. If everything is in order, we can celebrate the beginning of a new relationship."

Four hours later, Mercedes and Don were sitting in the back of a privately chartered government plane headed to Los Angeles. They were leaning against each other, holding hands, sipping champagne, and silently enjoying the moment. The canister of film was safely packed in her suitcase.

The two were wakened from their trance when the stewardess came by to refill their champagne glasses. Mercedes lifted her glass. "Ever since my parents were killed in the Spanish Revolution when I was 15 years old," she said, "I've been forced to fend for myself. From the minute we left Los Angeles until right this moment, you have no idea how safe and protected you have made me feel. I know it's been less than a week since we first met, but I feel very drawn to, even indebted to, you. You are giving me a second chance to reinvent my life."

They clinked glasses, and Don wrapped his arm around her shoulders as best he could and gave her a reassuring hug. He took her hand in his once again and tightened his grip. "Nothing would give me a greater pleasure than to be a part of your new life, Mercedes."

It was all the reinforcement she needed. Her last thought before drifting off to sleep was of Don, wondering what role he might play in her future life.

CHAPTER 28

Least Bad Decision

MEXICO CITY, JUNE 1949

Three weeks later, Manuel was still trying to understand Mercedes's abrupt departure and how he was going to salvage his film when the intercom on his desk crackled. "Señor Arena," his secretary said, "there are three men out here without an appointment asking to see you. A Mr. Stone from Stone City Bank, a Mr. Matthews from the *New York Times*, and Mr. Cerreta, the same man who accompanied Miss Velasquez on her recent return. May I show them into your office?"

As the introductions were being made, Manuel, turning on the charm, said, "Mr. Stone, I have been a longtime, loyal customer of your fine bank. Welcome to Mexico. I've looked forward to meeting you for a very long time."

Turning to Walt Matthews, he said, "I regularly read your articles. For a long time, I have appreciated the objectivity and accuracy of your reporting."

Saving Don for last, Manuel said, "I didn't think I would ever have the opportunity to see you again. Maybe you will help me to understand what went wrong during your last visit?"

Once they were all seated around Manuel's desk he seemed to become taller. None of the three men were able to see the six-inch pedestal built to elevate the height of his sitting position.

Mike Stone started the discussion. "I want to thank you for seeing us on such short notice. We're here to ask for your cooperation. We need your assistance in finding a way to stop Jordan McWilliams and his military-industrial clients from implementing their plan to escalate the rearming of the American military."

Surprised by the statement, Manuel took his time before responding. A calm but cautious moviemaker finally asked, "Why would you believe I would know anything about such an outrageous scheme? I'm afraid you have come a very long way for no purpose."

Mike continued. "Señor Arena, I'll cut right to the point. I have copies of the files we have compiled on your movie house skimming operations, along with the indictments we plan to hand over to an already-impaneled grand jury."

Pausing to open his briefcase, Mike took out a thick manila folder and slid it toward Manuel. "In that file, you will find copies of information we have compiled on your movie house skimming operations. Actually, it contains two reports. The first details the difference between the receipts you were observed collecting and what was reported to the state taxing authorities. It was compiled at the direction of Myron Goldman, one of your Hollywood competitors. You will note that the differences match deposits you made to your personal account in Stone's New York bank.

"The second report demonstrates the same results conducted by the U.S. Department of Justice.

"According to our computations, when spread over your hundred theaters during just the last 3 years, you have underreported your taxable sales revenues and pocketed approximately $1,500,000—money owed your Cuban investment partners."

Manuel prided himself in not reacting to bad news. Remarkably, he did not give evidence of the tremendous fear he was feeling. "Wait just a minute!" he calmly said. "You expect to come into my office, unannounced, show me some files, and expect me to cooperate? I know my rights, and you have no authority in Mexico!"

Mike, responding in a similarly calm but firmer manner, said, "Mr. Arena, I assume you understand the procedures banks are required to follow when it becomes evident that acts of fraud have been committed. Once the tax authorities file their suit, Stone City Bank becomes legally obligated to freeze any and all accounts of yours and those of any affiliates. Not only will this action disrupt the transfer of your personal funds, it will also prevent you from making regular distributions of revenues to your Cuban investors."

The three visitors watched Señor Arena pick up a small brass sculpture from his desk and nervously start to rub his thumb and forefinger along its polished surface.

Walt Matthews had seen such breakdowns many times in his investigative work. He was unmoved by these efforts to bluff one's way out of trouble. He started his part of the conversation by saying, "Mr. Arena, do you understand once the government files its lawsuits, the information that's been compiled becomes part of the public record? When that occurs, I won't have any legal prohibition from reporting this story in the *New York Times* and the 32 other newspapers that syndicate my columns. News is news!"

Despite his efforts to appear calm, Manuel had already dropped the small sculpture twice.

Responsibility for driving in the final nail into Manuel's coffin was left to Don Cerreta. "While we have been able to successfully document your skimming operations, we still lack the evidence we need to prove how your members have been conspiring to manipulate the military spending and decision-making process of the American government.

"I hope you will believe me when I tell you that you are not the primary target of our investigation. The Justice Department takes it very seriously when your friends attempt to compromise the congressional process for their own self-interests. If you were to provide us with the information we need to document the identity of the contributors and the recipients of the funds, I think we might be able to dissuade Mr. Stone from turning his evidence over to the Treasury Department and Mr. Matthews from writing the newspaper articles he described."

The next 30 minutes would turn out to be the worst half hour in Señor Arena's life. No matter how hard he tried to argue or convince his three visitors of the fruitless nature of their quest, he knew he had no practical alternative but to cooperate. Once he accepted the reality of the situation, Manuel realized he was being forced to make a *least bad* decision. While having his hands spanked and losing the patronage of the wealthy American industrialists would be most unfortunate, it would not be nearly as devastating as alerting his Cuban investors and the IRS of his skimming operation. It was at that precise moment when he realized the files that had once represented his "insurance policy" had become his hangman's noose.

CHAPTER 29

Cecelia's Big Dance

NEW YORK, MAY 1949

Once again, Cecelia found herself alone in her New York apartment. Mike had left for Mexico City to join Don and Walt. Claudine and Jacques were living in Geneva. Natalie was in England. David and Juan Pablo were in Riyadh, helping the Saudi government renegotiate their petroleum agreements with the British and American oil companies.

To fill up her extra time, she began to focus her attention on pursuing the Sentinels' growing continuity problem. Lying awake at night, she couldn't get her mind to shut down. *Somehow we need to attract and train new crops of qualified and motivated Sentinels. To be successful a new university must have a broader purpose than to train future Sentinels. How extensive might the market be for high-powered doctoral students trained to think and act in terms of identifying and solving Power-Cycle problems. Why have so many people chosen to be of assistance each time we have tried to solve one of our problems? If we knew the answer, maybe we would better understand what the requirements of a new university need to be.*

It was early in the morning. The alarm clock read three o'clock when she suddenly sat up in bed. She had been dreaming of an important idea. Worried if she went back to sleep she might forget what she had concluded, she got out of bed, made her way into the den, turned on the desk light, removed a fresh yellow legal pad from one of the desk drawers, and began to make notes. She had filled almost all the first notepad with her recollections about all the different problems they had solved, who had been involved, and what the particular circumstances were when they interfered with the German industrialists' attempts to utilize their "fortunes of war" to fund a new Reich.

Over a strong cup of coffee, two slices of toast, and a glass of freshly squeezed orange juice, she began to study her notes. By the time she poured herself a second cup of coffee, she concluded, she had decided to perform the same exercise with their efforts to prevent seven oil companies from monopolizing control over 90 percent of the world's oil supply. When she stopped for lunch, she noticed her notes had filled a second notepad.

Still in her pajamas, she decided to take a shower and get dressed. Standing under the warm-hot stream of water, she thought of the charts Armando had organized to help him analyze the possible meaning of all those scribbled notes. *Maybe if I used the same technique, I might discover how much interest our "Friends of the Sentinels" might have in helping us to fund the "Sentinel Institute."*

To help her organize her thoughts, she decided to visit the local stationary store and purchase several of those corkboard panels she had previously noticed. Lugging her purchase back to their apartment was no easy task for the diminutive woman. Determine to complete her task, she half-carried and half-dragged her precious cargo back to her apartment building. With the help of the doorman, she succeed in unpacking the corkboards and setting them against the wall where she was prepared to hang them. After removing the large paintings, she set about assembling the panels into one very large surface.

Having completed the assembly of the wall-size cork panel, taking advantage of her notes, Cecelia began to print the names of everyone who had cooperated with the Sentinels, along their two previous journeys. She wrote each name, organized by region, down the left-hand side of her big chart. Four days were required before she could complete the first leg of her project.

Returning to her files, she began to record her interpretation of the problems they had been asked to solve. Working from her notes, she began to list each of the problems along the top portion of the chart. When she was finished, referring to her notes, she started to make little x's at the intersection where the solved problem corresponded with the people who were involved. After days of meticulous work, she finished placing the last of her marks in the appropriate space.

Standing back to study the results of her work, she could easily understand which problems affected the highest number of parties. Armed with the information arranged on her big chart, she had identified the top 10 problems and the names of the principal beneficiaries.

She now possessed the information she would need to determine the depth of interest of those who had most benefited from their efforts. After removing another painting from an adjacent wall, she taped a large world map in its place. Flipping through the pages of both pads, she began to place colored pins in the map that identified the location of each beneficiary. The color of the pin identified the solved problem. The work was slow and tedious. Two more days were required before she finished the next step of her analysis.

The next day she visited the camera shop located across the street on the next block. With the assistance of the courteous clerk, she learned how to operate the wide-angle camera, understand what film to purchase, and how to arrange the artificial lighting. An hour later, with the roles of exposed film in hand, she returned to the same shop.

* * *

ARMED WITH HIGH STACKS OF DEVELOPED PRINTS DEPICTING THE two charts she had formulated, she began to summarize the results of her findings. Using her conclusions to support the list of objectives proposed for Sentinel Institute, she was now ready to start her world tour. She planned to meet with each of the designated beneficiaries, show them the results of her research, describe her vision of the proposed Sentinel Institute, and discuss their potential interest in participating in its funding.

CHAPTER 30

Building a Bridge

LONDON, ENGLAND, MAY 1949

From London, Natalie's friends were calling to inform her that her presence was needed. "You need to meet personally with the leading casting agents before they are willing to seriously consider becoming interdependent with your new program," they advised.

The school year was drawing to a close. For the next 3 months, Natalie would be free to devote her complete attention to developing the British segment of her bridge. Making time for David no longer seemed to be of importance. With increasing frequency, he had found new excuses not to accompany her to Los Angeles. On the weekends when she was able to remain home in Berkeley, he would claim to have made "other arrangements." During the middle of the week when their work required them to remain at home, he appeared to be only politely interested in any of the news she was excited to discuss. Whenever she tried to discuss her concerns with him, he was quick to change the subject or withdraw into his impenetrable shell. After a time, she quit trying. They simply had become two independent people who occasionally occupied the same home.

* * *

IN LONDON, THE NEWS OF NATALIE'S PENDING ARRIVAL IN LONDON quickly circulated through the movie and theatrical communities. Curious people were talking. "Why would Natalie after two years' absence suddenly announce she would be spending her summer in London?" Was she returning to the stage? Was she rehearsing a new show? Was she accompanying David on some kind of a business trip? Her friends were curious to learn what they could do to help her.

Only her closest friends in England's motion picture casting community knew of her intention. She needed to test the feasibility of completing the other half of her "Bridge." She was responding to their suggestion, "Natalie, we believe if you can convince two or three of our most successful producers to sign a few of your best candidates, we think the dam of inertia will be successfully breached, but it's going to take your presence."

Even her friends who knew of her true intentions were confused. They were wondering why Natalie, who never had a political bone in her body, had become so interested in the Hollywood blacklisting problem. Their curiosity was further heightened when they learned she, together with an old friend, Sir Colin Meyer, were planning to hold a reception for her friends, agents, casting directors, and successful movie producers. When they heard she would be accompanied by two traveling companions, Gloria Adams—the much publicized "Heroine of Hollywood" and Mercedes Velasquez, the former Miss Universe, their idle curiosity was transformed into determined interest.

When invitations to Sir Colin's soiree failed to include many of his aristocratic friends, they concluded Natalie must be planning something very different. The list of invitations had been limited to Natalie's friends from the theater, influential members of England's film community, and certain members of the press.

The night of the reception arrived quickly. A quintet, specially selected from the London Philharmonic Orchestra, was seated just inside the entrance of the grand ballroom, playing a medley of tunes from some of Natalie's old shows. The men were dressed in their traditional nighttime black-tie tuxedos, and the women had used the occasion as an excuse to wear their finest gowns and their most exquisite jewelry.

Mercedes, looking as glamorous as ever, was circulating among the guests, introducing herself and making careful mental notes of everyone she met. Not knowing what to expect, to a person, they were pleasantly surprised by the interest she seemed to show in them. Although, it would have been impossible for them to not be conscious of her size and physical beauty, they were impressed by how skillfully she steered the conversation to talking about things they were interested in.

Gloria, with a glass of vodka firmly grasped in her left hand, was saying hello to her old friends, tactfully acknowledging the people she knew by reputation, and graciously allowing herself to be introduced to the others. Their conversations seemed to center on their own experiences involving obstruction of personal liberties. Colin's guests were discovering how intelligent, friendly, and brave this former movie actress really was. Although they didn't realize it at the time, telling Gloria stories would become a future pastime.

At precisely nine o'clock, Sir Colin Meyer stepped up on the small stage. After asking for silence, he said, "Thank you for accepting Natalie's and my invitation. I hope you will become as excited as I have to learn what Natalie and her friends hope to accomplish. Before Natalie sings a few songs, she has something to say."

Dressed in a pair of faded blue Levi Strauss jeans, a red and white checkered shirt, a bright red neckerchief, highly polished high-heeled cowgirl boots, and a broad-brimmed cowboy hat, Natalie emerged from stage left, accompanied by music from *Oklahoma!* The crowd greeted her with the kind of enthusiastic ovation a fine star and an old friend clearly deserves. Taking her place in front of a grand piano, the only prop on the stage, Natalie flashed her famous smile, kicked up one of her heels, and patiently waited for the applause to die down.

"Thank you for coming. As most of you know, one of the nicest things that can happen in the life of a musical actress is performing for her friends, which is exactly what I plan to do tonight. But first, I would like to tell you a little story."

As briefly as possible, Natalie described the essentials of the American situation: the HUAC trials, Gloria's performance, and the ongoing efforts to blacklist and terrify prominent members of Hollywood's filmmaking colony. "My message is quite simple: I have come here to ask for your cooperation in constructing a bridge—a bridge that will connect Hollywood talent with your filmmaking employment opportunities here in London."

After waiting, once again, for the applause to die down, Natalie said, "I would like to introduce you to a special person and an important new friend of mine, Miss Mercedes Velasquez. Some of you may recall that she was a former Miss Universe from Toledo, Spain. After I return to Los Angeles, Mercedes will remain here in London to be available to meet with you, discuss your employment needs in greater depth, and communicate her understanding to me so that I can organize a short-list of commercially proven, qualified, and motivated candidates for your review. Once a perceived fit has been established, Mercedes and I will be prepared to work with you in making whatever arrangements are necessary for you to meet face-to-face with the appropriate candidates. I only hope you will find working with Miss Velasquez as interesting and rewarding as we have."

A brisk round of applause broke out. A voice from the audience could be heard, "Love, tell us what you need." Responding, Natalie said, "That will come later. Now, without further delay, I would like to introduce another friend of mine and my most recent song-and-dance partner, the 'Heroine of Hollywood,' Mrs. Gloria Adams." And before beckoning the older actress to join her, she said, "Gloria really needs no introduction. The testimony of this brave woman before the House Un-American Activities Committee has made it possible for future witnesses to avail themselves of their constitutional rights, as provided by the First and Fifth Amendments of the American Constitution. Properly armed with their rights and given proper legal representation we would like to believe the tyranny of the government attacking its citizen can be stopped.

"Gloria's many contributions have hit a nerve with the American public and the working press. By so courageously standing up to the intimidating tactics employed by members of the HUAC, Gloria's remarkable performance reminded the American public of its need to remain vigilant to threats that could compromise their personal liberties and be prepared to voice their opinions at the ballot box. I hope you'll be interested to hear, straight from this self-described 'pissed-off old broad,' some of the experiences she's encountered along the way."

With the aid of a small footstool, Gloria climbed up and perched herself on top of the piano. The inveterate storyteller regaled the crowd with tales of her appearance before the HUAC and her never-ending romance with the fascinated press. The guests were spellbound by the feisty woman who held a glass of vodka in one hand and a cigarette in the other.

Worried the questions would never stop, Natalie stepped forward and spoke. "Okay, everybody, it's time for you to allow a couple of song-and-dance women an opportunity to do what we enjoy most . . . singing to our friends."

Thirty minutes later, Natalie, amid the applause, whistles, and the cries of encore, thanked the audience for their gracious response. "Before we depart, I would like to tell you the real question we hope we are asking. Why shouldn't English movie producers take advantage of the recent availability of box-office-proven American actors, writers, and directors? These Hollywood blacklisted people are the same people who would ordinarily be engaged in the making of new movies expected to generate large box-office receipts in America. Should you have an interest, please call upon us. As the name 'Natalie's Bridge' implies, we are here to assist you in connecting with Hollywood personalities who have expressed interest in working in England. Why shouldn't you take advantage of Hollywood's short-sightedness?"

Excited members of the audience could be seen gathered around each of the three women. When they weren't asking questions, they were handing out their business cards; it took a long time before the excited crowd began to file out of the big ballroom. David Marcus had been standing, unnoticed, on the outer periphery of the large crowd. He was waiting for the last of the people to leave. He was hoping to have a private conversation with Natalie.

As she was completing her conversation with some of the last people to leave, Natalie couldn't help but notice his presence. His red hair seem particularly bright. Surprised by his appearance, she was talking and thinking, *Why would David, after all this time, make an appearance at Sir Colin's reception? He certainly wasn't on my guest list. How could he have been admitted without showing his invitation to one of the guards? Now I remember . . . He and Sir Colin are old friends. David must have convinced Colin it was important for him to see me. I don't know whether I should be happy or sad that David would go to so much trouble.*

When David suggested she join him for a late-night dinner in the Grille at the Claridges Hotel, she understood they were about to have a very serious conversation.

CHAPTER 31

Dinner at Claridges

LONDON, ENGLAND, MAY 1949

They were sitting at the same corner table in Claridges Grille, where they had resumed their relationship 3 years ago. David was doing all the talking; a cool and reserved Natalie sat quietly listening. *I wonder if this discussion is going to be another one of those "Statue of Liberty" conversations like the one I had with Jacques when he told me he was leaving me for Claudine.*

* * *

DAVID ORDERED A BOTTLE OF THEIR FAVORITE WHITE WINE AND TWO orders of fillet of sole. Attempting to pull her into the conversation, he asked, "Isn't this the same table where you were sitting that night when I wandered into the Grille?"

* * *

RECEIVING NO RESPONSE, DAVID TRIED CHANGING THE SUBJECT. "Natalie, you had to be pleased by everyone's response to your little talk. I wouldn't be surprised to learn that your idea for a new play is going to receive a lot of support. I'm amazed at how far you have brought your program in such a short period of time. From my vantage point in the rear of the room I could watch people's reaction. You certainly held their attention, and from listening to what they said, I'm quite certain you will be receiving their cooperation."

* * *

It was at that point when the waiter arrived with the wine, a basket of rolls, and a small dish of unsalted butter. Pausing to sample the wine, David continued. "Natalie, I can understand why you must be very upset with me. Please bear with me. You have no idea how difficult it was for me to come to your party and have this conversation. There have been many times when I thought of disappearing and not trying to help you understand what has happened. If I didn't love and respect you so much, I wouldn't be sitting here, hoping you will understand what I am about to tell you.

* * *

"Natalie, your silence isn't making this situation any easier for me. But, what the hell, here goes. I think my problem began the night we were driving over the Bay Bridge, on our way back to Berkeley. I remember thinking how threatened I was by the idea that you might want to find out what it was like to star in a musical. Knowing your aversion for returning to the life of a 'dancing bear,' I assumed that the best way to ensure that our life together would not be interrupted by what was happening was to let things run their course and be as supportive as possible.

* * *

"I think, emotionally, each time I took you to the train, I was secretly holding my breath until I saw you step off the train when you returned. You have no idea how relieved I was that day when you returned so thoroughly upset with those Hollywood producers."

* * *

Pausing to pour himself a second glass of wine, David continued. "It was when I perceived your growing interest in the 'Hollywood

Ten' that I really became alarmed; you were starting to develop an independent interest in helping those people. If you recall, I don't think I missed one of those early trips to the dinner parties in Southern California. I even rearranged some of my trips so that they wouldn't interfere. I always thought that your interest was a passing fancy and in time, would resolve itself. Looking back, I guess I was guilty of wishful thinking.

* * *

"ONCE I BEGAN TO REALIZE HOW SERIOUS YOU WERE BECOMING, I knew that things were going to change. That is when I began to think back through the second phase of our relationship, the one that started at this very table. Try as I might, I could never figure out a way to explain how upsetting I found having to share you with your new interests. How does a grown, intelligent man say, I can only be happy when you are fully devoted to me and my interests?"

* * *

INTERRUPTED BY THE WAITER SERVING THEIR DINNER, DAVID concentrated on his meal. Still no comment from Natalie. Understanding that she wasn't going to respond, he continued. "The more I thought about these last 2 years, the more I realized that we reduced two separate lives into one, one where you were my friend and research assistant, and lovers. Without realizing it, I became totally dependent on your constant attention and your love. Before you, I devoted my life to my work; women were options to fill temporary voids. For the first time in my life, I learned to enjoy sharing my life with one woman.

* * *

"AT FIRST, I COULDN'T UNDERSTAND WHY I WAS SO UPSET. I STOPPED joining you for all those dinner invitations. I started scheduling more trips to England and the Middle East, hoping the distraction would make the hurt go away.

* * *

"UNFORTUNATELY, BEING AWAY FROM YOU ONLY MADE THINGS HURT all the more. That is when I sought professional assistance. With help, it didn't take long for me to realize that as long as you were totally devoted to me, and your life was my life, and I didn't have to compete with any of your outside interests, I was completely happy."

* * *

Finishing the last of the wine before continuing, he said, "Now comes the most difficult part. Knowing you as I do, I had to consider how you would react when I explained all of this to you. Believing that there was the possibility that you might agree to give up this new interest represented the risk I was unwilling to take. Being honest with myself, I knew that I wasn't prepared to take the chance that the same problem might arise again. As hard as I've tried, I can't seem to work my way around that problem."

* * *

Having finished saying what he had to say, David sat back, waiting for Natalie to respond. He watched as she seemed to be rolling what he had just said through her mind.

* * *

Finally, she asked, "David, is there another woman? Either tell me the truth or don't answer. I don't want you to lie to me."

* * *

Now it was David's turn not to answer.

* * *

"What is it about you men?" Natalie said. "This is the second time in my life when someone I loved destroyed a relationship over his concern about something I might do. Why didn't you talk to me before coming to your conclusions? How do you know that maybe the one thing I want more than anything else in life is to be able to support and love a good man the way I have always dreamed?"

* * *

"Natalie, I've had a lot of time to think; I don't want to lose you. Is there any chance that you would forgive me and provide me with a second chance?"

* * *

"David, that is a question you don't want me to answer!"

* * *

As disturbing as David's message had been, Natalie realized that he had provided her with the clarity she needed to embark on a new life. *He has set me free. David will always be a good friend, a person who has helped me generate more meaning to my life, and a professional colleague. For that I am very grateful.*

CHAPTER 32

A Little Chat

NEW YORK, JUNE 1949

The report Jordan had received from his security company was a difficult one to digest and even more troublesome when he began to consider how to report the results to his clients. *How am I going to explain what had been planned as a simple kidnapping of three people had turned into the killing of three and the wounding and/or capturing of five highly skilled and experienced professional operatives employed to complete what appeared to be a simple assignment? Preliminary reports indicate the local police were tipped off, the three subjects were no longer in residence at the appointed time of their attack. Their carefully planned trap had been converted into a trap set to interdict our operatives as they were leaving the property. A second report indicated that FBI personnel were involved, and the entire operation had been supervised by a high-level Justice Department official.*

* * *

*I*F THE JUSTICE DEPARTMENT IS INVOLVED, DON'T I NEED TO ASSUME *the federal government has learned of our plan and is actively supporting the Sentinels' opposition? What have the police been able to learn from the captured operatives?*

A LITTLE CHAT

* * *

FOR AS LONG AS HE COULD REMEMBER, J. JORDAN MCWILLIAMS HAD lived his life in accordance with a carefully orchestrated calendar. He went to bed promptly at 10:30 p.m., slept in a separate room from his wife, set his alarm clock for 6:00 a.m., finished his floor exercises by 6:30, and was showered, shaved, and immaculately dressed by 7:00. When he emerged from his Upper East Side co-op apartment at 7:05, he was greeted by his driver, who handed him a cup of coffee, a small bag containing two croissants, and a copy of the *New York Times*, before he ducked into the backseat of the long black car.

At 7:30, he would be greeted by his loyal secretary of many years, who handed him a second cup of coffee before taking her regular seat next to the left side of his desk. At 7:45, he would begin dictating whatever thoughts had occurred to him during the previous evening or while he was studying the morning paper on his drive to work.

On this particular morning, his dictation was interrupted by the ringing of his private telephone. Annoyed, he picked up the receiver preparing to crucify whoever was calling. The few people who had this number knew very well not to call until after nine o'clock.

When he heard sobbing on the other end of the line, he held his tongue. Amid the babbling Jordan could tell the caller was Manuel Arena, sounding inebriated and inconsolable. The moviemaker rambled on, offering apologies and excuses. Jordan had to ask Manuel to repeat his story twice before he finally understood what his longtime friend was trying to tell him. The little bastard had given the Manuel's Club files to Mike Stone, Don Cerreta, and Walt Matthews.

Familiar with each man, Jordan couldn't conjure up a worse group of people who could have in their possession so much sensitive information. Afraid of the answer to his next question, Jordan hesitantly asked, "Manuel, think carefully, is there anything else missing from your safe?"

Assured that the Mexican war chest remained intact, he knew one thing for sure. *I need to immediately speak to Ben Holt and the five other attorneys.*

Two hours later, he had completed his calls. The reaction he had received ranged from calm acceptance to blustering outrage. After patiently waiting for their emotional outbursts to subside, Jordan calmly questioned if a second meeting to be held in his office was in order.

Concerned about how widespread the news reporting Manuel's robbery and the killings may have become, Jordan walked over to the bookshelves and turned on his small television set. After switching between the different news channels and failing to find anything of interest, he turned to his radio. Once again, he failed to hear anything about a killing in Mexico. Finally, he walked over to the teletype machine that he kept in the small cubicle located in the far wall. For the next 15 minutes, he monitored the reporting of the different news agencies. Failing to find anything of interest, he returned to his desk.

Confused why such an event would remain unreported, he wondered, *What kind of game are Mike Stone and his friends playing? If they already possessed the information they wanted, what would they stand to gain by killing Manuel? Why would bankers and government agents want to steal all our money?*

* * *

AROUND 2:30 P.M. THAT SAME AFTERNOON, JORDAN WAS SITTING alone in his office. He could feel his orderly, predictable world collapsing around him. His recent bout of depression was beginning to return. Never one to give up so easily, he was wondering if he had missed something. By 4:30, he had assembled all the data contained in his different security reports. It was scattered all over his normally immaculate desk, and he was totally absorbed in studying each of the reports, one after another. The more he read, the more convinced he was becoming that, although he didn't know what he was looking for, he would recognize it when he saw it. Without thinking, he had selected the next report that lay on top of the high stack of material. It had been prepared on the American Maintenance Company, the building maintenance company employed by several of his clients. He was studying the fine print and the footnotes when he discovered a seemingly unimportant notation describing the company's credit references. It mentioned the name of Mr. Michael Stone, executive vice president, Stone City Bank. *It doesn't make sense. Why would a big-money bank be doing business with such a small and relatively new building maintenance company?*

His interest piqued, he flipped back a few pages and started reading the report more carefully. There it was again . . . Clearly printed were the names Marco Tancredi, president of American Maintenance, and Mike Stone, executive vice president, Stone City Bank. Jordan was obviously aware of Mike Stone, but Marco Tancredi was a new name.

Jordan didn't believe in coincidences. Instinct was telling him he needed to learn more about Mr. Marco Tancredi. The break finally came when he decided to look deeper into his personal history. Scouring every word of the small print, he learned Tancredi had attended grammar and high school in "Little Italy."

Researching Don Cerreta's personal background was much easier. His résumé was included in the Justice Department's Annual Review. Jordan's review revealed the federal prosecutor and Marco had attended the same schools at the same time. Although he had no way of understanding why these three men were connected, he instinctively knew he had found the link he was seeking. Jordan's brilliant mind was kicking into high gear. If the company removed the daily trash from the offices of some of Manuel's Club members, it stood to reason cleaning personnel must have discovered some sort of information that described their Mexican activities. It didn't take much imagination to assume Marco had passed his information on to Cerreta. Knowing of Cerreta and Stone's history of working together opposing the efforts of the "Oil Club's" attempt to monopolize the production and distribution of 90 percent of the world's oil production, Jordan surmised, *So that is how the Sentinels and the Justice Department have been getting their information!*

At 9:35 the next morning, Jordan was sitting behind his big desk contemplating how best to use his new information when the intercom buzzer indicated his secretary needed to speak with him. "Mr. McWilliams, there is a Mr. Michael Stone standing in front of my desk without an appointment. He has suggested you would probably want to see him."

Entering the office, Mike formally introduced himself, before handing Jordan a large manila envelope, then he said, "Mr. McWilliams, enclosed you will find a copy of what Walt Matthews is planning to print in tomorrow's *New York Times*. It documents the names of the contributors to your Mexican war chest, the names of recipients, and the amounts of campaign contributions, as well as their voting records on military appropriation bills."

As Jordan took the article, Mike was studying him the same way, in his youth, he would assess an amateur boxing opponent.

Jordan, the wily old pro, was doing his best to ensure that his relaxed countenance and steely blue eyes didn't betray the many thoughts racing through his mind.

Once Mike felt he had let Jordan squirm long enough, he said, "Why don't you take a few minutes to study the contents of the article before we have a little chat?"

Mike felt he had let Jordan squirm long enough, before he said, "Now that we and the Justice Department have, in our possession, multiple sources of evidence we need to indict, we have been wondering, with your assistance and your other lawyer friends, if we could come to an understanding and we could provide you with an opportunity to stop all of this before things get out of control."

The sight of the article had shaken Jordan, but his mood lifted as he remembered he might still have one card to play. *Assuming my hunch about Marco Tancredi and Don Cerreta might be true, although I don't know all the details, maybe I can bluff my way out of this predicament.*

"Mr. Stone, I suggest that you listen very carefully to what I am about to explain! Did you really believe we were unaware of your, Cerreta, and Tancredo's efforts to illegally obtain information from executive offices? If you plan to publish that article, I can't even imagine the amount of the damages you and your friends will be charged with for publicizing detrimental information illegally secured! And if that isn't a good enough reason, we can add the fact that you have attempted to coerce Señor Arena by using the threat of exposure to convince him to turn over sensitive data against his wishes."

* * *

"NICE TRY, McWILLIAMS! PERHAPS YOU WOULD PREFER TO STUDY these affidavits I am about to hand you. They have been signed and witnessed by employees of his studio who state Señor Arena *voluntarily* provided us with the files stored in his safe. Or, if you would prefer, we would be willing to ask him to testify."

Mike patiently waited for Jordan to finish processing what he had just been told before continuing. "How do you think the public will react when it learns that the House Un-American Activities Committee was engaged in punishing innocent people and abusing the rights of Americans for the benefit of impressing the public with the threat of spreading Communism? How do you expect the courts to react when they learn of your attempt to manipulate the congressional appropriations process as part of a plot to unnecessarily accelerate increased military appropriations? How do you expect the consumers of the products produced by your clients to react when they learn of their willingness to take advantage of the American people?

"Then there is the question of the Washington lobbying effort and its attempts to obtain the voting support of the to-be-named congressmen. Do you *really* wish to expose all your dirty linen to the public?"

* * *

"MR. STONE, I DON'T THINK YOU UNDERSTAND THE '*BIGGER PICTURE*.' If we were talking about a couple of military contracts here, I doubt the risks you have so eloquently described would justify our continuing. Unfortunately, we are discussing the economic health of the United States economy. When the entire story has been told, do you really believe your seedy little contentions would withstand the pressure of the entire military-industrial establishment?"

* * *

"MR. MCWILLIAMS, YOU AND YOUR FRIENDS HAVE 72 HOURS TO provide us with conclusive proof of your terminating Manuel's Club, repatriating any remaining funds in that war chest to the original donors, canceling all lobbying contracts, and evidence informing all political recipients there will be no further contributions made to their campaigns. Your 72-hour clock is running."

CHAPTER 33

Something of Importance

NEW YORK, JUNE 1949

It was one in the morning when the phone on Armando's bedside table began to ring. Only half-awake, he picked up the phone. He heard the familiar but panicked voice of Frank Majors, one of his building maintenance managers. Struggled to understand what Frank was trying to say, it took a moment before Armando was able to understand the seriousness of what we was hearing.

"They scared the hell out of us!"

"Frank, calm down. Count to 10 and then slowly explain what has happened."

"There were seven guys, each of which was carrying a gun. They were dressed in dark clothes, wearing ski masks to cover their faces, and carrying what looked like very large bags. After they scooped up all the trash and stuffed it into those large bags, they started interrogating us, one at a time. They were asking us questions about you and Mr. Tancredi and people we'd never heard of.

"When they suggested we had been separating executive notes out of the trash, we mentioned the exercise was an ongoing practice we had engaged in for years. Reading them and speculating on what the important people might have been discussing was our way of regularly entertaining ourselves during our midnight lunch break. I explained once read, they were deposited in the incinerator along with the rest of the trash. I even showed him some of the notes we had separated out that night."

"Frank, you should call the police department and tell them everything you have just told me, less your last comment."

* * *

At 10 minutes to twelve, Armando entered the restaurant and walked past the bar and into the restroom. After the customary 5 minutes, he emerged and slowly made his way to Marco's table.

As he patiently listened to Armando, Marco was becoming increasingly concerned. Not quite certain how to react, the normally in command secretive streetwise executive didn't immediately reply. He was busy thinking. *Could Jordan have discovered the connection between me, Don Cerreta, and Mike Stone? If so, he might be trying to determine if our cleaning company might be the source of their information. How else could they explain why we seem to know whatever they are planning? From Frank, the connection between me, Don Cerreta, and Mike Stone?*

What's their motive? Are they trying to send us some kind of message? Are they preparing to put the three of us out of business? Or are they only trying to learn how Don and Mike have been obtaining their information? Whatever their purpose, we would be wise to take all necessary precautions to protect ourselves and warn the others.

* * *

Two days later, Marco and Armando were enjoying a specially prepared lunch, well complemented with one of their favorite Tuscan wines, when the yellow light mounted over the bar began to flash. Calmly, they, together with the other patrons, rose from their tables, leaving their partially finished meals, and proceeded to the rear of the restaurant where a large floating paneled wall protected a set of stairs that led to the basement wine cellar. When the last of them had entered, a heavy iron door was closed and locked.

The flashing yellow light had been triggered by one of the men employed by Marco's friends, who was staked out behind an open window in a third-floor apartment directly opposite the entrance to the restaurant. His presence was part of a longer term security precaution afforded the colorful regulars of the popular Italian restaurant.

* * *

ABOVEGROUND, TWO HEFTY MEN EXITED FROM A BLACK CAR THAT had suddenly pulled to a stop in front of the restaurant. Carrying automatic weapons, they made their way into the now-vacant restaurant. Confused by the vacated restaurant and the unfinished meals left on the tables, they immediately started yelling to the driver sitting in the waiting car, "Someone must have been tipped off. The tables are covered with partially eaten food. No patrons, no waiters, no bartenders."

* * *

AT ALMOST THE SAME MOMENT, TWO POLICE CARS HAD SCREECHED to a stop, blocking any possibility the waiting car might escape. Standing behind the protective cover of the squad cars, the officers trained their guns on the emerging gunmen and the man sitting in the idling car. Realizing they were caught with no opportunity to escape, they dropped their weapons and raised their hands.

* * *

FOR THE SECOND TIME IN A WEEK, JORDAN'S HOME PHONE BEGAN TO ring. Only the head of his security company had his private number and was authorized to call at any time in case of an emergency. Expecting to hear his deep gravelly voice, Jordan didn't immediately recognize Mike Stone's voice.

"Jordan, apparently we failed to understand each other. We have just arrested three more of your hired killers. As we speak, they are sitting in isolated jail cells where your lawyers won't be able to find them. They're waiting to be questioned. Twelve hours of your 72-hour grace period has expired. Unless we can work out a solution, all hell could break loose. Be in my office at nine o'clock tomorrow morning. You might conclude we have something of importance to discuss!"

CHAPTER **34**

Across the Atlantic

LONDON, JUNE 1949

Assured that Mercedes had met and received the contact information of London's more active casting agencies, Natalie returned to Los Angeles. Based on the expressions of interest she and Mercedes had received, she needed to finalize her list of Hollywood's most promising candidates who might fill the specific needs of potentially interested employers. Her last instruction to Mercedes was, "Why don't you call on the people who attended Sir Colin's soiree and begin to qualify which ones have the highest sense of urgency to fill a vacant position. Once you're able to prioritize your list, I'll know how to better focus my work."

* * *

Two DAYS LATER WHEN THE ENORMITY OF HER RESPONSIBILITIES WAS becoming clearer, she began to experience her first fears of failure. Naturally, her first thought was to call Don and ask him for his support and assistance.

Don, pleased to hear from her, found himself patiently listening to Mercedes as she excitedly described what she had been asked to do. The longer he listened, the more he found himself thinking about how rapidly Mercedes's life was to change.

Wanting to be very careful how he responded, Don asked her to explain, in detail, what it was she had been asked to do. The longer he listened, the more he found himself thinking about how rapidly she was transforming herself from the glamorous actor-model to a serious working professional. He didn't have to be told that professional success and the reinventing of her life were highly interdependent.

Responding to her plea, he said, "Mercedes, the best way I can help you is to share your burden and remain a good and trusted listener. It's important that you not be excused from having the experience of struggling to solve these problems on your own. It's part of the process we have all been required to endure. It's important for you to realize the successful implementation of your assignment could create the opportunity you need to propel yourself out of your modeling and acting world."

Without thinking, Mercedes replied, "How do I not know I am not in way over my head? How do I not know that I have been set up to fail?"

As tempted as he was to yield to the request, Don was convinced that Mercedes's personal success depended upon her learning that it was her efforts that had made it possible for great things to happen. "Mercedes, as much as I would like to be your lover, I can't be your business partner. Learning how to solve all these problems has to come from within you."

Not expecting that kind of answer, Mercedes had the good sense to not immediately react. After taking a moment to consider what she had been told, she said, "Knowing you as I do, I know that you wouldn't have said that if you didn't respect my intelligence and abilities. The confidence you are showing in me helps to provide me with the confidence I am going to need. I will be forever grateful. Thank you!"

After letting out a sigh of relief, he said, "Mercedes, I do have, however, two pieces of unsolicited advice I would like to pass along. First, always remember that the dynamics of London's film colony are most likely very similar to what exists in Mexico City and Southern California. *Beware of the predators.*

"Take advantage of what you've recently learned. Verify everything, and don't let any of those *sons a bitches* push you around.

"Second, always remember to avoid becoming a wet paper bag full of marbles hitting the floor and exploding in all directions. Take the time to interview each of your most promising candidates before you make any commitments. Find out what motivates them and what problems they are hoping to solve. Pick your targets carefully. Take your time and concentrate your initial efforts on the most motivated. Make absolutely certain that your early efforts are successful."

* * *

"Don, on our trip to Mexico, I was growing hopeful we were experiencing the start of what I hoped would be a meaningful relationship. I'm worried that with all our mutual distractions, we might lose something very important. If I understand my job properly, it will require me to return to the United States to screen the prospects Natalie has tentatively identified for each of our orders. Would you like me to arrange, on at least one leg of my trips, to spend a long weekend with you in Washington?"

* * *

Fascinated by the prospect of spending 3 days of uninterrupted time with Mercedes, Don answered, "Just give me a little advanced notice and I will make all the arrangements."

Laughing in the hearty way Don had grown to appreciate, Mercedes said, "Don't worry—I'll make all the arrangements. Do you really think I would leave the romantic details to some stuffy attorney? All you will have to do is show up and wear green!"

"Wear green? I don't even own a green tie. What the hell are you talking about?"

"By the time I finish making restaurant and hotel reservations, you are going to need a lot of green!"

CHAPTER 35

An Alternate Approach

NEW YORK, JULY 1949

At precisely 9:00 a.m. on the day following the arrest of the two gunmen and their driver, the immaculately dressed dean of Wall Street corporate attorneys marched up to the desk of Mike Stone announcing he was there to see Mr. Stone.

Noting the hard set of his jaw and the steely intensity of his penetrating blue eyes, the middle-aged woman hesitated before removing her finger from the intercom button. Rising from her chair, she retreated to Mike's big wooden office door. After politely knocking on his door, out of force of habit, she entered his office, and in her shy way, she said, "Mr. McWilliams is waiting to see you. He looks mad, like bear with a hurt paw! Would you prefer I call security?"

Before Mike could answer, he watched his door being pushed wide open and an agitated J. Jordan McWilliams came striding into his office. Mike stood up from his desk chair. Across the big desk, the two adversaries were silently sizing each other up. To Mike, the scene reminded him of his days as an amateur boxer, when the two opponents, from their respective corners, would size up each other before landing the first blow.

Predictably, the excited lawyer threw the first punch when he asked, "What makes you think you can order me around? Why should I care about whatever you alleged to have happened in that Italian restaurant? I've never heard of it, been there, or know where it is! Unless you summoned me here to issue an apology and explain why you found it necessary to disturb me in the middle of the night, I am planning to leave!"

"Apologize? Planning to leave? Are you out of your mind? I strongly suggest you sit down and become prepared to have a civil conversation. You should thank me for not exposing what we have learned about you and your pals thus far. By now, the feds are aware of your clumsy attempt to cause trouble in that small Harlem restaurant.

"I've invited you here in the hope that we might find a way to help each other. You might be surprised to learn, my colleagues and I are not attempting to make judgments about the need for all the military procurement you are seeking. That is your right.

"It's the *way* you are going about it that has us concerned. Once you attempted to use your wealth and influence to circumvent well established congressional approval procedures, you threatened the very essence of our government's authority. That is something we can't allow to happen.

"Let me be clear. It is not within our capacity to determine the worth or validity of any particular proposed new weapons program. We are, however, concerned that your group is undermining the deliberative process established to make certain the objective evaluations are not circumvented or compromised," Mike said. "Why, when you could have asked your clients to contribute to the election funds of national political parties and political action committees, did you find it necessary to move offshore and create your own political war chest?"

Jordan stared at Mike warily. After carefully considering his course of action, he said, "It's not so complicated. For obvious reasons, my clients had independently determined it was economically necessary to bring forward the manufacturing of aircraft and weapons systems that would most likely be approved at some later date. By acting in concert, our clients became convinced they could exercise greater influence over the country and its government."

"Jordan, take a minute and consider what I have just said. No one is objecting about the restoration of military spending. Our bone of contention involves the methodology that you have chosen to pursue your objectives. By collaborating with one another and funding an offshore secret political war chest, your clients have not only broken a whole bunch of laws, but they have circumvented well established procedures which must be satisfied before the government is authorized to spend the public's money.

"Before things are allowed to get out of control, I am proposing your clients consider changing your methods of operation. Why shouldn't they modify their approach to one of working above the table rather than beneath it?

"Jordan, I want to make our position indelibly clear. Should I or any of my friends ever hear of a whisper, a hint, or even an unsubstantiated rumor of any further attempt on your part to pursue your agenda outside of prescribed channels, you can be assured the information we've collected will be immediately released to the press, to Congress, to the White House, to the SEC, and to the Justice Department. We will be prepared to let the chips fall as they may!"

CHAPTER 36

Mercedes Returns

LONDON, ENGLAND, SEPTEMBER 1949

Rarely did something happen that was of significance that didn't become common knowledge in London's small moviemaking village. Agreements between British studios and several high-profile Hollywood actors, writers, and directors had been consummated, filming was underway, and early praise was being regularly reported. Natalie's Bridge was successfully launched, and its legitimacy established.

Mercedes was no longer required to sell local filmmakers on the value of the service she and Natalie were attempting to provide. She was able to concentrate her energies on establishing a proper fit between employer and applicant and solving individual problems.

As word of her success spread, interested employers began calling her. Sometimes, they expressed legitimate employment needs, and sometimes they wanted to use the excuse of employment needs to meet and spend time with the former Miss Universe. The experienced actress from Mexico City was able to quickly identify and politely separate herself from the predators and concentrate her attention on the more genuine people who were seriously in need of her casting services. She was becoming widely respected and appreciated. Word of her success and professionalism was spreading. Mercedes was regarded as a hardworking professional, dedicated to helping London's filmmaking industry to improve the quality of its pictures and its revenues. Regardless of the nature of her invitation, Mercedes quickly realized she was expected to dress and play the role of a former Miss-Universe-turned-serious-working-professional. With each passing week, she was finding her need for a greater variety of clothing was rapidly expanding. She was having to spend more time shopping for dresses, shoes, belts, jewelry, sweaters, and coats. The arrangement of her hair and the application of makeup required more time. Responding to the growing number of inquiries demanded more time. Retaining sufficient time to meet with clients, to greet and organize the introduction of qualified candidates, and to remain available to solve problems was becoming an issue.

Within a month, Mercedes required the services of a personal assistant, a driver, and a secretary. The one-woman band Natalie had left in London had become a small, well coordinated, highly professional team.

The triweekly trips to the United States never happened. When Don offered to fly over to London for a long weekend, Mercedes could never fit a visit into her schedule. The time came and went for her to complete and submit her application to law school and take her entrance examinations. She rarely had time to think about what might be happening to her relationship with Don or her dream to attend law school. She was just too busy.

By early September, in Europe, the Hollywood Blacklist barricade had been breached. London filmmakers were gradually beginning to employ Hollywood actors, writers, and directors.

Mercedes, from her ringside seat, knew the lost Hollywood revenues would place growing pressure on the studios to make new movies and re-employ many of the same people she was securing work for in London. Rather than becoming threatened with the someday termination of the Hollywood's blacklisting, she could foresee the day when the competitive interest of moviemakers in international markets would increase the value of her clients. There were times, at night, when she was waiting for sleep when she would think about her playing an important role in the emerging casting profession. *As effective as I seem to have become in fitting the needs of the moviemaker with the skills of movie personnel, I need to recognize how many of the problem-solving demands require assistance from a legally qualified expert. Is the time approaching when I need to return to Washington, attend law school, and pay more attention to Don?*

When she booked a cabin on the USS *Constitution* for the Atlantic crossing, Mercedes was hoping to have the quiet time she needed to reflect upon all the different experiences she had enjoyed during the 4 months since she had left Los Angeles. She needed quiet time to arrange all her notes, her correspondence, and her growing volume of files. *These are things I need to complete before the distractions of Don and law school enter the picture.*

* * *

FOR WEEKS, PRIOR TO HER DEPARTURE, RUMORS ABOUT MERCEDES'S return to the United States and law school had been flying around her insular village. The questions from her friends, her acquaintances, and people with whom she had worked, and the people who looked forward to working with her, were endless. Would she still be available if they had problems? What type of law was she planning to study? What were her plans after law school? Was there a man in her life? Would she ever return to acting?

* * *

BY THE SECOND DAY FOLLOWING THE OCEAN LINER'S DEPARTURE from South Hampton, Mercedes learned she had booked passage on the one ship members of the London and Southern California's motion picture industry habitually used to cross and recross the Atlantic Ocean.

* * *

BY THIS TIME, MERCEDES HAD BECOME A RISING CELEBRITY, WELL recognized for her work to bridge the two entertainment industries together. Any hope that she might have harbored in spending quiet time alone was quickly interrupted. The attention of successful casting agents was always coveted by almost everybody involved in the making of a movie. Invitations for an early stroll around the deck, a late breakfast, a cocktail before lunch, lunch, another afternoon stroll around the deck, a cocktail before dinner, dinner, or an after-dinner drink were constantly being delivered by the ship's purser.

Not wishing to appear impolite or uninterested, Mercedes accepted as many of the invitations as her time would allow. For the next 5 days, she was busy meeting with clients or prospective clients and then using the late-night hours to carefully catalogue the results of each encounter and systematically store them in her growing volume of files.

On the morning of her last day on board, while the other passengers were standing on deck admiring the approaching New York skyline, the Statue of Liberty, and all the other ships that were arriving and departing New York's harbor, Mercedes was below deck feverishly packing her extensive wardrobe into a very large steamer trunk, her jewelry into a small suitcase, and her cosmetics into a third bag, and making sure all her records were properly filed in her traveling file cabinet.

Knowing Don would be waiting, she wanted to look her best. More time was required to dress, put on her makeup, and arrange her hair. By the time she made arrangements for her luggage to be taken ashore, she was among the last of the passengers to appear on deck. They were anxiously trying to spot the people whom they were expecting to greet them upon their arrival.

The dock was crowded with people anxiously waiting for their friends, their loved ones, or to see any celebrities who might be disembarking. They were busy trying to identify their arriving friends among those who were standing next to the rail. The ship had docked, and passengers were already disembarking.

A group of reporters had crowded in front of Don, making it difficult for Mercedes to spot him. His waving finally attracted her attention. When she smiled and waved back, he knew she had spotted him.

The line was moving slowly. Gradually, she made her way to the gangway. Wanting to appear as attractive as possible for Don, Mercedes had selected her favorite Paris-designed business suit, a high-collared silk blouse, and some of her highest heeled shoes. She had paid particular attention to how she applied her makeup and arranged her hair.

As she slowly moved to the entrance of the gangway, she noticed how precarious her descent might become. The downward angle, the jostling of the crowd, and the separation between the planked surfaces of the decking could cause trouble for the thin pedestals of her 3-inch high heels. Wanting to avoid the possibility of last-minute embarrassment, she gradually inched her way over to one side of the wide gangway, where she could hold onto the rail and remove herself from crowded congestion as she carefully managed her way down the far side opposite from where Don and a group of reporters were anxiously waiting.

They were less than 20 feet apart before it became evident that the group of reporters standing in front of Don were waiting to interview her!

Unbeknownst to her, infringement on civil rights had become big news. Walt Matthews had been faithfully reporting news of her European employment progress in the *New York Times* and its 32 syndicated newspapers. Whenever another member of Hollywood's blacklisted filmmakers was employed in London, a running total would prominently be displayed in Walt's daily column.

The public, aware of the civil rights abuses that were disturbing the lives of so many of its citizens, was becoming excited by how the brave efforts of two women could make such a difference. Walt's readers had begun to keep score the same way they followed baseball players' batting averages. If the papers weren't reporting Mercedes's latest employment success, they were describing Gloria's one-woman town meetings.

Before she could finish stepping from the gangway onto the dock, the first reporter asked, "Miss Velasquez, given your success, how long do you estimate it will take before Hollywood is forced to abandon its 'Blacklisting' policy?"

Frustrated by the unexpected interruption, Mercedes took time considering her answer. Having made up her mind, she replied, "Unfortunately, the people who have benefited from Miss Cummins and my work represent a very small proportion of the people whose lives are being adversely affected by the trespassing on personal liberties we have allowed to take place."

Another reporter asked, "What will happen to your efforts you and Miss Cummins have been working so hard to accomplish when Hollywood decides to terminate blacklisting?"

Mercedes looked at the reporter. She recognized him to be one of those who had enjoyed making life so uncomfortable for the Hollywood witnesses required to appear before the congressional hearings. Aware of his vicious attacks, she said, "I am very pleased you asked me that particular question. Has anyone stopped to consider what the eventual effect of talent moviemaking personalities will have achieved when the market for their services has been expanded beyond Hollywood? I'm sure you understand, and Hollywood executives are about to learn when the agents of these talented people develop competitive bidding for their clients' services."

Standing unnoticed on the outer periphery of the crowd of reporters, Walt Matthews raised his hand. Recognizing her old friend, Mercedes pointed toward him signifying for him to ask his question.

"Miss Velasquez, what are *your* future plans?"

Smiling at Walt, Mercedes said, "I hope to be able to continue to develop my craft as an international casting agent. My only problem is I have learned that I need to develop legal skills and experience before I can hope to service a more complete range of client needs. Right now, I hope to qualify for admittance to a leading law school."

After pausing to look directly toward Don, she said, "And, there is one more thing I hope to add to my list. There is a certain man in my life who deserves my overdue attention. Now, if you will excuse me, I think the time has arrived for me to start my new life."

CHAPTER 37

A New, Clear Voice

For years, Gloria had been accustomed to being passed over for movie roles on account of her age. Despite all the compliments she had been recently receiving, she still assumed her acting days were long past. Now, the "Heroine of Hollywood" was overjoyed to have the opportunity to audition for new roles for films that were already in production in England. At the same time, she realized she was not being invited to play supporting roles for her acting abilities. The producers were interested in taking advantage of her current publicity value and its ability to improve revenues at the box office.

Fortunately for Gloria, the same British film producers who had issued her their earlier invitations were in attendance at Sir Colin's reception. They had been able to see, firsthand, the inspirational, highly poised, and the charismatic way she had developed for introducing a very serious problem.

In recent years, a limited number of British film distributors had found a promising market in American boutique theaters located in the East Coast college towns and cities. The small theaters were locally owned and operated well beyond the influence of the Hollywood studio system and the network of theaters dependent upon its production.

* * *

Wʜᴇɴ Gʟᴏʀɪᴀ ᴀᴘᴘᴇᴀʀᴇᴅ ꜰᴏʀ ʜᴇʀ ᴀᴜᴅɪᴛɪᴏɴ, sʜᴇ ᴀʀʀɪᴠᴇᴅ ᴏɴ ᴛɪᴍᴇ and well prepared. The directors were even more pleased with her consummate on-set professionalism and her ability to provide more than one interpretation for each character. One director, upon seeing Gloria's film tests, became so impressed with her performance, he decided to include her in the film he had recently finished shooting. New scripts were prepared. The cast was recalled, and the new scenes incorporating Gloria's performances were spliced into the recut master.

Distribution of the film was delayed, movie houses were required to reshuffle their schedules, the replaced actress was upset, the studio had to reschedule use of its sound stage, and the film was going to come in over budget. When people complained to the director, the only response they would receive was his knowing smile.

By the end of summer, arrangements were made to premiere the recut movie at Covent Garden, home of the Royal Ballet, and long appreciated for its extraordinary acoustics. News of the unusual event began to permeate through London's entertainment community. Budgets for advanced promotion of the film were doubled, and then doubled again. Enthusiastic movie fans were beginning to submit requests for reserved seating.

On opening night, the sight of Sir Colin Meyer helping Gloria step from his Rolls-Royce limousine and escorting her along the red carpet had a captivating effect on the large crowd assembled to see the celebrated and much-admired American actress.

Impressed by the people's reaction to the forgotten actress, British moviemakers were watching as the film's director decided, at the last minute, to escort Gloria out onto the stage before the curtain was pulled open. With a spotlight focused on the two of them, he signaled for quiet before introducing Gloria Adams and briefly explaining how Miss Adams and Natalie Cummins had come to London as part of their effort to find work for Hollywood's blacklisted unemployed.

Before he could finish his remarks, a strong voice in the audience was heard shouting, "Gloria, love, tell us about Hollywood blacklisting."

Unafraid to respond to unrehearsed, spontaneously asked questions, the seasoned veteran found herself comfortably replying to the wide array of questions being asked by different members of the audience.

Concerned people in the audience who had come to see the movie were growing impatient. The theater manager said, "Who has the last question for Miss Adams?"

The film critics present that night were generous with their review of the film, but they reserved their stronger praise for Miss Adams's preshow performance. One critic was moved to say, *"Rarely in recent history have I had the pleasure of witnessing a more entertaining and timely presentation of satirical wit and humor. In a time of global adjustment and change, Miss Adams's voice has emerged as a clear reminder of our need to remain vigilant of the values and ideas we most cherish."*

* * *

By the time Gloria's film was released for showing in the small New England movie houses, her preshow town meeting services had been contracted. Filmmakers in Hollywood, London, Paris, Berlin, Madrid, and Rome were paying close attention. The improved size of audiences, the higher ticket prices, and the longer runs were not going unnoticed.

CHAPTER 38

Fall from Grace

A difficult phone conversation with Manuel was unavoidable. When he was informed of the need to shut down the Mexican operation and return the war chest funds, Manuel had reacted more reasonably than he had anticipated. Later, however, when Jordan casually mentioned the necessity of providing a final accounting, Manuel immediately adopted a defensive tone.

When he first began to object, Jordan interpreted it as the normal resistance to a task that would be something of a hassle. As he continued to press for an audited report, Manuel's hostility rapidly intensified. Finally, Jordan offered what he thought was a constructive suggestion. "Why don't I send a team of auditors down there to help you organize your books and produce the properly documented reports we will need?"

Manuel blew up. "Jordan, I don't need any of your goddamn bookkeepers down here snooping around in my records! I'll send you a check and you can prepare whatever documentation you think is necessary." Then he slammed down the receiver.

A lifelong cynic, a confused Jordan had been long trained to assume the worst. "What is he concerned about? Has he failed to account for all the expenditures? Is some of the money missing? What am I going to tell all the clients who are bombarding me with phone calls regarding how much money they could expect to recover and when it would be returned?" The depressed leader quickly decided he would leave the problem of communicating the news for another day.

After a long, difficult day, Jordan decided to stop at the health club, well before his flight to Washington was scheduled to depart. He needed to release the tension in his system and shift his thoughts from his problems with his wife and his work and begin to imagine how delightful his 3-day weekend with sweet Amanda might become. On previous occasions, he had learned to appreciate the seagoing hospitality of his old college friend Stanley Victor aboard his luxurious yacht.

An hour later, refreshed after the penetrating bite of the strong hands of the club masseur, the relaxed lawyer slowly made his way to the sauna and its hot, steamy atmosphere. Seated in the foggy chamber, he let his mind wander to thoughts of Amanda, the young and sensuous younger woman and her voracious appetites. He had been introduced to her during the previous weekend he had spent on Stanley's seagoing yacht. Afraid the wrong question might interfere with his delightful experience, he never summoned the courage to ask how it was that she was one of Stanley's yacht guests.

His thoughts were interrupted by a voice from the next bench. "Jordan! Nice to see you at the club. Would you like to join me for a drink when we're through?"

Looking up, Jordan saw Alex Farrand, a fellow classmate at Harvard Law, a senior official in the Justice Department, and his regular partner in his Saturday morning golfing foursome.

There was something in the tone of Alex's voice that suggested the invitation was not entirely voluntary. *Senior officials in the Justice Department didn't extend casual offers.*

"Okay," he said, "but it will have to be a quick one. I have a plane to catch."

A short while later, they were seated at a remote table in the far corner of the Men's Grill, well out of earshot of other members. Alex wasted no time coming right to the point. "Jordan, this might not be the appropriate place to tell you what I have to say. If it weren't so important, I could save it for another time. But the word around the office is that your Mexican friend, Señor Arena, is suspected of skimming the top off his movie receipts. Should that be the case, the IRS will become interested in his fraudulent reporting taxable income. Perhaps of greater importance is the risk he will incur should his Cuban investors learn of his efforts to steal monies to which they are entitled.

"I thought you might want to warn him."

* * *

JORDAN MAY HAVE HAD A DIFFICULT DAY AND HAD SPENT THE LAST 2 hours trying to relax and relieve some of the pressure, but his instincts were telling him there was much more behind what Alex was telling him.

If the Justice Department has heard about Manuel's possible skimming, other people have to know. If other people are aware, the chances must be pretty good the Cubans are already aware or will be shortly. What can I do? It's late Friday afternoon. Why don't I worry about it on Monday?

* * *

ON BOARD THE EAST COAST FLIGHT FROM NEW YORK TO WASHINGTON, Jordan was relaxed. He was leaning back in his chair. He had removed his shoes and was enjoying his Old Fashioned, when the thought flashed through his mind. *Why would Alex warn me about Arena unless he knew of my prior relationship with him and of our Mexican war chest activities? Was Alex trying to warn me the Justice Department was aware of what my clients and I have been attempting to accomplish?*

Not even a second drink, thoughts of spending a weekend on Vic's yacht, playing gin with his interesting friends, or the prospect of spending two complete evenings with *"Sweet Amanda"* could prevent him from thinking about the world that would be waiting for him when he returned to New York.

CHAPTER 39

The Head of the Serpent

Alex Farrand and Don Cerreta were engaged in one of their customary walks through one of Washington, D.C.'s, many public parks. The park was almost vacant of its normal complement of tourists, landscape workers, small children, and nannies pushing a pram. Reasonably confident they would not be observed or overheard, the two men were engaged in serous conversation. Clearly, they were pleased by the progress that had been made interrupting the Manual's Club plan, but they both knew there was much more that needed to be accomplished.

Alex was leading the conversation. "We may have prevented these industrial prime contractors from achieving their initial plan, but what will happen if they fall back and initiate a second plan, one that we are not privy to? One thing for sure, they may be frustrated by their initial failure, but they had to have learned by acting in concert, they are much more effective than when they act independently. Shouldn't we assume that it will only be a question of time before they conceive a second plan?"

Don relied, "Alex, let's face it. These CEOs still remain in charge of their companies. Their companies' transitional problems haven't changed. And, their aggregated power is still a source of incredible influence. To me, as tarnished as he may appear, I still regard Jordan's leadership as a necessary ingredient to any new plan. If they plan to move in concert, who else would they trust to organize and lead a second attempt?"

The two men had walked more than 100 yards when Alex asked, "Can you think of some way we could remove Jordan from the equation? If we cut off the head of the serpent, how much difficulty would we be able to cause?

"When I think about how much influence these fellows have succeeded in inserting into our government, I wonder if our success in stopping them this time represents the end of the threat or the start of what could become a continuous problem. Would McWilliams's removal slow things enough that we can become better prepared to identify and oppose their next effort?"

"Boss, you may know him socially, but I can assure you, from an operational viewpoint, he would be a tough nut to crack. There is, however, one approach I would like to try. Challenging him head-on could prove very difficult, but there may be a way he might be 'persuaded' to withdraw."

"Now *that* is an original thought. How can you possibly believe there is a reasonable probability that he would voluntarily choose to retire?"

* * *

"Boss, we have received word that he is being openly criticized by some of his clients. The disclosure of their records and the loss of their invested working capital has been very upsetting. In addition, they are frustrated by their inability to work from the shadows.

"How do we not know Jordan is having his own misgivings about continuing? In addition to being underappreciated, he has to be concerned about his law partners believing *he* could be the cause of the loss of a substantial amount of legal revenues.

"Then there is the problem of his knowing he is officially a subject on the Justice Department's radar screen. When I think back over the course of his career, I have to conclude that his effectiveness depends upon the degree of trust his corporate clients, members of New York's investment community, and high officials in the government have in him.

* * *

"At work, he has been canceling appointments, not returning phone calls, and spending long hours sequestered alone in his office. Aren't these characteristics of a disturbed, unhappy man? If that isn't enough, it's been reliably reported, on weekends, he has been visiting an old friend, one Stanley Victor, in Georgetown. Together, with other friends of Victor's, they have been enjoying weekend cruises in the company of a very attractive younger woman.

"For some, that kind of behavior might not be considered so bizarre, but for a highly structured, all-work, high-profile attorney, it is really strange. How do we not know, under the right circumstances, he might 'voluntarily' choose to resign, take a long vacation, and channel his career in another direction?"

"Don, I don't want to be a pessimist. In a situation as serious as altering the appropriations process of the American government, doesn't our opposition need to depend on something a bit more tangible?"

"Absolutely. I think there may be a way whereby we can 'encourage' Mr. McWilliams to reach our desired conclusion. But before you ask, I will need a few days to work out the details of my plan."

CHAPTER 40

The Fifth Estate

CAMBRIDGE, OCTOBER 1949

Following the multiple delays in the distribution of the modified and recut movie, its American fall premiere was finally scheduled to open in Cambridge's boutique foreign movie house located near Harvard Square in late October. To capitalize on the interest of the college set, the preopening promotional program announced Miss Gloria Adams, the "Heroine of Hollywood," was scheduled to recreate her highly acclaimed London preshow town meeting and accept questions from the audience. Ads promoting the coming attraction ran in the *Cambridge Chronicle* and the *Harvard Crimson*.

When opening night arrived, to a packed audience, Gloria confidently walked out to the lectern placed in the center of an empty stage. Behind her, the curtain was closed, and on it was pinned a blown-up image of a *New Yorker* cartoon depicting Gloria hanging "Slick Dick" Bailey.

Dressed in her trademark simple smock and chalk-white tennis shoes, she announced, "Hi, there, is there anyone in the audience who would like me to describe how it feels to defend your constitutional rights before the House Un-American Activities Committee? Please . . . by the whistling, clapping, and whooping," the feisty lady said. "OK, but here's the deal. I will tell you *my* version of what happened if you promise to ask me questions!"

Not knowing what to expect, an excited audience stood up and provided the modest and unassuming little old lady in tennis shoes with the first of what would be several standing ovations. Fascinated by her stories describing some of the more memorable incidents of her appearance before the "Big Bad Wolf," with her quick wit and sarcastic sense of humor, one question after another cascaded from the audience.

Concerned that the audience was growing impatient to see the movie, the movie house manager ascended the stage to announce, "One more question and then we will start the movie."

A strong voice from the rear of the audience asked, "Miss Adams, what is your most vivid memory of all that you have been able to accomplish?"

Taking her time to mentally scan all the drama that had been part of her more recent life, she smiled before saying, "I guess it's my amazement of what an *old broad* can accomplish if she really becomes pissed off!"

* * *

IN THE FOLLOWING WEEKS, SIMILAR EVENTS ORGANIZED UP AND DOWN the East Coast began to adopt the character of town hall meetings. Frequently, the showing of the movie had to be delayed for as long as an hour because the discussion was so lively. In Gloria's wake, theaters continued to play the film, drawing healthy crowds week after week. In many towns, the film was shown in larger theaters, and more showings were scheduled as ticket prices increased.

The "Heroine of Hollywood" was fast becoming the "Paul Revere" of the motion picture industry. *Variety* magazine reported: *"Hollywood's Loss is American people's gain."* Miss Adams's remarkable accomplishments served to warn grassroots America what can happen when fear of *"isms"* is allowed to override common sense.

* * *

REGARDED AS MERELY OVERNIGHT SUCCESSES, THE GENERAL PUBLIC was unaware of how much time, thought, and sweat had been required to generate large audience attention. Their unawareness was not shared by the small group of people who traditionally were searching for new material upon which they could create new Broadway musical shows.

* * *

Oɴᴇ ɴɪɢʜᴛ, Nᴀᴛᴀʟɪᴇ ᴀɴᴅ Gʟᴏʀɪᴀ ᴡᴇʀᴇ ᴇɴᴊᴏʏɪɴɢ ᴛʜᴇ ʜᴏsᴘɪᴛᴀʟɪᴛʏ of George White, the same Broadway director who had been responsible for directing Natalie's first New York Broadway show. He had waited until the dessert had been served before asking the question, "How would you two feel about playing yourselves in a play written to tell your story? There is certainly no shortage of fresh material. Providing you agree to play yourselves, I think we could attract the cooperation of New York's finest composers, choreographers, and best playwrights.

"Think about all the people who are already familiar with both of you and your work. When you add it all up, when has there had to be a very large audience who would be interested in attending a properly produced show?"

Gloria was intrigued with the idea. Natalie's first reaction was not so positive. "George, this old actress would enjoy working with you one more time, but it's important to me you understand I have moved on. Returning to the stage is not something I wish to do. For the first time in my life, I am living a life where people I admire respect me for my intelligence and regard my efforts to help others as a very serious endeavor. I can't even begin to imagine what could persuade me to give up 'Natalie's Bridge.'"

Pleased with his former student's response, George continued, "How would you react if I suggested we name the play *Natalie's Bridge* and organize a musical around the idea of providing the Sentinels with the voice they need to reach grassroots America?"

Caught off guard, the surprised Natalie reflexively asked, "Could we tell the *real* story? Do you think the American public is prepared to accept the story behind the story of how concentrations of wealth and influence conspire to abuse the privilege of Democratic Free Enterprise for self-serving purposes?"

"Natalie, the real question you might be asking is, 'Has the musical stage made sufficient progress in adapting itself to presenting subjects of social commentary where it is practical to believe they are ready for your satirical brand of commentary?' I guess that is a question we will need to answer. Certainly, audience reactions to Gloria's town meeting tour provides us with some indication, but it's important you realize there is a world of difference between a movie audience and someone who has to pay a large price for the privilege of attending a live show.

"There is a good example of what we are discussing that is currently being performed. The play is called *Call Me Madam*. It was written and composed by Irving Berlin and it stars Ethel Merman. I seem to remember both of them are not only good friends of yours but are great admirers of your work. If you wouldn't mind staying an extra night, why don't I get some house tickets, and the four of us can see the play, and then you can decide for yourselves if the musical stage is ready for what we are discussing. I'll phone Sardi's for a reservation at my private table, and after the show, we can enjoy an excellent dinner and talk about the show. I am very interested in learning of your opinions. I might even be able to convince Irving and Ethel to join us for an after-theater dinner."

Somehow, George's talking about the theater and old friends lit a spark of curiosity. For more than 2 years, Natalie had managed to block the musical stage, her theatrical friends, and any curiosity about new productions from her mind. *Here I am talking about the theater, considering returning to the stage, and anxious to visit with old friends. What has changed?*

The memory of her earlier conversation with David flashed through her mind. *Didn't we talk about the possibility of developing the musical stage into what we referred to as the "Fifth Estate"? Doesn't George's idea represent a more pragmatic discussion of the same concept? Why couldn't the American musical stage become a continuous running satirical voice designed to tell the story of the past, present, and future reoccurring Power-Cycle threats? What an excellent opportunity to inform the American public about what was and is really happening in our world of ever-increasing concentrated wealth and power.*

CHAPTER 41

Aren't You Going to Say Hello to an Old Friend?

GEORGETOWN, NOVEMBER 1949

Normally, Jordan McWilliams prided himself on being disciplined about time. He seldom found it necessary to rush. Over the years, the nature of his work required him to hide any emotion or excitement he might be feeling. Sitting in the back of the cab, he knew it was only going to be a matter of minutes before he would step out of the cab and join his old friend Vic and Sweet Amanda. *Something is different. For the first time in days, I am not feeling the constant pressure of the burden I have been forced to carry. Could it be, the farther I get away from New York the more relaxed I become?*

Having previously made the same trip, Jordan estimated the amount of the fare and, after adding a generous tip, he paid the cabby prior to his pulling up to the curb. Stepping from the cab with his overnight bag slung over his shoulder, a grinning man quickly approached the revolving front door, waved at the doorman, and walked directly toward the elevator bank. Impatiently waiting for the elevator to arrive, his attention was focused on watching the hand on the floor indicator's gradual descent. He was only vaguely aware of the woman standing beside him.

When the elevator arrived, Jordan waited for the woman to proceed before entering the elevator. As the car began to rise, he heard her say, "Jordan, aren't you going to say hello to an old friend?"

Caught completely by surprise, Jordan quickly took notice of the woman standing next to him. She was tall, probably 5 foot 10, with an olive complexion, short, curly black hair, and was dressed in an old maroon sweater, well-worn Levis, and dirty-white tennis shoes. On first impression, he judged her to be one of the Georgetown law students who frequent this area. After taking a second look at the face of the smiling young woman, he realized it was Mercedes, the glamorous former Miss Universe he had spent such an amazing night with in Acapulco.

He said, "Mercedes! What are you doing in Georgetown? I thought you would be in Mexico making movies with Manuel."

Before she could answer, the elevator stopped at the ninth floor and the door was beginning to open. She paused long enough before she stepped through the open door to shake his hand and say, "Jordan, the next time you are in Washington, why don't you call me. We could catch up on old times."

* * *

IF THE VISION OF MERCEDES HADN'T GONE THROUGH HIS MIND, THE 3-day cruise would have been exactly what he had envisioned. The days were warm and sunny. The conditions were perfect for lounging on deck, scuba diving, or playing gin on the covered deck. He consistently won at the high-stakes gin game they had played. The scuba diving off a new reef provided him with the opportunity to swim among a variety of colorful fish and photograph the coral structures, replete with their own habitations of fish and plant life.

The carefully planned meals and the quality of the served wines were only improved by the constant amusement that came from the witty conversations with all; each of the other men were self-made men who had founded and managed their companies. They were high-energy problem solvers who lived their personal lives in a similar way they managed their companies. The excitement of gambling, spending time with beautiful, younger women, and partaking in fine food and rare wines were an important ingredient to how they spent their private time. But it was the wide-ranging witty conversations about things of importance that made the 3 days at sea so unusual.

Wives were never invited on Stanley's stag cruises. The younger female companions reminded Jordan of some of the women he had met, over the years, during his prior visits to Acapulco. Everyone on board was there to have a good time. There was no room for business talk, complaining, or talking religion or politics.

During the day, his growing awareness of Amanda and her interest in the stories he would tell, her occasional participation in far-ranging conversations, and her suggestions of what they should do next, pleasantly contrasted with what he had learned to expect at home.

Laughing her hearty laugh, Amanda said, "I wondered how long it would take before you asked me the question everyone wants to ask: 'What's a nice girl like you doing in a place like this?'

"What alternatives wait an attractive, intelligent, career girl from the Midwest, a graduate of a small Ohio college and George Washington Law School, who is employed as a paralegal normally have but to submit to the attention of young men of limited interests who want to get married, raise children, and employ their wives as behind-the-scenes home managers?

"Don't misunderstand. It's not as if I don't look forward to marriage and children, but this moth just wants to fly closer to the flame of a more exciting life before settling for a lifetime of more serious living. How else would a woman like me have the opportunity to spend weekends on such a fabulous yacht, meet such interesting men, and enjoy the comfort and excitement of your marvelous lifestyles?"

* * *

Accustomed to rising early in the morning, Amanda and Jordan were enjoying breakfast at a two-person table situated on the rearmost portion of the deserted aft deck. Following an evening of passionate lovemaking well punctuated by periods of personal talk, Jordan and Amanda had discovered almost endless topics of conversation they both could relate to and enjoyed discussing.

For 3 days, Jordan felt like a free and reborn person enjoying the lifestyle of a younger, carefree man. It wasn't until they were returning to port when he began to think about New York and the different world to which he was returning. For a brief moment, he considered what the consequences might be if he failed to return. *Do I really believe the people in my world would understand why, as the mature, middle-aged, managing partner of a leading New York law firm, I would choose to resign, sacrifice a lifetime of building up a world-class group of prominent industrial clients, in an attempt to learn how to best apply my talents and experiences to something else, something that would have more meaning?*

* * *

Knowing such an abrupt change was practically impossible for reasons he couldn't explain, he started to think about Mercedes. *After I leave Stanley's condo, why don't I accept her invitation? If nothing else, a pleasant conversation would provide me with an excuse to delay returning to New York.*

* * *

When Stanley's yacht was firmly moored to his private dock, Jordan arrived back in Georgetown physically refreshed but mentally disturbed by the prospect of having to return to New York and the problems that would be waiting for him. When they entered the lobby, Jordan, feigning fatigue, asked if he could excuse himself, and get an early start to the airport. After waiting for his host and his friends to disappear into the elevator, he walked over to the bank of mailboxes imbedded in the opposite wall of the lobby. Remembering Mercedes had exited the elevator on the ninth floor, he crossed the lobby to inspect the names. There was an M. V. Ordonez, listed for apartment 908.

Taking a deep breath, he marched back to the elevator, rode to the ninth floor, and rang the bell of apartment 908. When she opened the door, he was surprised by her transformation. Dressed in workout clothes, not wearing any makeup, she hardly resembled the beautifully dressed and carefully made-up woman he remembered meeting at Manuel's movie night party. Looking past her, he could see stacks of books and papers scattered all over the living-room floor.

Noticing his look, she said, "Oh, don't mind the mess. I'm studying to take my entrance examination for law school."

To break any awkwardness, he asked, "Mercedes, how would you like to buy an old sinner a cup of coffee?"

Thirty minutes later, Jordan was quietly listening to Mercedes describe her exit from Mexico, her problems with Manuel, and her experiences with Natalie Cummins. Watching the way her face lit up when she started to describe her work in Europe, her thoughts of becoming a qualified international casting agent, and her interest in law school, it caused him to focus on what he had been considering 2 days ago. Fascinated by her tale of personal reinvention, he was thinking, *If this young woman, who was so terribly mistreated, could rebuild her life, why can't I do the same thing?*

Two more cups of coffee and an hour later, her story was winding down. Taking notice of the time, Jordan knew it was time for him to leave. Standing awkwardly, contemplating how best to say good-bye to his new-old friend, he was relieved when she firmly embraced him before kissing him gently on the cheek. As a parting comment, she said, "Talking with you about my problems has been most enjoyable. Do you think we might become just good friends?"

CHAPTER 42

Dinner at Sardi's

NEW YORK, NOVEMBER 1949

George White, his wife Betsy, and their two celebrity guests had arrived at the theater early. They needed to provide George with the extra time he would need to pick up the four, third-row-center complimentary house tickets. The three ladies were standing near the right-hand wall of the theater entrance, well away from the anxious people who were crowding their way into the sold-out theater performance. Talking quietly among themselves, they failed to notice the people who had recognized Natalie and were alerting anyone who happened to be standing near them, and who were pointing in their direction.

Tickets in hand, with the assistance of a special usher, they entered the theater. It didn't seem to make any difference whether they had been spotted outside or by members of the audience who recognized George or the surprise appearance of the famous star of New York's musical stage. Their progress down the aisle and past the other seats was constantly interrupted by fans and old friends of Natalie's who wanted to say welcome home. The unexpected commotion only started to subside when the orchestra in the pit began to play the overture.

For the next hour and a half, Natalie and Gloria's uninterrupted attention was focused on every detail they could possibly absorb of the three acts. Miss Merman's performance, Irving Berlin's words and lyrics, and the satirical message had been laughingly accepted by the approving and appreciative audience.

Emotionally drained by what she just witnessed, her hands sore from clapping, Natalie turned to whisper to George, "Why don't we sit here for a few minutes before leaving. Maybe we can avoid some of the earlier congestion?"

Flashing his infectious grin, George said, "Oh, I don't think that will be necessary. Ethel and Irving are waiting backstage to say hello to an old friend, thanks to your old friend, Walt Matthews, and your efforts to help Hollywood solve a very nasty problem. As you are aware, Hollywood and Broadway are two very separate centers of entertainment that are somewhat connected by similar investors. Although it's never been discussed, there is the unspoken fear that the anti-Communism inquisition might extend to Broadway. Apparently, they have been following your progress with your 'Bridge' attempts to limit the damage in Hollywood. In addition to spending time with a valued and respected colleague, they are anxious to hear what you have learned."

An hour later, the six exhilarated friends arrived at Sardi's an hour late for their reservation. Somewhat familiar with the hectic demand for late-night tables at the famous after theater restaurant, Natalie was surprised when the six of them were warmly greeted by Vaughn, the maître d' and grandson of the original owner of Sardi's, and were escorted to the celebrity table located in the center of the restaurant. As she was preparing to sit down in the chair Vaughn was holding for her, Natalie felt the touch of George's hand on her arm, followed by, "Before you sit down, let's examine the walls and see if your picture is still hanging on one of them." Remembering the approximate location of George's three-person table, Natalie was slightly amused when he insisted they begin their search on the opposite side of the restaurant.

Seeing the cartooned images of old friends, actors, directors, and prominent theatrical angels was bringing back many old memories. Even when their progress was impeded by their having to stop and say hello to familiar friends, Natalie didn't mind the interruption and the attention. They had completed their inspection of two walls and were beginning to work their way along the third wall, the wall that would eventually lead to George's table, when she suddenly realized, she was no longer upset by the fact that she was being recognized for her theatrical success. *Could it be with my recent accomplishments, I am no longer so sensitive about not being recognized as a serious woman interested in solving serious problems?*

About the same time she had become aware of her unknowing transformation, they arrived at George's personal table. His picture hung directly above it, and her picture still hung next to it. Instantly, she realized keeping her caricature next to his was his way of expressing how much he still cared for her and respected her both as a friend and a talent.

Ignoring the public attention they were receiving, she turned to George, and after kissing him softly on his cheek, whispered in his ear, "I will never be able to express how much I treasure your respect and friendship. Seeing my image still hanging next to your caricature means more to me than you can possibly understand!"

Before they headed toward their table and their waiting friends George pulled her to one side. "Natalie, knowing you and working with you has been the single greatest experience of my theatrical career. I want you to believe me when I say, nobody could be more proud of your recent accomplishments and nothing would give me greater pleasure than building a show around all the marvelous things you and your friends have been able to accomplish.

"Before we join the others, I should warn you, I've taken the liberty of informing Ethel and Irving about our idea. Get prepared; you are about to become part of what I suspect will be one of the most exciting dinner conversations you will ever have."

George was right. The dinner conversation was one of the most intelligent and far-reaching discussions of the contemporary musical stage Natalie and Gloria had the privilege of participating in. Natalie was convinced. Listening to Ethel Merman speak in private was the second best thing to attending one of her performances. There were times when she was having difficulty distinguishing between what the reigning queen of the musical stage was saying and the character she played in *Call Me Madam. Only a strong willed, intelligent woman with a booming voice could have so convincingly portrayed the life of Perle Mesta, a widowed, very rich contributor to the Democratic Party who had been appointed by the president to be the United States of America's ambassador to Luxembourg.*

She would always remember Ms. Merman saying, "Listen, honey, when they told me I was to play some rich babe who would use her influence with her friends in Washington to provide all the money needed to acquire the cooperation of a small country, I thought everybody was nuts. I watched in amazement when they didn't censor out the best lines and insisted on adding new material that would more fully emphasize the underlying theme of the play. And here we are with the hottest show on Broadway."

"She not kidding," said Irving Berlin, the composer. "Can you imagine my reaction when they gave me the script to study? Did they really expect me, long associated with the production of patriotic musical plays, to compose the music and lyrics for a story that cast American diplomatic practices in such a questionable light? Although the play was set to take place in a small fictional country somewhere in Europe, the references to current practices in the United States were unmistakable."

Fascinated by Irving's revelation about the play, Natalie asked, "Tell us how you were able to produce a play that informed audiences about serious problems and didn't upset them?"

"Aha, *that* is the trick, or if you will, our *secret magic sauce*," George answered. "We learned, some time ago if the entertainment quality exceeds the audience's expectations, and you avoid any practice of malice, they will concentrate of the entertainment quality they are witnessing and not immediately think about the less obvious message they are being exposed to."

Intrigued by the conversation, the animated discussion continued until the last of the other patrons had long since departed. If Vaughn had not politely informed them their taxis had arrived, they might have failed to notice the waiters silently standing motionless, not wishing to distract the remaining guests with their late-night cleaning chores.

Natalie, still consumed by the dinner conversation, only stopped talking when the last of her friends had said good night and stepped into one of the waiting taxis. At the last minute, she paused and said, "I prefer to walk. The Algonquin is just a few blocks from here. Maybe the walk will give me an opportunity to reflect on all the things we have been discussing. One thing for certain, you have started me thinking. I haven't been so excited since we started talking about some of the ideas that became the foundation of the 'Bridge.'"

* * *

Sometimes at night, when the concept of sleep didn't seem probable, she would wander into the Algonquin Bar to see if she could join any of her old friends for a final-final and talk of old times in the theater. Tonight was one of those nights, when she hoped to be able to discuss George's new ideas with her theatrical friends and witness their reactions. "Maybe a drink and good conversation will make it easier for me to go to sleep."

CHAPTER 43

Impending Doom

NEW YORK/WASHINGTON, D.C., NOVEMBER 1949

Returning to New York, Jordan opened his apartment door to find his private phone ringing. Dropping his coat and bag and ignoring his wife's hostile glare, he rushed across the room to answer it. He was greeted by the familiar voice of his legal colleague from Los Angeles, Dale Pennington.

"Jordan, I have just received word that Manuel Arena has been killed, gangland style. His safe has been cleaned out. I think it is safe to assume our money and our files may be in some very strange and dangerous hands."

Jordan found himself gasping for air under the crushing pressure of impending doom. He hung up without another word. His years of transatlantic cartel work evaporated overnight. He immediately thought, *The only other time when I felt this much pressure was the day Germany declared war on the United States and years of work literally disappeared like a puff of smoke.*

Maybe I better take the time to sit down and rethink what has been happening. The federal government has become involved. Somehow, the Sentinels seem to be aware of our every move. Our plans are being tipped off in advance. Security agents have been killed or captured. Who knows what they have told the government? Our plans to accelerate rearmament have been exposed. Stone and Matthews are in possession of the financial details of our contributions and disbursements, and now the funds we were planning to use for "Plan B" are missing. Soon, I am supposed to meet with both national political committees to determine how much money is required to acquire our needed influence.

* * *

"J" NEEDED TIME TO THINK! WITHOUT SAYING A WORD TO HIS WIFE, lost in his own thoughts, Jordan made his way into his library, poured himself a generous portion of his favorite scotch whiskey, selected a cigar from the ever-present humidor, and sat down in his big comfortable chair. *J, has the time arrived when it is necessary for you to question what you have become involved in? Are you certain you want to be responsible for whatever they have planned next?*

After all these years, how do I continue to practice law, manage our law firm, and exercise the authority my position requires? If I abandon the needs of my client base, what will happen to me if I just walk away, the same way Mercedes did? Am I really prepared to sacrifice all the support and influence I have spent a lifetime building?

I am too young and have too much energy to retire. What could I do to sustain a useful, productive life, one that I would enjoy and find fulfilling?

Wait a minute. Why should someone who has spent so much of his time serving the needs of others expect to know the answers to his own questions? That doesn't mean better solutions don't exist. I just don't know what they are.

* * *

IN THE DAYS THAT FOLLOWED, JORDAN SPENT MUCH OF HIS TIME thinking about his problem. *My orderly world and my reputation lay in ruins. I can't confide in my wife, my law partners, my clients, or my friends at the club. Could Mercedes be the only one who might appreciate discussing my problems with me?*

* * *

AT WORK, HIS PARTNERS WERE BEGINNING TO QUESTION THE APPARENT decline in billable charges of Jordan's clients. Longtime clients weren't returning his calls. Lunches were being canceled.

Trying to distract himself from the disasters that had befallen him, Jordan decided to call Stanley Victor. He needed some way to disguise his true intention of meeting with Mercedes. The thought of spending a weekend in the Virginia countryside with his *new-old best friend* made Jordan smile for the first time in days. He'd become so detached from his work, he didn't think twice when he tossed a scrap of paper with notes on the trip into his office wastebasket.

CHAPTER 44

Gift from a Friend

CHARLOTTESVILLE, VIRGINIA, DECEMBER 1949

Accustomed to Jordan spending weekends in Washington, his wife rarely questioned him about his frequent trips and had learned not to talk to him about his work. Any communicative rapport they might have previously enjoyed was dissolving into a highly polarized relationship. Life in the McWilliams's household was rapidly becoming that of two old friends living separate lives in the same house.

With all the changes taking place in his life, thinking of Mercedes represented the high point of his day. Instinctively, Jordan understood the quality of the time they would be spending together on their first weekend countryside tour of the battlefields of Virginia, which would determine if he would be able to spend other weekends with her.

Familiar with her firsthand experiences with the Spanish Civil War and her interest in Early American history, he had visited the local bookstore near his office, and with the assistance of the highly knowledgeable clerk, spent more than an hour selecting three books set in the period of America's War of Independence in the 1700s, and the Civil War in the 1800s. He also purchased a large, well detailed foldable map describing the route his itinerary called for the two of them to follow.

Returning to his office, he asked his secretary to hold all calls and reschedule his afternoon meetings. Left alone, he spread the big map out on his desk and began to trace the route he had planned. First, he marked the location of the two country inns where he had made reservations. With the help of the books he had purchased, he marked the locations of the more interesting sites they would be visiting. Next to each mark, he placed two notations. One referenced the book that was the source of the information describing the background and the history of that particular site. The second notation contained the number of the page where the information could be found.

It was late in the afternoon when his work was completed. He wrote a note of explanation, signed it, and asked his secretary to wrap the three books, the map, and place his note into a nicely decorated package and have it sent by special delivery to Mercedes's apartment in Georgetown.

* * *

Several days later, when he was helping her with her luggage, he noticed the three books and the map had been placed into what looked like a heavy canvas bag with two sets of heavy leather handles. Watching Jordan take notice of the sack and its contents, Mercedes hastened to say, "Jordan, thank you for your thoughtful gift. I was so pleased you signed your note 'professor' and 'old friend.' I do not recall anyone taking the time to give me something like this. I will enjoy it, and hope to remember it for a very long time. But I have to warn you, if I appear crabby, I became interested in studying your map and reading about all the sites we will be visiting. That was when I decided to read the entire three books. I'm afraid I haven't had much sleep. But don't worry about my falling asleep. Your newest student has a lot of questions!"

* * *

For the next 3 days, they toured the countryside. Mercedes would take advantage of half their travel time between sites to ask questions about what they had just seen and the other half to inquire about what they were going to see. Each time she would ask a question, she was holding the appropriate book, opened to the proper page.

Jordan enjoyed playing the role of the professor to the curious student. Mercedes was learning to treasure the opportunity to talk about subjects that had nothing to do with her experiences as a model or an actress, nothing that related to her schoolwork or her international casting work. Very simply, she was enjoying the opportunity to discuss subjects of personal interest with a very intelligent and charming friend.

Each time they would stop, she would, with book in hand, lead the way to, through, and around whatever it was they were expected to see. Jordan was struggling to keep up with this long-legged woman who had grown up walking over the hills of Spain. Catching his breath and answering her unending stream of questions was proving to be a delightful challenge.

No matter how interested he appeared in accompanying her as she vigorously walked around each of the sites, he knew that it would be only a question of time before he had to determine if there was an opportunity to reintroduce romance into their relationship. In the next moment, he would pause to think, *One wrong statement, and the entire relationship could disappear like a puff of smoke.*

The first evening when they checked into the charming country inn outside of Charlottesville, Jordan was careful to clarify he had reserved two rooms. As he slowly filled out both registration forms, he hoped Mercedes would suggest the second room wouldn't be necessary. When no suggestion was forthcoming, he was careful to hide his disappointment.

Three days and two long dinner engagements studying America's early history appeared to have succeeded in creating a new kind of personable bonding between the two very different companions.

Jordan was pleased by how well his idea of touring the old battlefields, the local museums, and restaurants had seemed to please his remarkable young friend.

Mercedes, always impressed with Jordan's extraordinary knowledge of so many people, events, and American history, felt like she was gaining a very unusual friend.

* * *

DURING A CANDLELIGHT DINNER ON THE LAST NIGHT OF THEIR TRIP, Jordan reached across the table and took both of Mercedes hands into his. Looking directly into her large brown eyes, he introduced the subject he knew not to mention. "Mercedes, I know that there must be more than 25 years' difference in our ages and that we've known each other for only a short time. Nevertheless,

I've never enjoyed such a wonderful sense of companionship. I find myself not only being attracted to you physically, but it's been a long time since I have truly enjoyed someone's company on a personal level. Is there anything I can do to persuade you to allow our relationship to grow to the next level?"

Having sensed his growing interest in her, Mercedes had suspected this moment would eventually occur. After withdrawing her hands, she asked, "Are you asking me if I would be interested in joining you for another one-night stand?"

Unprepared for such a direct response, Jordan found himself in strange territory. After a career of asking the disarming questions, he suddenly found himself at a total loss for words. In a fumbling attempt to respond, he stammered, "Well . . . uh, I guess I'm not sure. I just want to have a more intimate relationship and spend more time with you. No matter how fond of you I have become and how much I treasure your company, I haven't been able to forget that incredible evening we spent together in Acapulco."

Not waiting for Mercedes to respond, he nervously continued. "As you have probably guessed, I am a relatively wealthy and powerful man and well connected to some of government's most powerful and influential official leaders. I enjoy, on a first-name basis, friendships with many of the world's top industrial leaders. There arc many things I could do for you, if you would allow me. I could help you finish law school and live comfortably. I could see to it that after you graduate you would be employed by one of Washington's leading firms."

Mercedes was disappointed, but not shocked. In the back of her mind, she had suspected that all along his renewed interest and empathetic talk was nothing more than a smoke screen to advance the possibility of revisiting the relationship they had shared that night in Acapulco.

As prepared as she considered herself to be when and if this unfortunate moment might arise, Mercedes realized she no longer wanted to follow the script she had rehearsed so many times. *Jordan, at least not in my eyes, is the enemy; he is a lonely, disillusioned man who needs a friend.*

"Jordan, things are not as they might appear. My meeting you in the elevator was part of a carefully orchestrated plan designed to take advantage of our previous relationship to put a sympathetic ear near you. The objective of our plan was to encourage you to talk to an old friend in the hopes, upon reflection, you would decide to remove yourself from your involvement with the members of Manuel's Club and all the activities it entails. My friends in the Justice Department believe, as upset as the members of Manuel's Club are regarding their recent disappointments, it will only become a question of time before they will realize they will still need your experiences, skills, and services if they expect to coordinate and implement their present goals and objectives.

"If you were to retire, my friends talk in terms of *cutting off the head of the serpent*. They are convinced, without your leadership, the coalition of military industrialists will no longer be able to advance their influence into the government, at least not in the short term."

Jordan sat very still as he listened. The impassive look on his face failed to reflect any reaction or thoughts he had spent a lifetime to conceal. To break the discomforting silence, Mercedes said, "I want to make certain you understand, in the short time we've spent together, I have learned to appreciate you as a trusted and good friend. None of the things you have confided in me will ever be repeated. No matter how you regard our relationship, I'll always think of you as a good friend!"

Jordan put up his hand to interrupt her. "I don't even care that our meeting wasn't coincidental. Tell Don whatever you want. If you'll allow me to simply withdraw my earlier comment, I would be very pleased if we could continue our friendship on its current basis."

"Jordan, there is a man in my life, and after I finish law school, I hope to work with Natalie to construct an enduring international casting company. I sincerely believe we may have succeeded in accomplishing more than merely finding needed employment for some very deserving people. Once the Hollywood moviemakers come to their senses, I expect transatlantic competitive bidding for the services of the same people Hollywood studios have chosen to threaten. When that day comes, I hope to be in a position to help my clients receive their just due.

"Along the way, I would like to get married, have children, and have to struggle with all the problems young marrieds have to contend with in building a solid relationship, raising children, and pursuing two separate careers, for myself and my spouse.

"Part of the problem of trying to reinvent yourself requires one to really think about these sorts of things. At this time, I am really convinced without achieving that degree of clarity, I wouldn't feel confident about completing my journey. The one thing about which I am absolutely sure of, my best interests are not served by permitting me to devote the time or temptation of what you are expecting and you deserve. I don't want to be under the control of a man who feels he can manage my life."

* * *

THE NEXT MORNING, AS JORDAN WAS PERFORMING HIS EXERCISE routine, he was dreading meeting Mercedes for breakfast. He had no idea what he would say—or what she would say.

Mercedes was already sitting at a small table near the front window when Jordan entered the restaurant. The sun was shining, and the table looked as if it were illuminated by some concealed floodlight. He couldn't help but notice her smile as he approached. He hoped the next few hours wouldn't be too difficult.

"Jordan, while I was walking, I was thinking about last night's conversation. I realize I was very direct—it's the way I've learned to talk to my close friends. I want you to relax; everything is fine. As a matter of fact, I was secretly flattered by your offer. There was a time when your offer of financial security, the pleasure of your company, and the protection of being under your wing might have been very tempting.

"As a token of my sincerity, I want to give you a present."

She reached over to the chair next to her and picked up a large, square, thin, white box wrapped with a red ribbon and a big red bow. Extending it toward him she said, "Enclosed in this box is the only known copy of a film which was shot the night of our intimate performance. I'm quite certain that Manuel was planning to use it to embarrass me and blackmail you. You will never know how much trouble I have gone to in order to rescue it from his safe. Please accept it as my gift from one friend to another. I strongly suggest you destroy it before it gets both of us in a lot of trouble!"

CHAPTER 45

Tony Garibaldi, a Fellow Dreamer

NEW YORK, NOVEMBER 1949

Tony Garibaldi, Natalie's old friend and fellow Sentinel, was seated near the center of the long and crowded bar. In her haste to make her way to the corner table beyond the far end of the bar, where the *"regulars"* might be seated, she failed to recognize him. Startled by the outstretched arm blocking her way, in panic, she turned toward the unexpected intruder. Just as she was preparing to lodge a protest loud enough to be heard by all the other patrons, she recognized her deeply tanned, handsome, wine-growing friend from the Napa Valley.

Before she could think of anything to say, he asked, "Where the hell have you been? I was beginning to think I had traveled all the way from California to see you and you weren't here! Do you have any idea how much scotch a man must consume waiting for his *'important friend'* to make her appearance?"

"You traveled all the way from California to see me? Have you lost your mind? Why would you do a thing like that? How were you able to learn where I was staying? At least, you could have called and warned me you were coming."

"And spoil the surprise or hear you say no to a question I have been composing for a very long time? That is a chance I didn't want to risk. Now, young lady, if you have a few minutes, there is something I have come 3,000 miles to ask you. If you would be kind enough to join me at that vacant table over there, there is something we need to discuss."

Excited to tell Tony about all the exciting things that had been occurring in her life, the instinctive actress could feel Tony's intensity and understood whatever had motivated him to come 3,000 miles must be very serious. Waiting for their ordered drinks to arrive, she cleared her mind, and watched her normally quiet friend wrestle with his thoughts.

When their drinks arrived, she was surprised when he failed to reach forward to raise his glass. Instead, he reached forward and clasped both of her hands in his before asking, "Natalie, I need to know if you were sensing the same kind of magic I was feeling for you at the Sentinels' last meeting?"

With her hands firmly clasped in his and his gaze focused on her eyes, Natalie understood this was one of those moments that could be a significant life changer. *He's expecting an honest answer.*

Withdrawing her hands, breaking eye contact, and reaching for her drink provided her with the needed opportunity to think about her answer and choose her words very carefully. With her mind made up, she slowly replaced her untouched drink on the table, reached for his hands, and after staring into his warm, brown eyes, she said, "Tony, I am so relieved to hear you were feeling the same way. I can't remember when I have been ever so impressed by a man, interested in what he said, and felt myself so physically attracted. Like you, I have secretly been looking forward to seeing you again when jealous ex-companions are not in the room and we could talk freely.

"But there is a problem! I don't trust myself to begin a new relationship with somebody I suspect I really care about. When David left, I concluded I am capable of loving a man I really care about, but at the same time, I am a person who is devoted to remaining a serious solver of serious problems. It would appear, after two failed relationships, I have learned the hard way that I don't seem to be able to pursue both at the same time. I don't want to risk a relationship with you by becoming seriously involved."

Any concern she may have felt hurting Tony's feelings with her direct reply dissipated quickly. She was surprised when he smiled, disengaged her hands, and reached for his drink. After lifting it up and inviting her to clink glasses, he said, "I'll drink to that. Knowing how you feel about me tells me what I needed to know. It's not my fault that Jacques and David never took the time to learn how to appreciate a fellow dreamer.

"Before you say anything, you are not the only one sitting at this table who has destroyed an important relationship by failing to combine chasing dreams with caring about someone you really loved. You might not be aware, but when we Sentinels were attending the University of California, Claudine and I could not have been a more serious item.

"Before we graduated, I had already started assembling land suitable for growing premium wine-quality grapes in the Napa Valley. My family needed to transfer their grape-growing and wine-making operations from Italy to the United States. Mussolini's fascist government was beginning to confiscate some of the more valuable vineyards in Tuscany and other regions in Northern Italy, and we needed to protect our family's heritage of fine wine production.

"During the weeks, still suffering from a language barrier, Claudine would help me with my studies, and on the weekends, she accompanied me to Napa and helped me survey and analyze all the different properties that were for sale. I think she has carried a heavy engineering transit over more than half the hills that comprise the wine-growing regions of Napa Valley.

"By the time we graduated, I was so involved with my dreams about creating a national premium wine-producing company, I failed to make room for her in my life. Even after she decided to remain in California and give up the brilliant European banking career that was waiting for her in Switzerland, I refused to make the time needed to better understand her needs. You have no idea how I have regretted my mistake. Ever since that time, more than 10 years ago, I have promised myself if I ever have the opportunity to fall in love with another highly intelligent, high-energy woman with serious interests, I will never make the same mistake!

"Now that I think I have met that woman, I believe we both understand the problem. I would like to believe, since we realize that conflict that can occur between chasing dreams and pursuing interests of importance, who can better understand how it is to walk in the *steps of a fellow dreamer* than the two of us?"

"I'll drink to that. But I do have one more suggestion. Since we are both sitting in a hotel where I have a room, don't you think this would be a good time for us to start building that relationship you have been discussing?"

CHAPTER **46**

Jordan Sails

NEW YORK, DECEMBER 1949

After his return to New York, Jordan felt like a man stranded in a foreign country, not knowing anyone, not speaking the language. Thoughts about his last conversation with Mercedes continued to dominate his thinking. *So many things she said really make sense. She might be right! Is knowing the path your present journey doesn't lead to where you wish to end up represent a sufficient reason for making what will undoubtedly be a difficult and uncomfortable change?*

For the first time in his life, Jordan was finding himself in strange territory. He would ask himself, *For a man who has carefully calculated, well in advance, his every move, is it possible that I am capable of initiating such a drastic change without knowing where my next journey may lead?*

He was walking along the wide passageway of the terminal carrying the white box in one hand and his overnight case in the other. His mind concentrating on other things, he failed to immediately notice as his wife stepped out of the crowd to greet him. Surprised, his first reaction was *What's she doing here? I can't remember the last time she met me at the airport.* His second thought was even more disturbing. *What am I going to do if she asks me about the white box with the red ribbon? Will she think I have brought her a present?* Just the vision of her reaction when she discovered the true nature of its contents made him smile.

Watching Jordan proceed toward where she was standing, wearing such a serious look, his wife was pleased when she noticed his look of surprise when he first recognized her, immediately followed by his big smile.

She thought she saw a sunnier, smiling man walking toward her. After they hugged in greeting, she was pleased. *Maybe I did the right thing by making the effort to greet my returning warrior. Should I have been doing this before?*

Sitting in the back of the cab, the white box wedged between them, about halfway through the 30-minute drive to their apartment, she finally confronted him. "Jordan, I hoped this trip would help make things better, but you seem as distracted as you were before you left. What could possibly be going on that we can't discuss? You used to tell me I was your best friend and your best listener."

Surprised by the directness of her question, Jordan felt trapped. Well aware of the white box and its contents, he said to himself, *Oh, what the hell. I might as well get this over!*

"You are right. You have been my best friend for a very long time. I can only hope that as my best friend you will be able to understand why I have found it necessary to change the direction of my life. I no longer am content to live a polarized relationship with a wife whom I care very much for as a friend, but with whom I no longer share the companionship and the adventure of life that I so highly treasure. For several weeks, I have attempted to explain my problems at work. When you failed to pay attention, unconsciously, I think I began to think of you as an enemy.

"Had I persisted, you would have learned, in an effort to best serve the needs of my clients, I voluntarily allowed myself to organize certain programs, employ ruthless private operatives, and direct the funding of activities designed to influence the introduction and passage of certain self-serving legislation. My friend, Manuel Arena, has been murdered, and the investment funds of my clients have been stolen. Now, I am being asked to approach old friends who operate the National Committees of both political parties. It will be my responsibility to determine what magnitude of political contributions will be required to influence the election of new candidates, the election of which will enable us to control the outcome of legislation considered critical to the needs of my clients.

"Finally, I have been provided the opportunity by the Justice Department to walk away from my Manuel's Club responsibilities, terminate my relationships with any former clients, and make myself available to testify should it become necessary.

"In the past, I might not have questioned what I am being asked to do. I used to believe *winning at any cost* represented the key to success. Now, as a result of spending many hours talking to a new friend, I have learned to appreciate the importance of dedicating one's energies to be consistent with my own values, which will take me in a direction I wish to pursue."

Having finished what he had waited so long to say, Jordan let out a relieved breath, sat back, and waited for his wife's emotional explosion. When she spoke, her voice was calm and even. "Jordan, I feel your pain. Somehow, I kept hoping things might improve. I even suspected that your trips to Washington might involve someone more than Stanley Victor, his business acquaintances, and fishing trips on his boat. Even if there was another woman involved, I was prepared to let things run their course and then do what was necessary to salvage our marriage.

"I can't compete with your desire for a new life. Until you discover who you are and what you want to do, there isn't much I can do. As strange as it sounds, I'm too set in my ways to play the role of the excited, enthusiastic supporter of you, your big dreams, and your desire to paint with a big brush."

* * *

SEVERAL DAYS LATER WHEN THE SHIP CARRYING J. JORDAN McWilliams sailed in front of the Statue of Liberty, it carried a man who was no longer confused or disillusioned. Standing at the rail, Jordan felt free—free to take deep breaths, free to seek out what interested him, free to use his skills and experiences to help out in situations of his choosing, free to find a new companion, one whom he could love, one who would enjoy spending quiet time with him, who wanted to meet his friends, and who would be interested in accompanying him on his new journey with a new brush. With a glass of fine champagne clasped in his hand and the white box with a red ribbon clasped in the other, he said a quiet good-bye to New York and all that it had represented to him for the last 40 years.

He then walked around the deck to the other side of the ship, the side that faced the open sea and all it might portend. Lifting his glass, he silently wished, *To whoever you are, buried deep inside me, may our journey be pleasant!* In the next moment, his free arm moved quickly forward, committing the white box with the red ribbon to the depths of the sea.

To Jordan, the experience of throwing the incriminating film over the side of the ship made him feel he had just discarded the last element of his former life. The smiling man standing by the rail for the first time in his life felt free… free to do whatever he needed to do, not fulfill someone else's expectations.

* * *

BACK IN THE UNITED STATES, IT WOULD BE DIFFICULT TO IMAGINE the rage of Manuel's Club former members created by the loss of their money, Walt Matthews's incriminating article, and the disruption the exposure had caused inside their carefully cultivated Washington lobbying system, along with their inability to blame the now departed lawyer from Wall Street. Unfortunately, they didn't have the luxury of indulging in self-pity. Almost daily, their attorneys were informing them about "Plan B" that required their attention if they had any hope of salvaging the introduction and passage of legislation required to fund pending military contracts. Without the appearance of any other feasible options, the stakes were too high not to consider the making of another level of expenditures and authorizing the "Voices in Front of the Curtain" to proceed.

The problems created by Jordan's absence began to appear. Unaccustomed to making principal decisions, the admittedly talented advisors' energies became entangled over their inability to agree over the best possible approaches, in the changing environment of uncertainty. Who among them was prepared or qualified to do the difficult work of communicating with third parties, and avoiding possible contingent liabilities. As they continued to argue among themselves, valuable time was being lost. It was becoming increasingly apparent, when the head of the serpent had been separated from the body, the loss of leadership was causing irreparable damage . . . the kind that might take years to repair.

CHAPTER 47

The Retreat

NAPA VALLEY, FEBRUARY 1950

The Sentinels were ready to celebrate. They were proud of their accomplishments. Their success was not the kind of work that created rooting sections voicing approval. Their only source of satisfaction was derived from their mutual inner understanding of what they had done to protect the privileges of Democratic Free Enterprise from those who would abuse them.

Mike and Jacques had prevailed upon Tony to host another reunion at their Sentinel winery in Napa, California. Consistent with historical tradition, the Sentinels and their new friends would gather together for the next 4 days and enjoy one another's company in the serene atmosphere of the Napa Valley. Hopefully, the 4 days of rest and relaxation would provide them with the opportunity to reflect on what they had learned, to discuss their concerns about any menacing clouds that may be forming just over the horizon, and talk about what changes needed to be considered to improve their future operating capability.

David and Juan Pablo were the only Sentinels unable to attend. David had notified Tony that his and Juan's presence was urgently requested in Tehran, Iran. No one questioned his decision.

What the others didn't understand was ever since Tony and Natalie had met one night in New York, they had been spending their weekends together. One weekend in Los Angeles and one weekend in San Francisco.

Step by step, they had been slowly building a relationship that was gradually evolving into one of deep romance. Mutually, they had decided they were comfortable enough about their feelings for each other, they were ready to expose their relationship to the other Sentinels.

* * *

Wanting everything to be perfect, Natalie planned to arrive at the ranch 2 weeks ahead of the others. She needed to use the time to search out the most interesting wineries, learn about their best wines, and sample the fare in recommended restaurants. She wanted to print information regarding her choices and their agenda into a brochure, one that would describe where they would be visiting, discuss the history of each facility, and summarize the heritage of the business and its founders.

Tony watched Natalie make full use of the days while he was attending to his regular ranch and winery duties. On her own, she would travel around the Napa Valley, locate the better vineyards and wineries, and introduce herself to their owners. She took the time to explain her relationship with Tony, and if appropriate, invite them for cocktails at some future date. It would have been impossible for them to misinterpret the actions of the famous star and their old and respected friend as anything but a friendly gesture.

She would politely enquire if they would be willing to show her their operation, explain its heritage, and permit her to take pictures. Rather than resent her requests, they believed her interest was a reflection of Tony's respect for them and their operation.

Natalie spent the second week transposing all her notes, pictures, wine lists, and menus into a multipage brochure that could be easily duplicated. On the back cover, she included a map with labeled marks clearly indicating the location of each of her selected wineries and restaurants. On the inside of the front cover, she had listed descriptions of each day's planned events. Providing professionally produced brochures for each of the Sentinels was Natalie's way of saying how proud she was to be Tony's *"companion"* and demonstrate her enthusiasm and support of his life's dreams.

VOICES BEHIND THE CURTAIN

* * *

O<small>N THE FIRST AFTERNOON OF THE DAY OF THEIR GUESTS'</small> <small>SCHEDULED</small> arrival, Natalie had planned the opening lunch to mimic the marketing format Tony had found so useful in introducing his new wines to national purchasers and distributors of premium wines.

Two long, heavy, oak tables had been set end-to-end near the mouth of the cave where they used the large handmade oak casks to age their wine. From sitting positions, visiting guests could look in one direction and see the long rows of the majestically maintained barrels placed along both of the chiseled limestone cave walls that ran deep into the mountain. Facing in the direction of the mouth of the cave, the guests were treated from an elevated position to a remarkable panoramic view of the Napa Valley, its vineyards, and its oak-studded hills framed by the pine tree-forested distant mountains.

After Natalie would finish introducing one of the invited guest chefs, she allowed him to describe in great detail the dish he was about to serve. The chef's explanation allowed Tony an opportunity to follow up and describe how the distinctive elements of the particular wine would complement each of the food's distinctive qualities the chef had described.

Jacques, the group's expert on wine, not for its making but for its drinking, said, "Tony, we couldn't be more impressed by all that you have accomplished. The day you suggested that the Sentinels invest $25 million into the achieving of your dream marked the day when we knew we had lost our sanity. Now that we can see the living proof of your dreams, I, together with all the original Sentinels, would like to congratulate you on a job well done and toast to the Sentinels for their particular brand of insanity."

Standing up alongside Jacques, Mike said, "I would like to propose a toast to Natalie. It couldn't be more obvious how much time and energy you have spent to ensure our enjoyment over the next 4 days."

Jacques, the inveterate teaser, said, "Natalie, now that we have finished recognizing all your fine work, there are some of us who would like to question your judgment. Would you mind sharing how you can be attracted to a tall, handsome, self-made, charming man who has been totally devoted to chasing his dreams? What could Tony have possibly said to convince you sharing a life with him might turn out to be a very lonely proposition?"

Appreciating how Jacques like to introduce a bit of sarcastic humor into serious questions of care and concern, Natalie said, "Having learned my lesson the hard way, on the evening when we met in New York, I asked him the same question. When he answered, '*Only another dreamer can understand how important it is to be sensitive and supportive of the same qualities in another person,*' I knew I was hooked. I'm just happy that I never took the opportunity to ask your question to you and David."

After waiting for the laughter to die down, Dr. Tom Burdick rose. "If you would allow your old professor to be serious for a moment, while all of us are together, I want to make a few observations.

"When I look around the room and see all of you, I couldn't be more impressed with how the six of you were able to provide so much greater clarity when you viewed the events of history through your Power-Cycle conceptual lens. But that's not what I want to talk about.

"When, in recent history, have six, independent, career-oriented friends, sharing a disgust for those who would abuse the privileges of free enterprise, succeeded in convincing so many responsible leaders to lend their support and cooperation to assist you in solving important problems? *That's* what I want to talk about!

"As I look around the table, I still see excited eyes, some of which have been tempered by 10 years of difficult and dangerous work. If any of you were to ask me what I have learned, it would be two things. One, the continued emergence of these Power-Cycle problems clearly indicates they are part of a continuing process.

"That's what I want to talk about. It raises the question, '*What should we be doing today to ensure tomorrow you will be able to expand your network of contributing Sentinel friends and to perpetuate what you have started?*'"

Hesitantly, a confident Natalie asked, "If we are going to discuss what the future configuration of the Sentinels should look like, I would like us to hear what George White has to say about why the production of a continuous running musical play needs to be part of our strategy.

"For those of you who are not familiar with George and his background, it might be productive if I explained. George is an acclaimed director and highly respected member of the New York theatrical community. He was my first American director. George is here to suggest why he believes the contemporary American musical stage can become America's Fifth Estate. By properly showcasing current attempts to abuse the privilege of free enterprise into well produced satirical musical plays, he believes as long as we refrain practicing the *presence of malice,* the musical stage can be used to expose and examine current threats to our system of free enterprise. Properly implemented, the musical stage might provide the Sentinels with a public voice, much the same way the press regards their role of being America's Fourth Estate. George, if you please."

When George had finished, Cecelia cleared her throat and looked up from all the notes she had been taking. The simple gesture attracted the attention of everyone present. "Looking at my notes, it seems that we believe it's important that we preserve what we have started and be prepared to add the discipline of theatrical production to our current list."

Jacques then asked the obvious question. "How much will all of this cost?"

Anticipating the question, Cecelia, as usual was prepared to respond. "One hundred million to construct the campus, and another hundred million to endow operations."

In shock, Claudine finally said, "One thing is for sure, we will never be accused of thinking small. Would you mind explaining how you plan to raise $200 million?"

Knowing the question was going to be asked, Mike leaned back in his chair, clasped both hands behind his neck, and waited for the fun to begin.

After reaching into her briefcase and withdrawing a rather thick folder, she passed the pile of multipage exhibits to her right, asking that everybody take one and wait for her to explain the content. "The first two pages contain photographs of the two charts I constructed that still hang on the walls of Mike's and my New York apartment. The next five pages represent different continents and contain the list of the names of people with whom I have discussed the Sentinel Institute idea and the approximate range of their indicated financial support. The regional totals are listed at the bottom of each page. You will note the sum of all the pledges adds up to $125 million.

"The eighth page lists the names of the New York theatrical investors who George believes might be interested in investing a total of $25 million into the ownership of a continuously running play. The ninth page includes a summary of the Sentinel Trust economics. We still retain approximately $75 million of our original capital base and the future earnings stream of the winery. I am recommending we consider contributing $50 million from the trust and

$25 million from the future surplus earnings of our winery. By my calculations, that funds the cost of the institute and provides us with a $25 million contingency fund."

Amused by their different reactions, Cecelia suggested, "In the next room, I have something of interest I would like to show you."

Moments later, when they had all gathered around the sheet-covered table in the adjoining room, Cecelia, with a firm, quick flick of her wrist, pulled the cloth off the architectural model.

"May I present the future somewhere campus of the Sentinel Research Institute."

The excitement over seeing the physical impression of how Cecelia envisioned the new campus and their amazement of her discussion of the investment economics was suddenly interrupted when Tony's secretary entered the room and handed Jacques and Mike copies of the same note. The note read: *Urgent we speak. There are serious problems emerging in Tehran that require our immediate attention.*

David and Juan Pablo